What they're sa

Perfect Disguise (as Lydia ...

Brooke Wills, Romance Junkies: "Lydia Hawke has created another terrific Civil War novel with her second book, PERFECT DISGUISE. Filled with tense excitement, tender moments, and a plot line that moves right along at a fast clip, this latest book by this delightful author is a terrific read."

Carol McPhee, Author of Something About That Lady, Undercover Trouble, Be Still, My Heart! And EPPIE Finalist Means To An End: Lydia Hawke has penned another winner with Perfect Disguise. Her three dimensional characters, vivid Civil War setting and intricate plot will fill a voracious reader's need for entertainment. The developing romance between Willa and Jeff will tug at your heart strings in hope of the elusive happy ending.

Firetrail (as Lydia Hawke)...

Renee Burnette, The Romance Studio: "This book is long and wonderfully detailed, but it flows so smoothly that you'll be finished before you know it. FIRETRAIL proves that Ms. Hawke is a wonderful writer and a gifted storyteller. I look forward to reading more of her work."
Romance Junkies Reviewer

Brooke Wills, Romance Junkies: Lydia Hawke's debut novel is a Civil War story that will touch your heart on all levels. It is beautifully written and rich in historical detail with characters that are memorable. FIRETRAIL is a story definitely worth reading and will stay with you long after you have turned the last page.
Getting It! (as Lydia Filzen)...

Brooke Wills, Romance Junkies: GETTING IT! by Lydia C. Filzen is adorable! Written mainly from Ruffian's point of view, this dollar download from Echelon Press is worth every single cent and more. It is quite short; you'll be able to read it easily in one sitting, but it packs a huge amount of enjoyment that will leave you feeling good when you are done.

SILENT WITNESS

Suzanne! Jump right in
and Enjoy the world
of dog agility trials!

[illegible]

All names, characters and incidents, except for certain trainers and clubs used wth permisssion, depicted in this book are totally the products of the author's imagination. Any other resemblance to actual events, locales, organizations, or persons, living or dead, is entirely coincidental.

ISBN: 0-9766449-1-6
Library of Congress Control Number: 2005938911

Published by Global Authors Publications

Filling the GAP in publishing

Edited by Barbara Sachs Sloan
Interior design by KathleenWalls
Cover Design by Kathleen Walls
Front Cover Photo credit: Ch. Foxfire Best Undressed, NAJ (Lark) by Tien Tran.
Back cover: Border Collie Lockeye Layel, MX, MXJ owned by Noreen Scelzo

Printed in USA for Global Authors Publications

SILENT WITNESS

BY

LYDIA C. FILZEN

Dedication page:

To my Collies, past, present and future, who speak to my heart.

Foreword

As I sit here at my computer my beautiful little tricolor Collie, Jetta, is curled up right behind my chair. I have to be careful not to forget she is there and roll the chair over her fur when I get up from my desk. She doesn't seem to mind the risk, as she makes it plain she'd rather lie on the floor beside me than park on the more comfortable couch. Such devotion is flattering as well as humbling, and I've learned to look before I roll.

Such preferences demonstrate the human-dog bond. For all their wolf-powered jaws, serious dog bites are rare. Dogs cheerfully participate with us in dog shows, which must be a colossal bore for them, obedience training, which only recently has evolved into a humane regimen, and agility. Finally, fun for the dogs too! We shouldn't forget the real work they do, such as pointing, retrieving, guarding, herding, various service functions, police work and search and rescue.

Personally I am convinced they speak to us. If only we could hear, life could run smoother for both ends of the partnership. Sometimes the messages crack through the wall of static. Like the times I wanted Jetta's company, and she just then padded into the bedroom to be with me. After 9/11, I sat stricken in front of the TV and she made it clear she understood something horrific had happened. I know she tried to console me. Or the times one of my dogs has been in distress, and the others let me know.

I've hung out with dogs for a long time. We always had a mutt when I was a child. I was obsessed with wanting a Collie. At the age of 13 finally saved enough money from a year's worth of allowance to buy one. My beleaguered parents agreed to let me have my Collie. I was able to take Gidget to a few dog shows. Together we earned a Companion Dog degree and a lot of Junior Showmanship and dog show ribbons. My poor husband probably had an inkling of what he was in for when we married, but he wasn't a committed (and I use that term advisedly) dog person in those days. Umpteen Collies later, he loves them and tolerates the inconvenience of a multi-dog household. They have a way of working their way into one's soul.

I can't possibly list all those wonderful dogs here, but a few stand out. Tipsy (Ch. Foxfire Blueprint of Sunquest) was smart, sweet and loved life to the fullest. Her daughter Erika (Ch. Foxfire All Aglow) was her mother's kid all over, plus a great show dog. Erika's grandson, Ch. Foxfire Hunter Lightfoot, CD, OA, NAJ got me started in agility. I enrolled him in classes for a confidence boost, as dog shows worried him. It worked. He finished his championship as well as a few agility titles, and got me hooked. Since then, several of my dogs have acquired initials at both ends of their names, My first smooth, Hawk, Ch. Talan's Rtwo, OA, OAJ and his daughter Lark, Ch. Foxfire Best Undressed, NAJ are carrying forward what Hunter started.

As I journey through life, I'm grateful to share life with such loving, intuitive and willing beings as my Collies.

Lydia C. Filzen
Foxfire Collies

Prologue

A blinding flash lit up the sky in front of Dani Sayer. The fireball illuminated the building behind it and reflected in the windows, turning the night into day.

She woke up sweating, knowing she had witnessed something awful. Trembling, she opened her eyes and stared at the green LED glow of the clock on her nightstand. 5:55, almost time to get up anyway. The explosion was only a dream. Waking reality came to her in reassuring waves. Yes, that was all it was, a dream.

Next she felt cold questing nose nudge her cheek. Soft warm breath feathered across her face. *What's the matter?*

"Nothing. Go back to sleep." Still not fully awake, she brought her hand out from under the sheet and touched the dog's silky head. She felt the soft thump of his tail against the bed. Next to her Jet, her Shetland Sheepdog, stirred and snuggled against her back. Safe among her canine pals, she felt the terror slide away. Their presence always steadied her. From early childhood, especially since her parents' death in an auto accident, she had found dogs easier company than most people.

The building in the dream was familiar. It resembled her former workplace, but it was puzzling that she should have felt so involved. She had no plans to return there, all ties severed two years ago.

The clock radio sounded, playing the acoustic version of "Layla." Dani lay there awhile, waiting for the news. She wanted to know what was going on in the world before she ventured out into it.

At the end of the song, the announcer started in with the usual bad news from around the world. War and terrorism, hate and pestilence. Then he said something about an explosion at a pharmaceutical firm in the Research Triangle area of North Carolina. No report yet on the extent of the damages, details yet to come.

Dani felt her fingertips go cold. It wasn't Crohn, but it was a similar company. Plus the Raleigh-Durham area was only an eight-hour drive away. Did that building in North Carolina look like the one housing Crohn?

Sometimes her dreams came true, such as when her grandmother died.

She shook her head. It was only a coincidence. She had no special powers, never did. She couldn't do anything for Gram, and she couldn't do anything to prevent a disaster at Crohn Pharmaceuticals, if that was indeed what she saw.

Chapter One

Dani felt a pang of apprehension, hearing the hum of the crowd and occasional excited barks. One more dog waited ahead of her and Crash before their turn at the start line. The exuberant Border Collie crouched on the grass at her feet. His deep brown eyes rolled, taking in the agility course laid out in the ring before them. *Run! Go! Hurry!* Dani sensed his active mind was playing truant. She whispered his name, trying to connect, trying to get him to focus on her, but his gaze locked on the dog in the ring instead.

Well-known trainer and frequent rival, Trish Smart, was running her red and white Australian Shepherd through the obstacle course. Dani caught her breath in admiration. After the dog flashed across the finish line, Dani joined the spectators at ringside in cheering his flawless run, a tough act to follow. Trish acknowledged the applause with a brilliant smile and called her panting dog back to her.

Crash also took in the action, every line of his body taut with anticipation. "Ready, Crash?" Dani spoke in an enthusiastic whisper. "We're next, after the black Lab!" She knelt down and stroked his tense body, but he hardly acknowledged her, his attention fixed on the dog and handler ahead of them, as though he wanted to give chase. She needed time to break off, take him out and work with him away from the stimulation of competition. She ruffled his fur and worked him through a quick routine of sit, down, sit, but sensed his impatience. He wanted to run, and that was a good thing. Uncontrolled zoomies once the collar and lead came off his neck would not be a good thing.

The Lab swept through the course and only had a few obstacles to go. The gate steward gave Dani an impatient nod and sang out to the ring crew, "Last dog!"

Dani took a deep, calming breath, cleared the negative thoughts and led Crash to the start line. She had worked with the dog for months and was convinced until now that he was ready to make his agility trial debut. The weather was as near perfect as northern Florida provided during late fall, cool and clear. The organized pace of the agility trial fostered a relaxed atmosphere at the show grounds. She had memorized the course, walked it and planned her strategy. Earlier she had warmed up Crash, massaged him, stretched him out and practiced attention exercises, then sent him over a few practice hurdles. Why shouldn't he perform with the same speed and precision he'd shown during months of training sessions?

Dani positioned Crash at a strategic distance from the first jump and told him to sit and stay. She removed the slip lead from his neck, tossed it aside and checked to make sure the ring crew and the judge were ready for her to start. Crash reluctantly held his "stay," vibrating with eagerness.

Praying he would behave himself, Dani led off a few steps, fist raised, then dropped her hand and said, "Okay, hup," giving him permission to take the first jump. He sprang forward and flew over the jump.

She swiveled, invited him to swirl around her and ran with him toward the tunnel. He slammed through the correct entrance with such force he pushed the flexible tube of conduit back at least a foot, sandbags and all. When he shot out the other end like a black and white cannonball, Dani caught his attention and motioned him over the next jump. She dared to hope they could hold it together through all fifteen obstacles.

Instead of springing over the jump, Crash ran to it, slid to a stop, grabbed the crossbar between his jaws, whirled and sprinted for the weave poles.

Dani sensed that if she chased him, he would play keep-away and bolt. Trying to avert a disaster, she called out, "Crash, come!" and started jogging in the opposite direction, hoping he would take the invitation to chase her. He didn't obey. He was on a tear, and like a horse with the bit between his teeth, wasn't of a mind to please her. She could have sworn she sensed him giggling.

The spectators gasped when Crash started through the upright poles, which were spaced less than two feet apart, carrying the four-foot jump bar lengthwise in his jaws. Dani pivoted and ran toward him, still yelling, "Come!" She was desperate to stop him but unable to do anything. It was like watching a train wreck.

To her amazement, he managed to drag and slam the bar back and forth all the way through all twelve poles. It wasn't a perfect execution; he missed a few of the uprights. But she had to give him credit for getting through the entire line at top speed without breaking his furry neck.

He emerged from the twelfth pole, still gripping the bar, and took off on a victory lap, playing up to the crowd's laughter. The judge blew his whistle, the signal excusing Crash from the course. The dog finally let Dani catch him at the ring exit. She smiled apologetically at the judge, who strolled toward her. Of course he had no choice but to kick them out of competition for complete lack of control.

"That's a first." Fortunately, the judge was grinning. "He is just too cute, isn't he? I hated for the entertainment to end."

"Yep, he's an original, all right." Dani held onto the squirming dog's nape a trifle too tightly. The leash runner met her at the gate and handed her Crash's lead. Dani spotted Trish Smart, who had smoked the course with her Aussie, laughing with another exhibitor. Worse, the woman getting the earful from Trish was one of Dani's new students, the one with the quick learning Jack Russell Terrier. Dani's humiliation deepened, along with the concern that Trish would steal her clients.

"Class clown," she hissed into Crash's ear, looping the noose around his neck. "I hope you enjoyed yourself, gigglepuss. Blew an entry fee and convinced people I'm a sucky trainer. Great job."

Fun. Big fun. She didn't have to read his mind to see that Crash was tickled with his performance, wagging his tail and lolling out his tongue in a doggy version of laughter. She took him to a fold-up chair she'd left a little away from ringside and settled into it, drawing Crash close. She checked him over, but he didn't seem to have injured himself. She ran her hands down his spine, stretched and flexed his joints. Fortunately, he didn't flinch.

"Dodged a bullet that time, Crash."

The dog gave her a look she could have sworn exuded smugness. The short exertion had warmed her too well, so she slipped off her jacket and deposited it beside her. "What ever possessed me to name you Crash? I should have named you something ordinary, like Spot. Or something sedate, like Slug."

"Crash fits him, Dani." The male voice sounded devastatingly familiar, part of a past she'd set aside long ago. To her dismay, her hearing had not deceived her, and she looked up into the face of Mark Vaughn. Uh-oh. Now she was up for a two-disaster day. He smiled tentatively, part of the nice-guy act that had fooled her before.

"Mark! What are you doing here?"

"Admiring your new dog." He reached down and stroked Crash's velvety head. The traitorous dog sniffed and licked the man's hand. His tail thumped a beat on the ground. "How about that?" Mark grinned. "He likes me."

"Crash, you hopeless suck-up," she said under her breath. She'd thought — wished — she would never see Mark again. The sinking feeling she'd experienced at the sight of him competed with a heady rush of excitement. Was that how reformed addicts reacted at the sight of their favorite intoxicant?

She hated to admit it, but he looked better than ever. Married life must agree with him. His lively dark eyes were rimmed with long eyelashes any woman would envy. His denim jacket fit casually over his firmly muscled but trim frame. She suppressed the urge to reach up and tidy his dark, windblown hair and clenched her fist instead.

Mark knelt to Crash's level and rubbed him behind an ear. The dog leaned into the massage, lips drawn back blissfully. "I found out about the agility trial on the Pals and Paws website, and what do you know? This weekend, right here in Jacksonville. I thought I'd look you up. Where's Jet? I want to say hello to him, too."

She tried to maintain her poise, relieved she could stick to the safe topic of the dogs. "Jet is resting in his crate. He already ran this morning, fast and clean. Wouldn't you know you missed it and caught this debacle instead?"

"Looked like Crash had fun."

"The fun was all his." She couldn't help letting out a rueful laugh. "I named him Crash, because whenever he wants to go from point A to point B, he kind of disregards what's in between. Anybody in his way runs the risk of being impaled by a Border Collie."

"I like his style and the way you kept your cool." He looked up, still grinning. "And you look terrific. I always thought you were the hottest item in the bio lab at Crohn."

"Liar." He'd found something hotter, or so he must have believed. She regretted her ultra-natural look sans makeup and wished he hadn't caught her at a disadvantage. Jeans or shorts were the norm for agility trials because it was an athletic sport, not a beauty contest. Besides, her time-crunched morning didn't allow for much attention to detail. She ran her hand through her sensibly cut hair. At least it was frizz-free, due to the dry weather, and the blonde color was all hers. She was hard-bodied fit from her active lifestyle, another asset.

"No, ma'am. I only speak the truth." Mark's glance leveled on the front of the Halloween-colored tee shirt Kevin, the groomer at her boarding kennel, had given her as a joke. What a day to snatch up this horrid shirt that read, "Vicious, Power-hungry Bitch" emblazoned across the bust line. The jacket would have concealed it, but oh, no. She just had to pick that moment to take it off.

He raised one of his neat dark eyebrows. "That's not how I remember you, Dani."

"Uh, I'm not really vicious. I only bite when provoked." She gave him a wry smile. "Don't risk it."

"Good to know you haven't changed after all. I liked you the way you were." His gaze returned to her face, and he appeared to suppress a smile. *Such a bashful guy. Yeah. Right.* "I'd like to train my dog in agility," he said.

"You finally got a dog? No kidding." She was interested in spite of her general disgust with Mark. "What breed?"

He nodded, eyes alight with enthusiasm. "Rebel's a smooth Collie. You know, I had a Collie when I was a kid and always wanted another one. This time I went for the variety with a buzz-cut."

Dani nodded her approval. "I hear they have good working drive."

"I'll say. I got him when he was a puppy. He's a year old now and still has energy to burn. I understand you teach classes at your boarding kennel."

"Uh, yes, I do." She let out a short laugh. "After that performance, are you sure you want to take lessons from me?"

"Absolutely. I watched you train Jet, and I want that for my dog, too."

Maybe it would be all right, as long as Mark stuck to business. She sure would. Besides, her creditors would appreciate any improvement in her cash flow. "You know where Critter Ranch is then? You know, the boarding kennel I bought just south of Orange Park after I quit Crohn?"

"Of course." He paused, and gave her a penetrating look. "Though I heard about it through the company grapevine, not first hand."

She ignored the dig, determined to keep her cool. Then she remembered last night's dream and the actual explosion in North Carolina. The pictures of the building that flashed on Fox News didn't resemble Crohn, as had the one in her dream. It was only a coincidence, that was all. *Stick to business.* "I've got a fully equipped agility field set up in back. Where's Jill? Do you two still live at that place you bought in Middleburg?"

"We're divorced."

Trouble in paradise? It would have been unworthy to gloat, so she said, "I'm sorry."

"So am I." Was that anger in his eyes?

"What happened?"

"It's a long story. Anyway, she moved out. I still live in the same house. I pass your place every so often. I remembered how much fun we had when I went with you to agility trials and thought I'd try it with Rebel."

"Just like old times, huh?"

He actually winced. Her flatly delivered comment must have hit a nerve. "I've missed you, Dani."

Here we go. "Oh, really. I got over missing you a while back."

"If you'd rather I train with somebody else…" He gave her a forlorn look.

She thought about suggesting that Trish Smart take him on instead. So what if she had to give up the income. But she wasn't sure she could in good conscience foist Trish's harsh methods on an innocent dog. A few sharp neck jerks did seem like a good plan for Mark, though. Unfortunately, she couldn't separate dog and owner. "Never mind, Mark. I'd like to work with you and Rebel."

She sighed, hoping she wouldn't regret saying that. "We might as well catch up on things."

He gave her one of his heart-stopping smiles, the one that crinkled around his eyes, but she managed to recover and continue in her professional persona. "I teach the agility classes, and Nancy Kleinhans comes in sometimes for seminars. She's one of the top people in this area. She's even competed at the World Agility Tournament in Europe. Tell me about Rebel."

"We got him when he was a puppy, soon after we moved into the house. After Jill lost the baby, I thought we could use the distraction."

"Oh, Mark. I didn't even know she was expecting." She wouldn't have minded the usual misfortunes falling upon the perfidious couple, like bankruptcy, for instance. But losing a child was something she'd never wished on them, even in the darkest corners of her soul. "I'm so sorry."

"To be fair, I guess you didn't have any reason to stay in touch with us. Not after—"

"The phone does ring on both ends, you know."

"Sure it does. But I got tired of leaving messages."

"Okay, you win. You're right. I didn't have any reason to speak to you." She heard herself getting snippy again and didn't like it. "Anyway, the kennel keeps me busy. Really busy." That sounded like a good reason, but the better reason was that she never wanted to see either of them again. And here he was, sniffing around like a bloodhound. She ought to tell him to find somebody else to work with him. Just looking at him brought unexpected pain. She hated that. She'd gotten over him two years ago, or so she thought. She took a deep breath and soldiered on. "You were telling me about your dog."

"His breeder taught me the basics and I showed him all the way to his championship. He finished his title from the puppy class." Mark radiated pride, and why not? That was quite an accomplishment and happy evidence that Rebel was a superior example of his breed. "He knows a few basic obedience commands, and I built a couple of PVC jumps to fool around with. Jill has him today, or I'd have brought him along."

"Well, Mark, you're in luck. I'm starting a new class of beginners Thursday night at seven, and I have an opening. You said Jill has Rebel. Does he live with her?"

"Sometimes. I have partial custody. Our biggest hassle was over Rebel when we parted ways. I guess her lawyer was better than mine. In the end I figured shared custody was better than letting the judge split him down the middle like a broiler chicken." His mouth twisted into a bitter line. "I usually have him during the week, so it should work out for class night. I'll push her for more time so I can keep training him."

"Why should she object to that? She used to come to the agility trials with us sometimes. You remember? The Gleesome Threesome? The Three Musketeers? The Three Stooges? Or was it two musketeers and a stooge?"

Mark gave her a long, penetrating look. "Dani, I should remind you we broke up before–"

"Never mind. I'll try to behave myself." She waved him off and took a deep breath. "If that time slot is a problem for you, I give private lessons, too."

The air buzzed for a moment as she considered how provocative that sounded.

Mark's eyes sparkled, but he kept a straight face. "That might work out better, if it's okay with you."

Thank God Mark didn't comment on the double entendre or she would have fallen out of her chair in embarrassment. "Uh, sure." She hoped she could remain civil, keep her mind on the lessons and keep the old fault lines from opening in her heart.

***

The next morning, Mark strolled into the spacious lobby at Crohn Life Sciences on the way to his workstation. As was his custom, he stopped at the reception station and wished a "Happy Monday" to Miriam. Instead of merely returning his salutation with her usual chirpiness, she said, "Mark, Mr. Snider at Security wants you to report to him right away."

"That's unusual. Is he in his office?" Mark's research tasks usually had little interface with Security. Did it have something to do with the infuriating stunt that got his ex-wife fired? He didn't bother to ask Miriam; chances were she didn't know either.

"Let me check." While she punched in the extension number, Mark idly glanced around her workstation. Pictures of her husband and two cute kids were mounted on the side of her computer monitor. He eventually wanted pictures of that sort in his office, too. All he had there now was a dog show win picture of a smooth Collie. He now realized his brief liaison with Jill was a detour that had sidetracked him from what he really wanted out of life. Seeing Dani again could be a step toward setting him back on course. Or not. It depended on whether they could heal the rift between them. He wanted it fixed. But did she?

Miriam finished a brief conversation with the person on the other end and turned her attention back to Mark. "Yep. He's in his office. You can go in right now."

"Thanks." Mark walked down the corridor leading to Security, his curiosity piqued. He'd been absolved of suspicion for Jill's cute little stunt, thanks to the good sense of his boss, Mr. Wickham. Nobody that knew anything about him would believe he could abet such an act.

He recalled hearing something on the car radio about an explosion at a drug company in North Carolina over the weekend. It was a disturbing report. The authorities claimed it wasn't terrorism, but their assurances in the face if so many incidents made him believe they were blowing smoke. However, the company victimized wasn't affiliated with Crohn.

The secretary at Security waved him into Mr. Snyder's office, who didn't get up from his desk but invited Mark to have a seat. The former cop got straight to the point. "Seems the eco-terrorists aren't just attacking West Coast companies any more. They're moving into the Southeast."

"I heard something about an explosion in the Raleigh-Durham area, but I don't know a lot about it. I've been out of the loop this weekend. Never turned on my TV once."

"It was nasty. A car bomb, like Oklahoma City, though on a smaller scale. At least one employee perished. If it had occurred during regular work hours, it would have been much worse. Naturally, we're stepping up security procedures."

Mark grimaced. "That's frightening. What is the problem with these nuts? Did anybody take credit?"

"Scuttlebutt says it's a nest of loons that call themselves The Cabal."

"Did they say why they're picking on pharmaceutical companies? Are they anti-progress or something specific?" Then again, why was he being singled out for an interview?

"You nailed it. They want to stop technology. I guess they don't think anybody should have electricity and running water, not to mention medical care. Personally, I think they should take their blowup toys and move to the Third World where they might feel more at home." Mr. Snyder scrubbed his hand across his face and Mark noticed the haggard lines around his eyes. "Do you think Jill might have had any connections to such a group?"

Aha. That was it. Mark kept his gaze steady. "She's turned into a real live animal rights fanatic, but I doubt she's been blowing up any buildings."

Mr. Snyder waved his hand. "Not her, necessarily. People she knows. She did her own act of sabotage, and we fired her for it. She might be angry with the company because she was fired, or who knows why. Also, I wonder who might have put ideas into her head in the first place. Does she have any suspicious contacts through her associations? We could use a little help here." Mr. Snyder paused. "Some of our people have been getting emailed threats telling them to resign or else. Is there anything you can tell us?"

"Threats?" Mark let out his breath. "I've gotten a few of those myself but didn't recognize the return address."

The security chief shot him a penetrating look. "Why didn't you report them?"

Mark smiled wryly. "I didn't take them seriously."

"I do. Forward them to me, okay? We're working on getting to their origin."

"Sure." He'd suspected all along that Jill and her boyfriend were the ones playing email head games, but Mark had resisted throwing around accusations. It was a nuisance he'd decided to ignore because he couldn't control it. "Jill's shack-up, Ted, seems weird, but I don't know much about him."

"Do you know his full name?"

"I can find out." He gave the security chief Ted and Jill's address on the west side of Jacksonville. "I think the house is a rental."

"That's no problem. We can look it up on the 'Net and find out who owns it. Anything else you can add? We have charges pending on Jill–tampering with lab animals is a federal crime–but

I can't sit around and wait for the FBI."

"I'll keep my eyes open. I have to go there after work to pick up my dog."

"Your dog?" A quizzical smile crossed Mr. Snyder's face.

"It's complicated." Mark shifted in his seat. Most people would think the tug-of-war over a dog beyond silly. "We share custody."

Mr. Snyder lifted an eyebrow. "Then you do have contact with her?"

"Twice a week." Mark quirked the corner of his mouth. "Believe me, it's minimal."

"I understand." The security chief's skeptical look said he understood not at all. "If you see anything suspicious, let me know right away."

"Sure thing." Mark paused. "Mr. Snyder, Jill and I didn't part on the happiest of terms. But I don't believe she would support an act of violence like that. She won't even eat meat."

"Yeah. Sure. Neither did Hitler. What do the neighbors always say about a mass murderer?" Mr. Snyder offered another of those arid smiles. "'He was such a nice polite gentleman. Quiet. Kept to himself. I'm so shocked he just went postal and blew away half a dozen people.' Mr. Vaughn, it's my job to keep this company safe. To that end, I must consider everyone a suspect."

Everyone. Including Mark Vaughn, no doubt.

Chapter Two

The cordless phone sounded like a Bronx cheer. Dani set down the hose nozzle, dried her hands on the towel draped over her shoulder, and dragged the device from her overalls pocket. She hit the answer button. "Critter Ranch."

Mrs. Wright wanted to schedule a grooming appointment for her Lhasa Apso. Too bad Kevin hadn't answered the phone and handled it himself; he probably had his hands full. She hated to inconvenience a paying customer by jotting down her number in the notepad she carried and calling her back. That could lead to a game of phone tag. Better to handle it on the spot and inconvenience herself instead.

"I'm sure he has an opening for tomorrow, but I have to go in and check the calendar. May I put you on hold for a moment?"

Dani swung open the gate and trudged across the driveway, onto the front porch and into the house. She walked past the display of pet items for sale and stuck her head inside the grooming room. The smell of shampoo failed to mask the musty odor of wet dog. The high-pitched racket of a yapping Yorkshire Terrier protesting its cage confinement assaulted her eardrums. She held up the phone. Kevin was up to his elbows in suds, washing a black Chow Chow. He looked over at her. "For *moi*?" He said it loud enough to carry over the canine din.

"Okay, I see you're indisposed," she hollered back. "Want me to schedule Mrs. Wright for you?"

"You bet, sweets," he said. "Bear waits for no man." He squirted more shampoo on his hand and worked it into the dog's thick coat. "He'd jump out of here in a nanosecond if I gave him a chance."

She closed the door on the grooming room and made the appointment. When she finished she went back to tell the groomer the details. Fortunately the yapper had paused in his commentary. "I set her up for tomorrow morning."

"Good-o. Business is picking up."

She nodded. "That's the good news. The bad news is Jim is feeling poorly. His mother called in. The treatment is really making him feel awful, and the docs wanted to inflict more tests on him."

"Tsk." Kevin started rinsing, and suds poured out of the Chow's fur. With his bright eyes, wiry frame and dapper Van Dyke beard, the groomer reminded her of a Schnauzer. "That's to be expected when somebody is on chemotherapy."

"I'm glad his mother made him go to the doctor and get checked out. At least they caught it early."

"You were nagging him, too, as I recall."

"Yeah. You know how guys are. Can't get them to admit there's anything wrong with them. I had a bad feeling about his feeling poorly all the time."

"Seems you were right."

"I don't enjoy being right about things like that." She thought of watching Gram waste away and felt tears well up. She blinked them away before Kevin witnessed her distress. "Sometimes I think I'm just a natural born pessimist."

"Or a realist. With Jim gone so much, you've been struggling to keep your head above water. Perhaps you'd better start trolling for new kennel help, sweets. It beats drowning."

"The economy is so good, nobody's looking for work."

"Have you advertised?"

She shrugged and didn't answer.

"It isn't disloyal," he said. "Business is improving. You could use a full-time person and let Jim come in whenever he feels like it, on a part-time basis."

"I wish I could reach in and get hold of the bad stuff and make it disappear. I keep thinking he's going to be okay and the problem will go away."

"Not any time soon." He tsk'd again. "I'd come out and help you this afternoon, sweets, but I'm booked solid."

"I know, Kev. We need to keep you focused on doing what you do." The grooming shop was a consistent moneymaker for both of them. It also brought in traffic and sales of pet-related items. "You're right, you know. If business keeps on increasing, I'd need more staff even with Jim working fulltime."

"More work means you'll be in the black soon."

"That's the bright side. In the meantime, know of anybody looking for a job? Hard work, sorry pay?"

"Honestly. Didn't that job description just now give you an itty-bitty clue why it's so tough to find and keep help? And I don't know any nice animal-loving illegal immigrants who'll work for peanuts. They simply don't run in my circles. Which is too bad, because some of those dudes are simply delicious." He sighed and ran his tongue over his lips while he squeegeed water from Bear's thick coat. The Chow tried to shake, but Kevin's firm grip on his head saved the room from a shower. "Anyway, they might try to make kitty cat stew out of some of your clients, if they love pets the wrong way."

"Please. Bad joke." She grimaced. "It ain't rocket science."

"Dahling, if I hear of any hot prospects, you'll be the first to know." He toweled Bear's face, and the dog wriggled into the terrycloth with transparent pleasure.

"By the way, I've got a private agility lesson scheduled for late this afternoon. It's a guy I used to know. We bumped into each other at the trial last weekend."

"Anybody I'd like?"

"You might like his looks, but I know for a fact he's not your type."

"Oh, poo." He flashed her a wicked grin from the other side of Bear's ears. "You know from personal experience?"

"You might say so. He's married and divorced since I last saw him."

"Oh, then he's available." The grin curdled into a smirk. "How private is your lesson going to be?"

"Maybe he's available, but I'm not," she snapped. "At least not for him. I learned my lesson, and I don't want another dose of Mark Vaughn any more than I want a relapse of the flu."

"Touchy, touchy. Too bad, sweets. Might improve your disposition if you took a lover."

"What would improve my disposition is ending this conversation." Dani eyed her desk's pile of paperwork. It seemed to her that papers left in the dark together procreated, making new stacks of full-grown bills. Nonetheless, they would have to wait.

Since she was in the house anyway, she went upstairs to her room to check on Crash and Jet. Both of them jumped off her bed and ran to greet her. Living alone, she could spoil her dogs as rotten as she pleased. With their actions they told her she was the most loveable person on earth, even if nobody else shared that opinion. She knelt down to hug her two best friends. Real friends, whose loyalty she could trust.

The bed was tempting, because she'd been losing sleep over the latest spate of fiery nightmares. "I'll let you two out for a romp a little later. Too busy to play right now."

She handed each of them a rawhide chew and left them to hang out on her bed. Then she returned to the kennel. With Jim unable to work, it was up to her to handle the entire morning chores. The kennel was at half capacity, as was the cattery. Still, the animals present took time to feed and clean up after, plus somebody had to see to their exercise and give them individual attention.

Dani returned to the partly cleaned run and went back to work. She peeked out and scanned the driveway every so often to check for customers, even though the doorbell rang in the kennel building as well as the house.

Though she had to do the work of two people, the simpleminded repetitiveness of the work left her plenty of time to meditate on her predicament.

Mark's appearance at the agility trial had unsettled her. She suspected his motives. To her annoyance, part of her was actually glad to see him. Certainly not the sensible part. Nor was it the part that had a lick of pride. It was just the basic, biologically inspired part. She'd have to keep those pesky hormones at bay.

If she had any sense she'd call him and cancel their appointment. She could use the cash, but she wasn't that desperate. It had taken her a long time to get him out of her system, and she wasn't up for another betrayal.

Business reasons aside, maybe she had agreed to work with Mark because of her curiosity about what he really wanted from her. In truth, she was more interested in meeting his dog.

Surely she could separate her professional life from her personal feelings.

After she finished cleaning the last run, she shut off the spigot, determined to climb out of the wet overalls and make herself at least look semi-respectable. Hadn't she heard that success is the best revenge? Her best revenge would have been a fine-looking fellow, her very own Hunka-Burning-Love, to oh-so-casually introduce to Mark. Unfortunately, Kevin was the only guy around, and in her opinion he hardly qualified, though other males of his persuasion might disagree. The best she could do was to look her best in a practical, casual dog-training mode. How spiffy should one attempt to look when training dogs? One swipe of a muddy paw, and there goes the sharp outfit.

Dani headed to the exercise yard, where she'd left the Golden Retriever whose run she just cleaned. The exuberant young dog brought her a tennis ball and placed it in her hand. It was good to see Dolly happy. Dani had taken her in after her owners were arrested on drug charges. Dolly had a home with her until new owners could be found.

She threw the ball, and Dolly gave chase. Dani sensed joy radiate from the dog in waves. As quickly as the feelings came into her mind, she quashed them. Everything she had been taught assured her it wasn't possible for a human to read a dog's mind. Some things just weren't for a person to know. So often the voice in her head seemed to echo an animal's thoughts, but it was only her own mind making assumptions, extrapolating what a dog might want to convey. She was sure of it.

Dani accepted the damp ball from Dolly once again and parted the fur on the dog's neck. Dolly accepted the examination stoically, as though she knew Dani's intentions were helpful. Any bruises on Dolly's body were fortunately long gone. The burns on her neck had also healed, but the scars they left would never support new fur growth. Shock collars were horrible enough when they were used with so-called discretion. Dani would have liked to be alone with the guy that misused one on Dolly, armed with a cattle prod.

Dani threw the tennis ball again. It always amazed her that dogs could so easily shake off the bad stuff. She continued the fetch game with Dolly for a few minutes longer.

Satisfied Dolly had exercised enough, Dani kept the ball after the Golden brought it to her. "I have to cut the recess short, Doll-face. Time to go back into your run." She slipped a lead around the dog's stout neck, careful to avoid the still-tender areas, and pushed the gate open.

When are my people coming back?

Dani stopped in mid-stride, her hand on the gate. She stared at Dolly, who was looking expectantly at her, tail waving to and fro. The voice in her head had sounded clear and unmistakable, more distinct and intrusive than the background mind-noise to which she was accustomed. It sounded like her own mental voice, yet apart.

"I didn't hear that." She shook her head, rejecting the way the words had beamed into her head, and walked Dolly back to her kennel.

The content of the thought disturbed her as well. It wasn't an obvious assumption, such as realizing that a panting dog was thirsty, or that an excited dog wanted to run. How could she harbor the thought that this poor, abused dog would actually want to go back to live with the guy who had treated her so cruelly? Where did that come from?

"Doll-face, do you suffer from the doggy version of Battered Wife Syndrome? Are you telling me you want the creep even though you were terrified of him? How could I make up something like that?"

Love and fear washed over Dani in a confused wave, and she shivered, feeling that it came from outside her, from Dolly.

Her rational, non-nonsense parents had discouraged, to the point of ridicule, her expressing such notions as knowing what animals were thinking. It was best to disregard them.

Still, sometimes she knew too much, such as her grandmother was about to die just before her illness came on. Though only her imagination, the premonition had devastated her just the same. Knowing such a thing ought to have allowed her to prevent it, right? But she couldn't stop the devastating disease that took Gram a decade before her time. So what good was such knowing? It only increased her grief.

Worse, if she was capable of those thoughts, she feared some part of her wanted Gram to die. That notion repulsed her, because she had fiercely loved Gram, her staunchest supporter in life, even in death, and no inheritance would ever take her place.

Gram had always told her she had a wild imagination. She wished she could drive a stake through the heart of such fantasies and bury them forever.

***

Ted Sturkey stared at the Crohn building, jumpy and bored at the same time. He stretched out his long legs as far as they could go in the passenger's side of Al's Honda. The seat was all the way back, but he wanted more room. He also needed something to calm his nerves. He remembered he had a small stash, already rolled, in his shirt pocket. He didn't have an extra to offer Al, but that wasn't his problem. He pulled the joint out, fished a matchbook from the same pocket, and lit the weed. A nice long drag didn't bring much of a hit. Weak, worthless stuff. He exhaled, then removed the home-roll from his lips He held it away and examined it, wishing it packed a harder punch.

Al reached across, plucked it from between his fingers and threw it out the window.

"Hey! What was that about?"

"For being stupid. You trying to get us busted?"

Bile rose in Ted's gut. His foot twitched. "Who you calling stupid? You think you can come down here and take over my whole friggin' life?"

"Can it, man." Al reached down by his seat and pulled out a pack of Kools. "Have one of these instead."

"It's not the same."

"It'll have to do. Let's take care of business. Think of it as surveillance 101. We gotta be inconspicuous, remember?"

Ted stiffly accepted the peace offering, lit it and inhaled a deep drag. He watched Al rest his head back and blow out a puff of smoke, aiming it out the driver's side window of the '97 blue Honda. Al's car was as nondescript as he tried to be. The Marlins baseball cap covering his short brown hair and the gray Jacksonville Jaguar sweatshirt over his stocky frame helped him blend in with the local rednecks.

Ted added his anger to his growing mental grudge list. He'd get Al back later, somehow. For now he'd better think of the bigger picture, concentrate on spying on the complex. They'd parked in an adjoining parking lot to watch the comings and goings at Crohn Life Sciences. He was showing Al, his new comrade, the security and the lay of the land.

Ted shifted his thinking to a happy track. He liked the way the three-story building's facade had more glass than concrete and steel. If Al delivered as promised, it would come down in a spectacular flash and a crunch of broken glass. He held onto his foot to make it stop jiggling, which gave him away when he got excited. "Ka-boom." He laughed out loud. "Now that's gonna be a real high. Clear out the man-made crap and let the woods take over. Set the natural order of things to rights. Let the jungle rule. Eliminate human polluters and save the planet."

"You really believe that crap?" Al wore a superior down-his-nose look. "Whatever floats your boat, man. To me, it's a job. Looks like this is as close as we can get without them noticing. The Cabal coulda picked an easier target, huh?"

"It'll work. We're still in the building stages." Still hiding his annoyance, Ted smiled at his own irony and studied the guard station at the parking lot entrance. A white Blazer, one of those gas-guzzling SUV's, pulled up and stopped. It had to be that Vaughn jerk. He drove an SUV like that one. The notebook toting guard came out and waved the driver through. "There he is now. Jill's ex, Mark Vaughn. Must be coming back from lunch fat and happy. Just another cog in the wheel. They're all the same. Nothing but capitalist swine. Leeches. Boo-jwa-zee. Polluters. Just like dear old Mommy Dearest, who divorced my old man so she could get herself a rich prick, live in a house with a guard at the gate to keep the riffraff out, and wrap herself in furs."

Al yawned, reached under his sweatshirt, and scratched his chest. "You got a special hard-on about Crohn. Got anything to do with that guy or your live-in?"

"He's A-1 on my shit list. I'd like to fix it so he goes down with the building."

"We got no room for personal vendettas. This project is too big for small stuff like that."

Ted didn't voice his disagreement, but he figured he could work it out to satisfy all his wishes no matter what asshole Al said. Soon he wouldn't have to content himself with mere threats. "I took up with Jill because she worked for Crohn. Hey, we clicked, and she was ready to leave Vaughn anyhow. Her pulling that stupid stunt and getting herself fired wasn't part of the plan."

Al snorted. "Stupid is an understatement."

"Canned her ass and took the pass card that gave her access. She thought I'd be happy about her striking a blow for animal rights." Disgusted, Ted added, "Like a one-woman army. It's a wonder she didn't get thrown in the slammer. She's gotta learn to take orders like a soldier and not go off half-cocked. It was all I could do to keep from slapping the crap out of her when she told me what she'd done. I let her know I wasn't happy."

"She's a weak link. The feds could still come after her, and if she knows anything she could be a problem to us. Why don't you get rid of her?"

Ted bristled. "Who are you to come in here and tell me to get rid of my woman?"

"She must be a good lay, huh?"

"I'd explain if you weren't too young. Anyway, what have you got to complain about?" Ted glared at Al, feeling a need to assert himself. In truth, he enjoyed her admiration as well as the other fringe benefits. "She cooks and she's washing that pile of laundry you threw at her."

"Cooks?" Al grimaced. "Who ever heard of making stew without meat?"

"What kind of animal rights advocate are you, anyway? Dead animals aren't supposed to be on the menu."

"Some animals got more rights than others." Al smiled broadly. "I like my critters just right. Medium rare."

Al was just a mercenary, not a soldier of true conscience. Disappointing. If Ted didn't need his expertise in things that go "boom," he'd have sent him packing. "Anyhow, Jill knows a few helpful things. The layout of the complex, who's who and where things are in there. I haven't told her the whole plan, though. She might not like it."

"Man, why'd you kick in with that bunch of losers anyway? Those animal-rights nuts? They aren't smart enough to find their butts with their own hands, much less help with a sophisticated project like this.

Ted was sick of justifying everything he did to this clown. Nor did he want to explain his anger over what the drug doctors had forced him to take. The cure was worse then the supposed disease. The drugs were what made him nuts. He felt saner without the poison bending his mind, but he still had meltdowns from time to time. It was all the fault of the doctors and their drugs that sent him over the top. Since then he'd discovered "The Unibomber Manifesto" and memorized every word. It was a revelation that had changed his life. His namesake, the more famous Ted

Kazinski, was a true visionary.

The makers of the poison must be punished for their part in confusing him, controlling him, diminishing him. He saw no inconsistency in his liking for pot, because that was a natural herb, unlike the manufactured chemicals. He hadn't found any bad side effects, either.

"Those groups are on the list, Al. They're connected with PETA. PETA supports ELF. Do they have any part of The Cabal? You tell me. I was on my own here till you blew in. I thought I'd find some allies there, but you're right about one thing." Ted dropped his hand out the window and slapped the already beat-up side of Al's car. "They aren't committed enough. The locals don't see the big picture. We need a bunch of freakin' radicals who want to raise a real ruckus, man, not sentimental pussies. A project like this is way beyond them."

"Too squeamish." Al nodded, but his sarcastic smile told another story. "All they want to do is free the puppies and kitties."

"They're still useful idiots, but the main deal is they're idiots. They wanted to picket the building, for Crissake. Now, wouldn't that draw attention? That's something we don't need, especially after that deal went down in North Carolina."

"That was so sweet." Al sat back, a dreamy expression on his face. "It'll be a long time before that facility gets rebuilt. It got fried good."

"The Cabal took credit. But the grapevine says it was your baby. They put you up to it?"

"I ain't talkin', man. I hear a night watchman got fried along with it. Some people got big mouths, but I got nothing to do with it." Al shrugged. "Can Jill get you an ID pass? Does she know anybody she can lift one off of?"

"Her ex."

Al laughed out loud. "You gonna ask him nice? You think he's gonna give you the time of day?"

Ted let out a low chuckle. "Ask nice? You take me for a fool?"

Al's sidelong glance said maybe he did. "Getting the pass will access the soft underbelly of the building, but the guards know what he looks like, and you'd trip their alarms for sure. You got any ideological objections to knocking off the guard?"

"He's nothing to me. It's his fault for being on the wrong side of the war."

"I'm just blowin' smoke up your ass, man. We don't need no freakin' access." Al smiled broadly and patted the dashboard. "All we need is a big old van."

***

Mark stopped by Jill's house after work to pick up Rebel. Fortunately, Ted wasn't home, so the brief visit had gone smoothly enough. He'd found out Ted's last name for Mr. Snyder, so he would be able to contribute that much to the investigation. He didn't believe it would lead to anything. Jill had gone nutty, but not nutty enough to become a terrorist. But if she had, he'd do whatever it took to stop her.

He shook his head ruefully when he saw the bumper sticker posted on Dani's Safari van that read "The more I know of men, the more I like my dog." How much had he contributed to that attitude?

As she had instructed, he parked near the gate. He took Rebel out of the crate in the rear of his Blazer and led the dog past the boarding kennel buildings. "Come on, buddy, let's see what's going on."

An inquisitive Golden Retriever strolled out into its run to watch. The Collie rushed to the fence to touch noses with the other dog. Mark spoke to the Golden but it eyed him suspiciously. Mark called Rebel away and continued through the gate that opened into the training field. The Collie bounded with eagerness, ready for anything new. Mark jogged with him the rest of the way up the path, knowing it wouldn't be enough exercise to take the edge off either one of them.

Various agility obstacles were scattered in a complex pattern on the lawn. He had gone to enough agility trials with Dani to name them and their functions: the teeter, A-frame, dog walk, plus those long pieces of flexible conduit the dogs ran through and a myriad of hurdles. He had deliberately arrived at Dani's kennel a bit before the appointed time to let Rebel familiarize himself with the surroundings. He wasn't sure about the need, though, because the dog made himself right at home, hiking his leg on every blade of grass after a thorough sniffing.

Who was he kidding? His urge to revisit her world was

compelling, like gravity, pulling him inward. He'd arrived early because he wanted to see Dani.

Dog agility would be just the thing for him to try with his own dog. Rebel needed a new interest. So did Mark, and he liked physical activity. He'd played football back in high school and he'd hoped to continue at University of Florida. However, his knowledge of physics led him to conclude that colliding with beefier guys aiming for the NFL was likely to land him in traction.

He recalled his encounter with Dani last Saturday. His interest in the agility trial had nothing to do with the possibility that she would be there, or so he told himself.

He'd proven that by not seeking her out right away. He recognized and spoke to old acquaintances, some of whom helpfully pointed out where Dani had laid out her gear before he even asked. After watching several dogs run through the obstacle course, Mark felt at home again with the high-energy atmosphere. He knew the basics and followed the action with the benefit of understanding what was going on. It was good, active fun.

Mark's level of excitement had risen when Dani brought her Border Collie up to the line. She filled out her shorts with firm curves and looked better than ever. She appeared fit, long legged, leaner than he remembered. Her short, sculpted ash-blonde hair framed a lovely tanned face that makeup couldn't improve. Knowing her drive to excel, he'd expected the dog's wild run to leave her frustrated, but her gravity tugged and he'd gone to speak to her anyway. Though her reception seemed chary, not especially warm, at least she hadn't sicced her dog on him.

He also told himself he was only renewing their acquaintance for the purpose of training his dog. Dani was an excellent trainer with an intuitive understanding of what went on inside a dog's brain. It had nothing to do with the loneliness he felt or his regret for past mistakes. Of course it didn't. Too bad nobody made the kind of Liquid Paper that would allow him to erase parts of his past so he could rewrite them.

He spotted Dani approaching from the kennel. Her red turtleneck sweater, tucked into the tops of her jeans, hugged her breasts. Her purposeful stride quickly brought her close enough for him to see her welcoming smile, and he dared to hope she was actually glad to see him. To his chagrin, he realized she was focusing not on him but on his dog, who was doing an excited tiptoe dance at the end of his lead.

"Hel-lo, Rebel!" She dropped onto one knee to greet the dog. Rebel pushed past her arms and poked his long muzzle into her face, an unusual reaction from him. Typically, the Collie was reserved with people he didn't know. Dani's laugh seemed to come up all the way from her toes as she pushed Rebel back playfully. "You are a lover," she exclaimed, while Mark stood there wishing she was telling him that. And wishing she would let him get his face that close to hers. Then she looked up, her expression shifting to neutral. "So you did make it."

"Dani, I really want to do this. No BS."

"All right, no BS. It's a deal." She gave his dog a final pat and stood up. "Ready to go to work? Did you bring some treats and toys?"

"String cheese and hot dogs." Mark set down his tote bag and pulled out a rope tug. "He likes this, too." He wiggled it in front of Rebel's nose then flipped it aside, tantalizing the dog. Rebel lunged forward, grabbed his end of the toy and hung on and shook, eyes intense, growling with mock ferocity. Mark leaned his weight back and swung the big dog around in a half circle, lifting his front feet off the ground.

"Excellent!" Dani smiled, and that pleased him even though her expression of approval was only a teacher's attaboy. "He enjoys playing with you, which will provide great reinforcement. You mentioned he has some basic obedience. Sit? Down? Stay?"

"Okay, boy, let go." When Mark released the tension on the rope, Rebel let it drop from his mouth but locked his gaze on it, those beautiful tulip ears alert. "We went through a puppy class where we learned do all that stuff." Mark put Rebel through a quick demonstration of their repertoire. To his pride and gratitude, Rebel responded enthusiastically and didn't make a liar out of him.

"I'm impressed. It looks like you've done your groundwork with him, and I like his attitude. We're just going to introduce him to a few things today, nothing at full height. We have to build up to that. The main thing is to make sure he's having fun."

"That's why we're here. To have fun."

Chapter Three

Despite Dani's conflicted feelings about Mark, she suffered no such ambivalence about his dog. She instantly recognized a willing and cheerful spirit wrapped inside a powerful, sound body. The Collie's face radiated intelligence, honesty and an inherent good nature, reminding her how much she preferred dogs to people.

She introduced the two of them to cavalletti work, a rhythmic circular sweep over low jumps intended to teach footwork. Then she had Mark call him through a shortened tunnel and walk him through the rungs of a ladder laid on the ground. She had to admit to herself that Mark seemed to have a natural affinity for working with Rebel. They appeared to be true friends. At least the dog liked him. Score one for Mark.

By the time the half hour was up, she decided that agreeing to train the pair was exponentially better than that relapse of the flu. She managed to get through the entire session without cutting loose with a single snide comment.

After the training session, she invited Mark to her office to take care of the business details. He sat down across the desk from her and pulled a checkbook out of his pocket. Rebel flopped at his feet. "You're a good teacher. I learned a lot in that short lesson," Mark's warm smile radiated his approval.

"So did Rebel. He's quick." Face to face, she found it hard to ignore Mark's guileless appeal. Was she that susceptible? She steeled herself against the danger of liking him too much.

"He looks beat." Mark nudged the dog with his toe. "Hey, you do more running than that when we go jogging. What a weenie." Rebel rolled onto his back, and Mark bent down to give him a belly scratch.

"He's mentally tired. Dogs work hard at figuring out what we expect of them."

"I can relate." His wry smile let her know something

meaningful lurked behind the comment, but she let it go and handed him enrollment papers. She poured each of them a cup from a coffee machine on the file cabinet. She remembered he liked sweetener in his coffee and tossed him a sugar packet.

Instead of diving into the forms right away, he took an appraising look around as he sipped from the steaming cup. She was glad she'd stuffed the worst of her unfinished office work into a drawer. The basic office space had been adapted from the living room. It contained the usual desk, file cabinets, a computer and fax/copier; a functional setup, nothing fancy. She was still in debt up to her eyeballs. The buzz of a blow-dryer from the grooming room, a converted bedroom, told her Kevin was working late. She still had the evening feeding to do.

The white noise of the blow-dryer cut off, and a moment later Kevin stuck his head into the office. From the way he checked out Mark, she was sure he approved. She groaned inwardly, anticipating the ragging that was sure to come. "Uh, Mark, this is Kevin, our groomer."

Mark stood, holding the questing Rebel by the collar, and extended his hand. "Pleased to meet you."

Kevin grasped his hand and held onto it a trifle too long. "The pleasure is all mine," he purred. He stroked the Van Dyke ornamenting his chin. "Dani is too modest on my behalf. I'm the chief canine coiffure artiste for the Critter Ranch."

She rolled her eyes. "Kevin believes in alliteration."

"That's not all I believe in, sweets. Anyway, my last client is on her way to pick up her puppy dog, so I'll finish up and see you in the morning." Kevin cut his eyes at Mark. "Ta." He blew her a kiss and oozed out the door.

"Ta," Mark said to the closing door, a bemused smile crossing his face. He let go of Rebel's collar and retreated back into his chair. "Colorful guy."

"Kevin worked here before I bought the kennel. He's an excellent groomer, and he's become a good friend. The clients love him."

"This kennel is a great setup. You've made quite the career out of it. Is the business all yours?"

"Mine and the bank's. I have five acres, so I hope that will provide a buffer against future encroachment by developers. You know how this area is exploding."

"This much property just outside Orange Park is a great location," Mark said. "Jacksonville has been growing this way for years."

"I was lucky to have the opportunity. I bought it as is, but it didn't require much renovation to bring it up to standard. The people who built it did it right the first time. Air conditioned buildings and covered runs. The kennel was closed for a while and lost most of the clientele. I had to start from scratch."

"You used to talk about doing something like this. I'm glad you found a way."

"Gram made it possible." She felt the familiar stab of sadness that always tainted the enjoyment of her windfall. "She left me enough for the down payment. I live here, too. Crash and Jet are relaxing in my room." She managed a smile. "Let me tell you, it's the shortest commute in town. A few steps and I'm at work, no sitting in Blanding Boulevard gridlock."

"I've avoided some of that since I moved to Middleburg. It's an easy drive to the Commerce Center now that they've cut through Brannon Field Road, but not as convenient as this. I'm happy for you, Dani." He looked and sounded sincere. She felt herself warming to him despite her resolve.

"It's a different life, that's for sure." She laughed to hide her inner war. "I've been busy. Up to my ass in alligators, to tell you the truth."

She caught his gaze shifting as though he were trying to view her rump, then back to her face. "That's good, isn't it? Lots of business?"

"Improving, for sure. But keeping up with the work has been a challenge. Today was a real bear. My weekday kennel helper is off sick so I had to handle the whole kennel. Business is good, so if I seem a little frazzled, that's why. Plus the holidays are coming, and that's going to be a busy time for us." She frowned, realizing she was confiding too much. "Never mind my babbling. You don't need to hear my tale of woe. How are things at Crohn?"

"I got a promotion. I'm running one of the cancer drug labs now."

"Congratulations. Not that I'm surprised. I always thought they underutilized you. Hey, maybe you'll come up with the next breakthrough."

"Curing cancer is my dream in life. We can always ask for a miracle."

"I know somebody who could use one. My kennel guy, the one who's sick."

"What's the matter with him?"

"Lymphoma." A dark look crossed Mark's face, and Dani remembered that was what killed his mother. Time to change the subject. "What about Jill? Is she okay?" Too late, she realized she'd merely traded one miserable topic for another. She did feel truly sympathetic for Jill. The same empathy she'd feel for any suffering creature. Losing a baby had to be rough and might have lasting psychological effects. Not that Jill was all that tightly wrapped to begin with.

"She isn't working right now." Mark's expression was controlled. "Say, maybe she could help out around here."

Dani blinked in disbelief. She wasn't the only one who was stepping in it, conversationally speaking.

"Or maybe not," he added.

Dani smiled sweetly. "Mark, don't ever let anybody say you're completely clueless." Jill was the woman who had triangulated Mark and Dani. The snake who'd hissed sweet poison into each set of ears and pushed them toward their breakup. The spoiler who had taken advantage of Dani's absence while she was away caring for her dying Grandmother, then claimed Mark as her prize. Daily contact with Jill would be unthinkable, and if she couldn't trust her with her man, how could she trust her with her charges? "Actually, doing all the work myself is looking better all the time. Who needs to sleep anyway?"

Mark let out a short laugh. "I guess Jill isn't one of your favorite people any more."

"Damned straight. What happened to her job at Crohn?"

"She got fired."

"No kidding." Dani lifted her eyebrows, surprised. "To get fired these days, somebody has to really work at it. What on earth did she do?"

"It's a long story. You remember how involved she was in dog rescue?"

"Sure. She took some of them home, and when her landlord

found out about it she had to give them back. How could I forget those gut-wrenching trips to the pound? That's where I found Jet."

"I know. He thinks he went to dog heaven."

"I suppose. Actually, the pleasure is mine." Dani recalled the shy, dull-coated pup that responded so gladly to care and attention. "I've continued doing some dog rescue myself. Not formally, but from time to time sad cases kind of thrust themselves at me and I try to find homes for the poor waifs. Right now I'm rehabilitating a sweet Golden Retriever that was abused. What does Jill's rescue work have to do with her getting fired?"

"I was all for the rescue activities, as long as she didn't try to adopt them all. Then she started listening to some animal-rights people. Dani, she's changed so much you might not recognize her if you ran into her on the street. She's attached herself to folks with extreme ideas–"

"Let me guess. A rat equals a boy equals a pig?" Dani wrinkled her nose. "Jill's latest fad?"

"Yeah, one of her many fads." He smiled grimly. "I guess I was only a fad, too, or maybe a convenience. "Animal Rescue Front. That's ARF, for short. Cute, huh? Anyway she objected to the use of lab rats and turned a cage full of the critters loose."

Dani threw back her head and laughed. "I can picture it! Little twitching noses peering out from under every cabinet. Scurrying rats all over the place." Then she thought of the ramifications and sobered. "Must have taken forever to round them up."

"Nope. She set them free outside. We safe-trapped a few with food, and we caught a possum, a feral cat and some wild rats for good measure. Most headed for the tall grass and disappeared. It set back a cancer drug research project by six weeks."

"That's terrible." Dani wrinkled her brow, trying to figure out somebody who valued the lives of rats over the lives of sick kids. She thought about Jim's life-or-death struggle with cancer, and her next reaction was fury. "Didn't she realize what a heinous act that was? Besides, isn't that considered a federal offense? Why isn't she in jail?"

"Crohn canned her immediately. I don't know the status of the legal charges. For me, it was a betrayal. You know how I feel about trying to beat cancer, and she sabotaged our work."

Yes, she knew how he felt about that insidious disease. He'd told her how he watched his mother die of it. "That was when you broke up?"

"Our marriage was already finished." Pain furrowed his brow. "Dani, the Jill you knew wouldn't have done it. She's changed. Gone off the deep end."

"As in gone nuts? I mean, really, freakin' nuts?"

"I'll withhold comment."

"Did it jeopardize your job? Considering she was your wife."

"We were divorced by then. Besides, she wasn't under my direct supervision. Fortunately, nobody seemed to give any credence to the notion I might have been an accessory. It could have been as bad a disaster for me personally as it was for the company. Worse yet for the patients awaiting the next effective cancer cure, and they know my feelings on the subject."

"And it crossed your mind I might hire her? What if she opened all my kennel run doors? Run free, pooches! Sure. Free to get splattered on the road." She suppressed a shiver. "What a nightmare." She recalled her own recent nightmares concerning Mark's workplace and gave him a sharp look. Was there a connection? Was he in some kind of personal danger? Was she crazy for taking the dreams seriously? "Sorry I mentioned her."

He cleared his throat. "What are you doing for dinner?"

"I haven't defrosted anything yet." She glanced at her wristwatch, then back at him. She could have sworn he was holding his breath. "Haven't even thought about it, too busy. Is this an invitation?"

"I could order us a pizza. My treat."

Again Dani weighed cost versus benefit. Free food versus spending more time with Mark. In truth, like it or not, she had enjoyed the evening session with him and his dog. Despite her distrust, the chary discussion of Jill, and the hurt she still harbored, the two of them had easily reverted into easy companionability.

"We've both got to eat," he said. "Who wants to eat alone?"

She'd been running at top speed all day long and was too weary to make the effort to object. Persuaded, she managed a smile. "It's a deal."

***

Left alone after Mark had picked up Rebel for his turn with their dog, Jill sank into a brooding, pissy mood. She kicked one of Ted's dirty socks along the hallway like a limp soccer ball. Now he expected her to do Al's laundry. Just because Ted was paying the rent, he thought he called all the shots.

Jill stared at the door to the room Al had taken over. Al kept the door locked, and the guys had ordered her to stay out. It wouldn't be hard to unlock it and get in. The doorknobs in houses like this weren't made for high security.

She found a screwdriver in the kitchen's whatnot drawer. A little jimmying brought a satisfying click. Simple. She turned the knob and slipped inside.

The room was neat. Actually, Al was tidy as guys went, despite the mound of unwashed clothes he'd brought with him. A laptop computer sat on the dresser, folded up like a tiny suitcase. That was about it, no printer, just a turned-off computer and an aluminum lawn chair pretending to be office furniture.

She didn't dare mess with the computer because Al might know if she did. Ted didn't even want her playing with his desktop in their bedroom without his knowing, though she still played Free Cell sometimes. The two of them had a little fun sending email threats to Crohn and to Mark, but he'd told her to cut it out now that Al was there. He was afraid the letters might be traced since that fascist Patriot Act could invade their privacy.

She looked in the closet, but Al hadn't hung any clothes in it. She peeked into the dresser drawers, but they were empty. Apparently all his clothes were in the washer. The guy believed in traveling light.

Maybe she'd forget to put them into the dryer for another couple of days. Would he even notice he was wearing the same things over and over?

As far as she was concerned, Al could go back to wherever he came from and leave her to work things out with Ted. Or he could blow his brains out. She didn't care which. His arrival made life too complicated, even if he had square-jawed leading-man good looks. She thought he was ex-military, though he was tight-lipped about his past.

When it was just Ted, Rebel and her, they got along fine most of the time. She loved Ted's zeal and fed on his energy.

His textbook-like knowledge of what terrible things people were doing to the environment made her want to set things right. That was why she had let the rats loose, and she was primed for more than symbolic action.

Still, Ted had his difficult moments. He was an edgy guy. At first his energy was a rush, but sometimes when he got really whacked, the craziness blew up in her face. She rubbed the sore spot on her jaw, a leftover from their last argument.

She could handle that, though. True geniuses were entitled to be a little nutty, and his angst intrigued her. Al was the one who really made her nervous. While Ted had too much adrenalin running through his veins, Al's system probably required antifreeze. What cold eyes he had.

She heard the roar of Al's clunker that announced the men were back, so she rushed out of Al's room and locked the door behind her. She stuck the screwdriver into the back of her jeans waistband and plastered a simpering smile on her face so they wouldn't suspect she was up to anything.

She heard them shut the car doors and hurried back to the kitchen to return the screwdriver and check on the pot of chili she'd started for dinner. It smelled pretty good this time because she didn't forget the chili powder. She'd made it with organic tomatoes and she'd soaked and cooked the beans herself. She was proud of her efforts, not too shabby for somebody who'd used to think a Big Mac was a gourmet meal. Now she would die before she ate dead cow.

Ted complained about her cooking, but she was learning. She noticed he usually ate whatever she tried on him. She didn't give a damn whether Al ate her food or not. He made it no secret that he didn't like her. Maybe she ought to break her own rules and get something special for him from the pesticide section at Walmart. Give him a bellyache or worse. What a satisfying thought. If only she dared.

The front door slammed open and she heard the men tromp into the little foyer that led to the living room. She drifted in to greet them, confident that they wouldn't suspect she'd been snooping.

To her disgust, Al carried a package from MacDonald's. The odor of hamburgers and French fries filled her nostrils. The meat smelled better than she wanted to admit, which made her feel a twinge of guilt. Her spirit had renounced eating flesh, but her body hadn't quite gotten the message. She ignored the tempting aroma and reminded herself that meat is murder.

Ted came in right behind him. She threw her arms around her man and kissed him. "I got supper ready, Teddy. Your favorite. Seven-bean chili."

He murmured, "I got dessert," and rubbed hard against her. She glanced at Al, letting him know he wasn't getting anything from her.

Al gave her That Look, the one that said she was stupid beyond belief. Lower than a slug. Something he'd later wipe off his shoe. The look that reminded her of the popular guys in high school who wanted to make out with her at night but were too good to speak to her during the day.

"Dessert! Mmm. I can't wait." She placed the flatware on the dinette table. She spooned herself and Ted bowls of the carefully prepared chili while Al flopped into a chair and unwrapped his burger.

Sitting across the table from Al, watching him eat that hamburger, made it hard for Jill to enjoy her chili. She wanted to punch him in the gut for eating meat in her own kitchen but figured he'd kill her if she did. Ted was dangerous, but Al was downright toxic.

He didn't even say boo to her but looked through her as though she were made of carbon monoxide — invisible yet noxious. The asshole treated her like that and still expected her to wash his underwear.

Jill fiddled with her soup spoon. "Al, how can you come in here and eat dead cow? I thought you renounced eating meat when you joined PETA."

Al chewed with a blissful expression on his face, then swallowed. "Doesn't PETA stand for 'People Eating Tasty Animals?' I'm a card-carrying member."

Ted snickered, and Jill felt her face turn red. How could he fail to back her up? "You think that's funny, Ted? I think you're looking like a hypocrite."

"Chill, Jill." Ted dipped his spoon in the bowl and blew on it. "Al may not be ideologically perfect, but he has other qualifications." He took the mouthful and started chewing.

"Qualifications for what? Thug school?"

Ted spewed some of his chili. Al shot her a calculating look. After Ted recovered, he said, "You'll see. Get off it, okay?" He poked into his bowl again with his spoon, furrowing his brow in suspicion. "Hey, these beans are crunchy. Beans aren't supposed to be crunchy."

"I cooked them for hours." Jill bit down on a bean and almost broke a tooth. Damn. She was never going to get this cooking gig right.

Ted turned to Al. "Hey, give me a bite of that burger, okay?"

Smirking, Al twisted off a small piece and handed it to Ted.

Jill was horrified. "Are you really going to eat that?"

"Why not? It's already dead."

Disgusting. Both of them were hypocrites. Now Al and Ted entered into a low murmured conversation that left her totally out. They mentioned something about Crohn. Evidently they'd been at the complex today. She gathered they were planning some kind of a guerilla attack against the company. That was fine with her, as long as they freed the rest of the lab rats while they were at it. She wished she were a real live computer whiz instead of a lowly data entry clerk. She'd hack into Crohn's database herself and mess the company up good.

Her curiosity got the better of her. "What about Crohn? I hear somebody blew up a drug company up near Raleigh. You aren't getting ready to do something like that, are you? You know how I abhor violence."

Both of their heads moved together as though connected by a steel rod. "What if we did? What would you do about it?" Ted's soft-spoken question was a warning. She'd heard that tone before, and the aftermath wasn't pleasant.

"Just wondering." Her hand crept up to her jaw again and she retreated into herself, not wanting to risk a Ted meltdown.

It had been that way ever since Al blew in early Sunday morning. Confidential looks between them and hushed conversations they didn't want her to know about. Last night Ted didn't come to bed until she'd given up and gone to sleep. He was busy with some project and refused to tell her what it was about. Had he gone queer on her? Now it was just Al and Ted, Ted and Al. No room for Jill. She'd talked to Ted about making Al move out, but he wanted him there, and that was that.

If she weren't scared of getting caught, she'd wait until they went away from the house for a while and see what was on Al's computer.

Men. She was beginning to doubt she could do a thing with any of them. At least Mark was a decent guy who didn't threaten her or make her feel small. Mark was one of the few decent guys she'd ever known. Too bad he was a speciest who didn't view animals the same way she did.

Ted used to hang out with her animal activist friends. In fact that was where she met him. But ever since she'd moved in with him, he wouldn't let her continue to associate with ARF. He seemed jealous of the other members and didn't want her bringing animals home. What a control freak. He told her animals shouldn't be in captivity and ought to run free. She agreed with him in principle, but she was afraid to let Rebel loose. As his guardian, she worried that the dog didn't know anything about the streets and might get hurt. Rebel didn't know how to fend for himself. Even if he did, he would end up killing other animals to eat, and that would make him a killer. Jill let out a deep sigh. It was a complicated issue.

For sure, Ted was starting to worry her. Maybe it was time to think about another change. Was it too late to go back to Mark? If she could, at the same time, she'd get Rebel back full time, and that would be another plus.

She wasn't ready to bolt yet, but it wouldn't hurt to keep an open mind.

Chapter Four

Mark noted Dani's qualifying glance before she excused herself to let out her own dogs for exercise. The pizza wouldn't arrive for half an hour.

His cell phone prodded his waist, so he took it off his belt and set it on the table. Might as well get comfortable. Then he filled out the form and wrote her a check for today's session. He heard her trot up the stairs then run back down with the clatter of the two dogs accompanying her. Doors opened and closed, and he realized he and Rebel were alone in the house for the moment, a condition to which he was accustomed.

She had mentioned that he could drop by and work Rebel on her equipment any time she didn't have a class in session. He had assured her he would take her up on that offer. That meant he'd be seeing more of her, too. That thought filled him with eager anticipation, and he felt better than he had for the past few unsettling, lonely months.

Was it possible they could pick up from the way they were before they they'd split up—at some happier point? Unlikely, but possible? He had given her plenty of reasons to doubt him, and he would be a fool not to realize he had a lot to live down. What had happened couldn't be undone. Nor could he adequately explain it over a cup of coffee, or even over a pizza. He'd take all the blame, of course, even though Dani's coolness and eventual abandonment of him had made the whole debacle possible. If she ever let him explain, maybe she'd see he wasn't the total jerk she thought he was. Maybe she would even agree she owed him an apology, too.

Dani returned to the office, a bounce in her step. "I let Jet and Crash out back to run around. I think I caught Crash just before he decided to rewire my bedroom. I've got some Merlot in the fridge. Would you like that with your pizza?"

"Sounds great." He followed her into the kitchen, admiring her trim backside, Rebel padding alongside. "Where do you want me to put Rebel?"

"You can let him hang out until the food arrives. Then we'll stick him in the grooming room. I don't do begging dogs. He'd end up with my whole dinner." She poured the wine and handed him a glass. When his fingertips brushed against hers, she recoiled as though a spark of electricity had hit her. He caught a look in her eye that resembled panic and refrained from following his urge to reach for her.

"It's just wine and pizza," he murmured. "I don't plan to spend the night."

"Good thing." She took a deep breath. "I don't plan to invite you."

"That's too bad." He sagged a bit, wishing for the old days, when he didn't need an invitation. "But at least we understand each other."

"Do we?"

He took a sip of the wine, ignoring her question, wondering whether it would be any use trying to explain why he had married Jill. As if an explanation would make any difference in the outcome, a misery for all concerned.

She opened a drawer, pulled out some flatware and set it on the counter. Then she opened a cabinet and lifted down a couple of plates. Her actions were still agitated.

"Let me help you with that. Where..."

She nodded with her chin toward the dinette table. "You can wipe it off, in case any dog hair has drifted in."

He dampened a couple of paper towels and scrubbed them across the Formica surface, glad for something to do. Maybe it was time to break away from the gravity, cut and run.

No, not this time. He was going to see it through. She was worth it.

***

The doorbell rang, signaling the arrival of the pizza. Dani welcomed the interruption. It gave her a chance to regroup while Mark went to the door. She restrained Rebel, who announced the deliveryman's arrival by sounding his formidable bark, and redirected him into the grooming room. "You can cool the guard-dog act now, you big fake," she told him as she shut him inside.

Her electric reaction to Mark's inadvertent touch had

astonished her and had set off in her a defensive, bitchy response. His acknowledging the undercurrent hadn't helped. The friendly, relaxed atmosphere was blown, and she wondered whether she would ever be able to view Mark with equanimity. "Get a grip," she mumbled to herself. "Like he said, it's just wine and pizza." She laughed to herself. "If we eyed each other, planted our feet and growled, we'd look like sparring pit bulls."

The source of her angst met her in the kitchen, carrying a large pizza box. He set it on the table. The rich aroma of oregano, cheese, tomato sauce and pepperoni teased her senses and reminded her she was famished. She sat down and fiddled with her wineglass while Mark served the gooey, steaming slices onto their plates. She watched him set an extra slice aside on his own plate. "I'm letting this one cool off for Rebel," he explained.

"As long as you don't share your wine with him. He's too young to drink." Glad for the detachment the banter provided, she carefully forked a bite-sized piece off the edge of her slice, slipped it into her mouth and savored it. The food soothed her jangled nerves. Maybe she was suffering from low blood sugar, and that's why she overreacted. Yeah, that was it. It couldn't be that she still felt some sort of animal attraction for Mark. Or could it?

"In that case, how do you feel about his eating tofu and soy milk?" Mark asked.

She swallowed. "Tofu? Soy milk? I guess a little won't hurt him." She wrinkled her nose. "You feed him that?"

"Not me. Ever since Jill went vegan she's been trying to make one out of him, too."

Dani frowned. "Dogs are carnivores, but they aren't picky. I hope she lets him eat something besides soy."

"Whenever he stays with her, it's vegetables, fruit, and bread cooked with sprouts."

She sighed. "It's not the best thing for him. She needs to forget the vegan bit and add meat. A dog's digestive system isn't geared for a vegetarian diet."

"That's what I thought. He's not very peppy after I get him back from her, and he seems to have digestive problems. I thought it might be the beans." He waved his hand across his face and grimaced.

"The *Blazing Saddles* reaction."

"You got that right. She says it's unethical to feed him meat and wanted me to switch him to the same kind of diet. I won't do it, though."

"Good for you. Maybe a couch potato pooch would do okay on that kind of diet, but a canine athlete needs to eat high-quality protein. I hate it when people inflict their political agendas on their animals." Dani rolled her eyes. "Maybe she ought to get a bunny rabbit instead of a dog."

"I hate sharing custody with her," Mark said softly. "It isn't just that I want him all for myself, though I really do. But I can't stand her boyfriend. She seems to be under his thumb and that's where she got her crazy ideas. Sort of like she's gotten mixed up with one of those nutty cults. Have you heard the rhetoric? Like he'd be happier as a free street scavenger than as an enslaved house dog?"

"Yeah, eating garbage is so satisfying. And getting squished on the road is the ultimate liberation."

Mark looked grim.

"You don't think she'd do that, do you?" Dani asked. "What about leash laws?"

"She wouldn't care about a mere law. You know Jill. Such a free spirit and all that. I have to work for a living. I can't be there all the time on the chance I'll catch her letting him run loose."

"Why doesn't she just let you take him? What's in it for her?"

He shrugged. "She has a lot of emotion invested in him, too. After she miscarried, I thought it would be a good idea to get a pup. As a distraction, you know. She wanted a rescue, but I wanted something more predictable, and I was interested in showing. Of course you can't show a dog of unknown background in conformation. I searched the Internet and found Rebel. We raised him together. At first she was as excited about his success in the show ring as I was, though later she complained that I was exploiting him." The bitter smile returned. "Also, I suspect she enjoys keeping her hooks in me."

Dani considered that. She and Jill used to be friends, or was it just that Dani felt sorry for her because she was so darned needy? Wherever Jill went, she seemed to use up all the oxygen.

Nonetheless, she wouldn't be a girl to cross. No, she'd gotten at Dani with a preemptive strike. "What are your chances of getting him full-time?"

"I'm working on it. But try convincing some judge that it's abusive to feed beans to a dog, and he'll laugh in your face."

"What about your vet? Can he make some kind of statement?"

"I have an expert, she has one, too. She even has magazine articles that back her up. Recipe books for vegetarian dogs. You name it." He speared a stray slice of pepperoni with his fork. "She tried to turn me into a vegan, too, but as you can see, she failed."

"And since you're a law-abiding kind of guy, you have to play the game and let her have her visits."

"If she pushes me too far, she'll find out just how non-law-abiding I can be."

His delivery was tight lipped and serious. So deadly serious that she felt a shiver of apprehension.

***

After Mark left, Dani finished the evening feeding and carried out other nighttime kennel chores. When she went into her office to shut down the computer, she noticed a cell phone in its case sitting on the table. Mark must have left it there. He hadn't changed a bit. She smiled, remembering how she always used to check behind him. Left to his own devices, he would leave bits and pieces of himself scattered around the universe. Funny how he could be so competent at his complex, precise and demanding work, yet lose personal stuff. How much help was Jill in keeping him organized? Heck, Jill needed a keeper herself. That must have been some pair. No wonder they couldn't make a go of it.

She knew the drill. He would miss the phone later and realize where he'd left it. She turned it off to save the battery and made a mental note to call Mark about it later if he didn't beat her to it.

She went outside and threw the frisbee to her own dogs to give them a good game of chase, now that she finally had some spare time. She had precious little of that and needed to create more. She was exhausted but too wound-up to sleep.

She decided to check on Jim, as he'd been occupying so many of her thoughts all day. Sure, it was inconvenient for her that he was off sick, but he was the one suffering the effects of illness and the horrific side effects of treatment. She picked up the phone on her nightstand and punched in Jim's number, feeling apprehensive. He picked up after the first ring. "How are you doing?" she asked.

"I'm okay now, but I can't believe I went through all those tests voluntarily. From time to time I thought I was in Saddam Hussein's torture chamber." He chuckled. "Did you really call to inquire about my welfare, boss lady?"

"Sure. I'm always interested in how my favorite employee is faring." His light attitude gave her some reassurance. "Find out anything useful?"

"If they did, they didn't say so. They mumbled about several possibilities and want me to come back later this week."

She didn't like the sound of that. "How are you feeling? Any better?"

"Bored with being sick."

"Then you're tired of sitting like a lump and watching daytime TV?"

"Nah. I'm using my time better than that. I've been knocking 'em dead on my Playstation."

"Sounds productive."

"For your information, I've been catching up on my school assignments, too. I dropped a couple of courses, but thought I could still handle one."

"That's more like it. Say, this is an SOS call. I can't keep up. How about coming in to answer the phone and handle the clients, at least? Maybe doing a few light jobs, whatever you can manage. If you get to feeling lousy, you can lie down in the back bedroom. The pay is still wonderful. Think you're up to it?"

He didn't even hesitate. "Sure. I'll give it a try. I'll come in tomorrow morning."

"Thanks, Jim. See you then."

She set the phone back in its cradle, hoping Jim was going to be all right. The college kid was a big help. He had a sure way with both animals and people. Because the treatments made him sick and weak, she would still have to do all the active or heavy jobs. It seemed so unfair somebody like him should be struck at a young age by such a horrific disease. Such a fate should only happen to bad people.

At least she wouldn't be running back and forth between the house and the kennel all day. Simply concentrating on one task at a time without constant interruption would greatly increase her productivity. Some of the tension drained from her body.

Unfortunately, not all of it. Despite her spate of unease, she had enjoyed Mark's company. Too much. Most of the time being with him felt cozy, like wrapping herself in a quilt by the fireplace. She wouldn't hesitate to trust him with her business or her animals, but he'd long ago proven she couldn't trust him with her heart.

And she wasn't sure she trusted her heart to stay out of danger.

***

It was well after dark by the time Mark drove through the woods and into the garage. His house couldn't be seen from the road, and he liked the privacy, even if it did get lonely sometimes. He didn't care for the new homes being built, boxes on postage stamp yards, where one could stand in the side doorway and throw a cat through the next-door window. At least he had a decent amount of land and no immediate neighbors. He enjoyed living in the one of the few rural areas left in the metro area. His job paid well enough for him to afford the luxury.

He fed Rebel, then turned on his computer. While the dog slurped up his supper and eagerly scraped his metal bowl from one end of the kitchen floor to the other, Mark sat watching the screen go through the upload procedures. Although he had turned his scant information on Ted Sturkey over to Snyder, he wanted to do his own checking.

A Google search turned up a website that chronicled depredations by eco-terrorists. Arson, bombings and vandalism on the west coast. A British firm targeted, its employees threatened, stalked and assaulted. Some of the threats were transmitted by email. He read through those posted on the website, and a chill ran down his spine. The hate mail resembled the messages somebody had sent him.

Could Jill or her boyfriend have anything to do with it? He'd already run down the email messages but didn't recognize their source. After talking to Snyder, he'd been able to forward them to the security chief's computer, as he hadn't cleared out his "deleted" folder in about a month. Maybe a law enforcement agency had the means to track them.

Eco-terrorism wasn't news to him because in his profession it was always a possibility. But he was a scientist, not a cop, and he'd never taken the problem personally or given it much attention until now. He resolved to do a little more investigating on his own. Was Jill's activism about to take a darker turn?

He checked his email and found no new hate mail, just spam and one of those scam messages about an African prince who wanted his bank account number, supposedly to send him money. Or more likely to clean out his account. He forwarded it to the FBI before he hit the delete button.

Rebel wandered in from the kitchen, licking his chops, and shoved his long muzzle under Mark's hand, scoring a free caress. The dog's presence brought back to mind his evening with Dani.

"What do you think, buddy? Am I wasting my time trying to crawl back into Dani's good graces?"

The dog belched, then licked his chops again. Mark grabbed a rawhide bone off the end table and tossed it across the room. He kept lots of chewables around to divert the young dog from eating his furniture. The coffee table legs bore scars from Rebel's recent puppyhood, and he still didn't trust Rebel alone and loose in the house. If he got bored he might munch the couch.

Rebel scrambled after the rawhide, skidded to a stop and snatched it off the hardwood floor. He pranced back to Mark, crunching it happily between his powerful jaws.

"Hey, look at it this way." Mark accepted the damp chew toy and waggled it in front of Rebel's nose. "If we spend more time with her, you'll have another person making a fuss over you."

He had made the blunder of his life by giving up on Dani and agreeing to marry Jill. He shouldn't have listened to Jill when she said Dani was no longer interested in him. He should have hung onto Dani with bulldog persistence, but Jill had made him think they were finished. Their re-acquaintance had convinced him his feelings for her were as genuine now as they'd always been. He'd been confused, overwrought, and stupid, stupid, stupid for getting mixed up in Jill's problems. Dudley Do-right had nothing on him for dim-witted virtue.

Who was he kidding? He was taking too much credit for

virtue. He'd drowned his sorrows then poured his confidences into a willing ear. One thing had led to another, and the mutual pity party morphed into a wedding party.

Had Dani shown the least inclination, he would have gladly picked up where they'd left off. But she wouldn't allow that. Not yet, maybe never. He'd made that dumb crack about spending the night with her and only increased the tension. He knew her well enough to realize the damage was possibly irreparable from the start. The old attraction was there, but not the intimacy. She had erected a brick wall between them, and he wasn't sure how to go about tearing it down or if he could. Even then, would they merely remain old friends?

He'd continue seeing Dani at the training lessons, keep working with his dog, and set about dismantling the wall one brick at a time if he had to.

He tossed the rawhide again, then glanced at his watch. When he saw that it was only ten o'clock, he decided to try another step in the demolition process. He fended off the playful Rebel and reached for his cell phone, because he'd programmed her number in it. The place on his belt was empty. He knitted his brows in annoyance then remembered taking it off in Dani's office.

That made a convenient excuse for calling her, anyway. It would also make an excuse for him to see her tomorrow. If he were a more devious sort, he should have forgotten it on purpose. He should have thought of that before. He took out the phone book, looked up her number, and punched it into his landline.

Dani's voice answered, and he savored the softness of it.

"Mark here. I hope I'm not disturbing you."

"I'm still up." Her voice projected warmth, no annoyance at all. "I found your cell phone. Is that what you're calling about?"

"You did? Good. It did come up missing." He thought of her lying in bed in a skimpy nightgown, and the sound of her sexy voice crept through his body. "Besides, I thought of something I forgot to ask you."

"What?"

"You said you teach evening agility classes. Do you mind if I come and watch from time to time?"

"Sure. No problem. Bring Rebel along and you can work with him before or after class. If you want to join, I have an opening.

Rebel would progress faster that way."

"Great." He hesitated. "I really enjoyed the lesson today. And getting together afterwards, too."

"Yeah, the pizza hit the spot. Thanks again."

He thought he heard her swallow.

"Class is tomorrow night at seven," she continued. "You can pick up your cell phone then. There's one Monday night, too. Come whenever you can."

"See you tomorrow." He ended the connection, grinned like an idiot and picked up the rawhide for another toss. "Rebel, old buddy, you're going to enjoy these training sessions if it kills you."

***

Jim did make it to work the next morning, much to Dani's relief. He came up to the run she was cleaning. "Want me to park myself in the office and handle things there?"

"Does a frog jump?" She grinned at him. "You look great." She wasn't lying, either. He'd lost a few pounds, but his color was good and he didn't really look outwardly sick, just his lanky self, a kid with a good-natured, freckled face. He must be having a good day.

He lifted his baseball cap, revealing his thinning crop of sandy colored hair. She also noticed the haggard look around his eyes. "Will you still say so when I'm bald as a cue-ball?"

"It makes you look older. Distinguished. Besides, it'll grow back. In the meantime you can pretend you're a skinhead."

"They say it'll grow back."

"You feeling okay?" She made it sound casual.

"Until I get the next round of chemo. I think they're going to try something new, though. The drug companies keep coming up with different experiments, and I'm the Guinea pig."

Dani thought about Mark's work at Crohn, and the setback Jill caused. If she already had reasons to dislike Jill, this was the topper. Jill's stealing Mark had only affected the three of them. When Jill released the lab rats, she hurt a lot of people in Jim's situation. "Maybe the next one will be a magic bullet."

"Let's hope." He rewarded her with a cheerful smile. "I'd better get to work, boss lady, before you decide to fire me."

She watched him walk to the office and offered a silent prayer for the brave young man.

***

Mark arrived the next evening an hour before Dani's class was scheduled, giving himself plenty of time to work with Rebel. With no one else there yet and distractions at a minimum, he planned to practice the moves he and Rebel had learned the night before. Though impatient to get to the real agility work, clearing jumps and obstacles at full height, he knew it would be best not to rush Rebel.

Dani was already in the field, working Jet. Sidelined in a crate, Crash crouched, his eyes following the action. Mark greeted him as he walked up with Rebel, but Crash appeared so focused on Dani's moves he hardly acknowledged him.

"I don't blame you," Mark said to the dog. "I like watching her, too." He shoved a tote bag aside to make room to sit on the crate. He let the dogs sniff noses through the wire grid while he enjoyed the view.

Dani paused after a short run with Jet, pulled out a long, floppy tug toy hanging from her belt and played an exuberant game with him. She glanced up at Mark, grinned and waved. Then she left the excited Sheltie on stay in front of a jump where he stood barking in excitement. She gave him a ready-set-go and raced him to the obstacle.

Naturally the fleet little Sheltie outran her, flew over the first jump bar and let Dani maneuver him through a complex series of jumps. Sheltie-like, he barked his way through the course. She appeared to dance with the dog, using her movements and an economy of motion to direct him. Mark found it hard to take his eyes off her. Dani's firm body moved in elegant ways that teased his senses. Less enticing but equally spectacular was Jet's ability to twist in midair, changing his direction before he hit the ground in response to her body language. Mark felt his pulse quicken as he watched the beautiful performance. The two seemed to move as one, linked by some bond of understanding beyond the visible.

Dani rewarded Jet with another round of tug. She walked over to Mark, Jet frisking alongside, and Mark rose to meet them. "You two looked great together," he told her. "That's how I want Rebel to work with me."

She smiled, breathing hard, her face slightly flushed. She

looked radiant, relaxed and friendly. "You'll get there. Then you can get Crash under control for me." She laughed out loud then picked up the tote bag atop the crate, dug inside and produced his cell phone.

"Thanks." He clipped it onto his belt. "I'm glad you found it."

"Business as usual." Dani gave a noncommittal shrug while Jet and Rebel circled and sniffed, making the usual unaesthetic canine getting-to-know-you maneuvers, nose to butt.

"Why don't you guys learn to shake hands instead?" Mark reached down and patted both dogs, then glanced up at Dani. "Maybe you just have to convince Crash it's better to get qualifying scores than laughs."

She looked at the Border Collie thoughtfully. "Yeah, he seemed to get off on playing to the crowd, didn't he?" Crash dug furiously at the door to the crate and barked, obviously wanting to join the party.

"I heard you call him a class clown," Mark said. "You were on the money."

Dani let Crash out of the crate. Needing no further invitation, the Border Collie sprang out and body-slammed the Sheltie, knocking him over. Jet rolled back to his feet and the two of them wrestled, growling, whirling and air-snapping with their jaws in a mock fight.

"Enough rough stuff, guys. Somebody's going to need a chiropractor if you keep that up." Dani grabbed Crash by the ruff, allowing Jet to scoot inside the crate. He drank from a small stainless steel bucket clipped inside.

His tackle dummy gone, Crash sprinted into the practice field, making a joyous looping outrun around the perimeter. Dani stood up and watched him for a moment, then called out his name.

Crash spun in his tracks and raced back to her. He threw himself at her feet, panting, eyes locked in a Border Collie stare. "Good boy." She smiled at him, and Mark could have sworn the dog grinned back, lips pulled back exposing shiny, sharp teeth.

Dani looped a lead around Crash's neck. "I'll hold him here for a bit while you work with Rebel. You don't need the distraction he'd create."

"You don't have to stop your practice for me," Mark said.

"I bought myself a little time for my own dogs today. Jim came into work and took some of the load. He felt well enough to answer the phone and kept me from having to be in two places at once."

"Okay. Tell me when I'm doing something dumb."

She laughed. "Hey, I'm a positive trainer. I'll try to catch you doing something right!"

It was about time for him to get something right, and not just with dog training. Too bad she wasn't around a couple of years ago to keep him from making his dumbest move of all. He took Rebel out to the field. Keeping Rebel on lead, he practiced letting the Collie find his rhythm over the circular series of low jumps.

Dani called out. "Now give him a treat, change sides and go the other way." He reversed direction, rotating in the center of the circle of jumps. Rebel may not have understood the logic of what he was doing, but he clearly liked the activity. Moreover, he enjoyed praise and the freeze-dried liver Mark slipped him at intervals.

Mark practiced a few more obstacles that were conveniently set at lower heights than standard in preparation for tonight's beginner's class. When Dani called out, "He's had enough for now," he gave Rebel more treats and jogged back to where she stood.

"Why don't you let him rest for a bit, then work him with the class like we discussed?" Dani suggested.

"Sounds good." Mark spotted an exuberant chocolate Labrador Retriever approaching from the parking area. He was digging in like a sled dog while the substantial lady holding onto the other end struggled to keep her balance. "Looks like your students are starting to arrive."

Dani glanced over her shoulder and smiled wryly. "I can see who's in charge of that team. I wonder if the Lab drove them here?"

"I hope he's not dog aggressive." Mark stepped in front of Rebel, blocking him from the Lab's view. "He's strong enough to break loose. Rebel won't pick a fight, but he'd sure finish one."

"The Lab just wants to play, and most of the others are nice. But watch the Jack Russell. He's a buzz saw, jaws like a piranha, and his owner seems to think it's cute. I've been trying to reeducate both of them. Should be worth it because the dog is talented." She slipped the lead off Crash. "Tell you what. I'll give the wild child a quick run through before everybody shows up."

She trotted onto the field with Crash and put him through the same routine as Jet. Mark wasn't surprised to note that Crash made even the quick and competent Jet look like a sluggard. Dani looked great with both dogs. Mark liked the idea of learning by observation and, as a bonus pleasure, watching Dani.

He could get used to this. He sure could.

Chapter Five

At the end of class, after Dani's students drifted away, Mark stayed. She hated the part of her that was glad he'd come and hadn't left yet. That part had lost its pride. And what of him? Why was he hanging around as though training his dog was just an excuse to be there? She had to give him credit, though. His efforts with the Collie seemed to be wholehearted.

"Rebel is working well with you," she told him. "He's going to be a great agility dog. His only competition for star student is the Australian Shepherd."

Mark bent over to give the Collie a vigorous rump-rub, and the dog's back arched into the kneading, squirming with pleasure. "He's having a good time. So am I. Thanks for letting me come."

"Teaching beginners class is a kick. In a few weeks, provided the owners do their part, the dogs will understand well enough to run a short, easy sequence off lead."

"Great." Mark laughed and gave Rebel a dismissive pat. "Okay, that's enough." He looked at her and said, "How long before we really know what we're doing?"

"You'd be surprised. All at once it seems as though the training and the practice suddenly click in. The learning curve seems to accelerate in a geometric progression."

He regarded her, a slight smile playing across his face, his eyes studying her. "My theory is, the instructor has a lot to do with making it happen. I noticed something while I watched class. You've still got that talent. I thought so before, now I'm sure of it."

Was he getting ready to ply her with a dose of flattery? She felt herself stiffen and go on guard. "What talent?"

"You can read those dogs like you know just what they're thinking."

She shook her head suppressing the start of panic in her chest, and she wasn't sure why she felt that way. "That's crazy. It's just experience and observation, that's all."

"I always thought it was more than that. You're extra intuitive. Like the way you understood the Aussie's problem. He wouldn't go around to his handler's right, and you pointed out he thought he was always supposed to be on her left."

"That doesn't take mind reading." She felt a thread of relief that she could easily explain that one away. "He's obedience trained. Formally trained dogs need some retraining sometimes because their routines are so rigid. That's not any intuition of mine at work."

"You do stuff like that all the time." He wasn't letting it go. "It's like you get inside their skins. Like you're connect–"

"Ooeeoo!" She forced a laugh to hide her discomfort that he'd nailed her secret. Not that she had anything to hide. She was being truthful when she told him she didn't feel any special insight. "Don't make me sound like I live in the Twilight Zone. It's all observation and experience, like I told you."

"Have it your way." He let out a laugh, too. "I think you have an extraordinary gift with the dogs. Did you have dinner yet?"

Fortunately, as before, a change of subject came to the rescue. At the mention of food, she became aware of how empty her stomach felt. All she'd eaten the entire afternoon was a slice of cheese. Who had time to eat? "Actually, no."

"That makes two of us. We could run up to the Woody's Barbecue on Blanding Boulevard. How does that sound?"

Her mouth watered and she had to swallow. Was spending more time with Mark jeopardizing her emotional equilibrium? Or was she secure enough to be comfortable with him? She had to admit she still liked being around him, even if he was a jerk. Not that he was acting like a jerk. Okay, she was hungry and he was good company. She knew better than to succumb to the little trembles of attraction she felt from time to time. Why should there be a problem taking him up on his offer? He wouldn't mug her or steal her virtue, such as it was. "Sounds good. Let's put up the dogs and get something to eat."

***

Mark sweetened his iced tea then took a long drink while he waited for his order of ribs. The restaurant was a rustic dive, comfortable in a basic way. Country music blared from a jukebox located near the counter. He was glad to sit farther away in a semi-isolated booth. By this late hour, the dinner crowd had thinned. He and Dani shared the place with a mere handful of customers. Their server, a perky young woman with a name badge stating "Jennifer" brought them their drinks, hastily scribbled down their order, and disappeared into the kitchen.

Mark reveled in the sight of Dani sitting across the scarred wooden table. She emptied a packet of pink sweetener into her iced tea and stirred it with her straw. Then she lifted the wet end to her mouth and licked off the drop that had collected there. The sight was too provocative for comfort. There ought to be a law against her looking so sexy.

But being with her felt good. And right. He wanted to somehow bring her into line with his way of thinking—that they ought to be back together. Should he continue to hang around her hoping for the best or come right out and state his case? Over time he'd realized that he'd been used and manipulated by Jill. Probably Dani had suffered the same treatment at her hands. He understood the distrust Dani felt, and he had to admit it was partially justified.

Jill had been artful in driving them apart. Casual quotes, things Dani had supposedly said, actions that may or may not have taken place, had caused him to give a more critical look to his relationship with Dani. They had drifted apart before her physical removal to Tampa. Nonetheless, Dani's apparent desertion bothered him enough to send him into an emotional bender.

Too many Margaritas later, he'd fallen for the rest of Jill's stories and let himself be persuaded into marriage. He knew it was unwise but thought it could work. He ought to get a Darwin Award for that one.

He was ready to stand up to Dani's anger and try to work through it. He could let her beat up on him a little, get it out of her system. He was strong enough to absorb her hurt and anger. After that, things would be cleaner between them.

Or else she would tell him to get lost. If she did, he would have to deal with it. But she wasn't going to shut him out so easily this time.

He squared his shoulders. "Dani, we used to have a good thing going, don't you agree?"

"I thought we did once." She jammed the straw back in her

glass, jawline hardening, suddenly testy. "I guess I was wrong."

"I think we still could."

She glared at him and tapped the edge of the glass with her index finger.

This is going well. He took a lighter tone. "Dani, as a biochemist, I'm an expert on the subject, and I can assure you the chemistry is still there."

"Sure. Cyanide." She rolled her eyes. "All right. Time to clear the air. There are other agility trainers around here and some are big stars. Stuart and Pati Mah, Nancy Kleinhans, the world class folks." She ticked them off on her fingers. "Then there's Lynne Wetherell, Lori Lewis and Vicki Ford, who are all more experienced than I am and have titled MACH dogs. Trish Smart, too, if you don't mind her methods. You came to me, and you've been sniffing around like it's more than dogs you want to play with. I'd have to be blind and dumb not to see that."

"Don't sell yourself short. Besides, you were the one who offered to let me bring Rebel more often."

"So I did." She frowned. "He's a good dog. He deserves to do well. In my not-so-humble opinion, I think I'm the right sort of trainer for him, at least for a start."

Never mind his owner deserved nothing but a kick in the teeth, was the part she left unsaid. Okay, he got that. "Dani, I'm sorry things worked out the way they did. Believe me, I never stopped caring about you."

She let out an unladylike snort. "Yeah, sure. You threw me over two years ago and blind-sided me by marrying Jill. That's some kind of caring, all right."

"There's more to it than that. Anyway, you made it clear you didn't need me, Dani. Jill did."

"Yeah, poor old needy Jill. She always did need something. Trouble is, she progressed from borrowing lunch money to stealing men."

"Dani, you convinced me we were history. I wish I'd fought harder for you, but after all the rebuffs—"

"I was going through a really bad time. I needed space."

"Like you wanted me in outer space. I was willing to provide support. You pushed me away."

"My grandmother was dying." She glared down at her drink,

stirring it fiercely with her straw. “That’s what mattered right then. Couldn’t you understand what I was going through?”

“I don’t recall it exactly like that. You started cutting me off before that. Before you went to Tampa.”

“Maybe I figured if you liked Jill so much you could have her.”

“I wasn’t interested in Jill, just you.”

“You weren’t interested in her, but you married her?” Color came into her cheeks and her eyes snapped blue fire. “That’s a real howler. Try again.”

“I’ll explain that, too. Give me a chance here.” Mark took a deep breath. “Look, I tried to call you while you were gone, but you wouldn’t return my messages. Then when I did get through, you acted like you were in a hurry to get off the phone.”

Dani looked away.

“I came down to see you, and you gave me maybe an hour of your time. Even then you weren’t with me. You were somewhere else. You started cooling off even before that. It looked to me like things were dead and over between us.”

Dani shifted her gaze farther away, out the window. “I didn’t mean to leave that impression. I was preoccupied. In a fog. I don’t remember that time of my life very well. I was probably in a depression. Not really myself.”

“So not yourself that you were completely absent. You didn’t give me much hope. What was I supposed to do, stalk you? I’m sure you would have loved that.”

She winced. “I needed time.”

“You never discussed that with me. Dani, you seem to be psychic, but I’m not.”

“Neither am I. Anyhow, you sure jumped on Jill mighty quick. Of course she got what she was looking for.”

“Have you ever got that wrong. Jill and I were friends. You knew that. And I wasn’t sneaking around on you. You acted like you wanted to call it quits. Then you took that leave to Tampa, and stopped talking to me. Jill was a good listener, and caught me at a weak moment.”

“Oh, I get it. You just wanted to marry somebody, and she was handy. I blow back into town, and you two are already locked in holy matrimony.”

"It was more complicated than that."

She smiled sweetly. "I just can't wait to hear about all those itty bitty complications."

"I'm sorry, Dani. I've never really apologized properly. I know I'm late, but I'm doing it now."

"Damn straight you're late."

He bit back a sharp retort. "It wasn't all about you, Dani. There was a reason I didn't explain. That was the way Jill wanted it, and I had to respect her wishes. She had this idea people would talk about her if they knew what was really going on."

"Like they weren't talking anyway? The twit had a reputation, you know." Dani cocked her head to one side. "Does it still matter to you what she wants?"

"It's old history, now." He let out a long breath and said in a low voice, "Dani, she was preg–"

Dani jerked upright. "You mean you were doing her at the same time we were—"

"No, no. It wasn't my kid. I never—"

"Then why did you marry her if it wasn't yours?"

"She told me she was going to get an abortion. I couldn't let her do that."

"Abortion is legal," Dani snapped. "Unpleasant, but legal."

"Not just unpleasant." He drew himself forward, locked eyes with her and planted his elbows on the table. "Dani, my mother wasn't married when she had me. She could have done the same thing, and I would have been discarded like a dirty nosewipe."

"Oh." A flicker of something - maybe the beginnings of understanding - played across her face. "I didn't know that. But your mother was married."

"Her husband is my stepfather, though he's been a real dad to me. I never met my bio father." He allowed himself a self-deprecating smile. "Though I'm sure he was brilliant and handsome, if unethical. I gather he was a nominally married doctor who got carried away with a patient, that being my mother. Anyway, I thought I should carry forward on the good deed."

"That's the story?" Her expression wasn't exactly lit up with belief and empathy. "Did you love Jill?"

"Love her? Not the same way I felt about you. I guess I was trying to save a small part of the world. Maybe watching my mother die gave me passion for saving a life. It didn't work out so well. She miscarried two weeks after we were married. She heaved a great big sigh of relief and started acting about as unmarried as anyone could. I tried to hold it together because I took my vows seriously. We were a terrible mismatch, but I'm not ashamed of what I did in good faith. Regretful, but not ashamed."

"Mark, all this nobility gives me a pain. You know, one woman's white knight is another woman's cad." Dani leaned forward just as he had, closing the space between them. "I cared about you. Really I did. And you dropped me like a hot rock without a word of explanation. It's hard to look at you without remembering."

"Hindsight is great, isn't it?" He let out a bitter laugh. "Marrying Jill was a mistake. And I should have tried harder to put things right with you first. It seemed hopeless at the time, and I wanted to do a good thing, misguided as that turned out to be."

Dani smiled grimly and looked almost sympathetic. "No good deed goes unpunished. Isn't that the way it works?"

"Now I'm trying to put a few things right, if that's possible."

"I guess we both blew it," Dani admitted. "When I think about it, I didn't give you much reason to stick around. I had some doubts about us. I seem to recall Jill fed me a lot of crap that made me wonder about you. Then you confirmed the suspicions."

"Fell right into it, didn't I? What was she telling you?"

"Stories not worth repeating. Seems there are enough hurt feelings as it is."

"On second thought, thank you for sparing me." He recalled Jill's insinuations that Dani had lost interest in him, that she didn't appreciate his qualities, that Dani's flight to Tampa and unwillingness to give him so much as the time of day proved it. She had him convinced Dani had found another man but wouldn't admit it. Now he was convinced that none of it was true. He sat back, relaxing now that he'd leveled with her. "I'd like to start over from square one. Is that possible?"

The server bustled up and set their dinner down in front of them. Mark knitted his brow, annoyed she'd chosen that moment to interrupt.

"You need anything else?" the girl asked.

Mark shook his head and so did Dani. Finally the waitress

flitted away.

Dani stared down at her steaming plate. The aroma of grilled pork and barbecue sauce filled the air. “I guess we’ll be seeing each other anyhow, since I’m coaching you and Rebel. I don’t know about anything more. I have to sort things out.”

“Fair enough.” Mark unclenched his hands and took a calming breath. “This time I won’t be so easy to run off.”

***

How had the conversation taken such a twist? Now Dani was the one who felt like apologizing. “Maybe I did treat you cooly. But I never meant to run you off. Nor did I imagine you wouldn’t be there for me.” She studied his face for signs of deceit, but his level gaze held no contradiction. At such times as this a gift for reading minds would be useful, but she had no insight, only a longing that he spoke the truth. “Mark, did she tell you who got her pregnant?”

His gaze was steady. “I believe there were several candidates.”

“That’s our Jill.” Dani studied the ceiling. “Anybody I know?”

“Maybe, maybe not.” He raised an eyebrow. “Does it really matter to you?”

“Not if you’re telling me the truth.”

“I never cheated on you. She was pregnant by someone else.” He spread his hands over the table. “That’s the truth.”

Dani had to concede it was possible he could be telling the truth, considering Jill’s free and easy attitude toward the opposite sex. Jill had often invited Dani to accompany her to nightclubs. Dani tried it once. A wolfish pack of men lurked at the entrance, inspecting every woman that came though the door. She was forced to run a gauntlet of leers to get inside. Then she ended up driving home alone after Jill hooked up with some drunken stud. She’d had similar offers, but the thought of bedding a bourbon-soaked stranger repelled her.

Dani had always been selective. To a fault, Jill had told her. Looking back, was it any wonder that Jill would covet a catch like Mark.

“Tell you what, Mark.” Suddenly weary, Dani scooped up some baked beans onto her fork. “I’m highly food motivated, and

I sure could use some positive reinforcement right now. Truce?"

"Sure. Truce." His face relaxed into a pleasant smile, no longer looking wound tight as a spring. Actually, he looked good enough to eat. The thought almost made her choke. She washed down an errant bean with a mouthful of iced tea.

He picked up a rib and bit off a chunk, a primal move for a refined sort of guy. Eating spare ribs lent itself to leaving off the Miss Manners bit and getting down to basics. She hadn't gotten down to basics with a man since she'd split up with Mark. That was fine with her. Not that she'd sworn off men; she was satisfied with her life and didn't need the drama.

He swallowed. "Have you been seeing anybody?"

Was he reading her mind? "I've been so busy I haven't been out looking. I dated a guy a couple of times, but he didn't like dogs, so that went nowhere fast. I figured there had to be something wrong with him, and he thought I was nuts. Talk about dysfunctional."

He laughed out loud. "No kidding. You really went out with a nonbeliever? Did you think you could convert him?"

She managed a smile. "I converted you."

"I already liked dogs. Remember? I even went to agility trials with you."

"There's another one this weekend." She picked up a French fry and nibbled the end, remembering the fun they used to have together at trials. She would end each day physically tired from contributing her labor to the trial effort and from running her dog. After a quick supper and a beer, she and Mark would find enough energy to enjoy a quiet, intimate evening together. Was it possible she could ever care for him enough to risk getting hurt again? "It's back at the Jacksonville Dog Fanciers property on Morse Avenue. They'll need ring crew, in case you want to volunteer to help. There'll have a raffle for the workers."

"Great. What time?"

"Our first walk-through is at seven thirty. I'll have to be there by seven to get situated."

"I'll meet you at your place and follow you over so I can help you unload your gear."

"You don't need to do that."

He grinned "Maybe I want to."

Maybe she wanted him to. It would be pleasant to have an

extra pair of hands to help her haul her dogs, her crates, her chairs, and her cooler under the arena. Strong, knowing hands. *Stop that, Dani*. "Okay. Bring Rebel along and let him get used to the atmosphere."

He frowned. "Jill is supposed to have Rebel for the weekend. In fact, I have to take him over there tomorrow after work."

"That doesn't make much sense, with you working and her out of a job. How are you going to ever show him? All the trials are on weekends."

"When we settled things, she was still working. Besides, like I said, I didn't have a very good lawyer." He let out his breath. "He was a friend of a friend. So much for the value of referrals. I've tried to get Jill to work things out, but she'd rather keep things difficult. Not much I can do about it until I take her back to court."

"Which is expensive," Dani pointed out.

"And even more annoying than the status quo, for right now." He stabbed into his coleslaw. "Never mind. I'll find some way to fix it."

She didn't doubt he would. The new Mark seemed more determined than the man she remembered, the one that didn't stick around when the going got tough. Maybe he was worth exploring, as long as she kept her defenses up, kept things cool, and didn't let herself get burned again.

Chapter Six

The next day, Dani had just finished the morning kennel chores when she spotted a UPS truck pulling into her driveway. She met the khaki-clad deliveryman at the gate, filled with the optimistic, childlike glee she felt whenever deliveries came.

"You brought me presents?" She flashed a smile at him. "And it isn't even Christmas yet."

The UPS deliveryman laughed and pulled the three cardboard packing boxes out of his truck. "Presents? They're from Pet-rite. How exciting can that be?"

"You'd be surprised. They sell cool stuff." She signed for the packages, and he helped her carry them to the front door. Inside, she set them on the bench in the front room next to the retail displays. On inspection, she found them difficult to open with her bare hands, because the packer had used about a mile of reinforced tape. She went into the grooming room to find a knife.

Kevin was just taking a cocker spaniel off the table and coaxing the cranky little dog into a crate. He carefully closed the cage door and glanced at her. "What's up, sweets?"

"We just got some supplies in. Didn't you order something, too?" Dani opened a counter drawer and pulled out a box knife. "Want to take a look?"

"Sure." Kevin followed her into the front room, where she slashed the tape and opened all the boxes.

She pulled out the packing slip and sneaked a look at the bottom line. "Thank goodness for plastic money. Maybe I can get this stuff sold before the bill comes due."

"If you're short on cash, you don't have to enter so many agility trials," Kevin pointed out.

"It isn't just an addiction. It's business. I have to be a shining example to my students." She checked the packing slip against the contents. She had purchased a bunch of bright plush squeaky toys, a package of colored tennis balls, and a package of rawhide chews.

In the second box, the heaviest, was a gallon jug of shampoo. Kevin pulled out the shampoo and set it aside, then unwrapped a newspaper-sheathed pair of thinning shears. He held them up, opened and closed them, and nodded his satisfaction. "These are mine. And the shampoo."

Dani checked the third box and found the colorful packages of freeze-dried dog treats, stainless-steel food bowls, plus collars and leashes of various types. "I'll get Jim to put price tags on these and add them to the display. Did he go to lunch?"

Kevin nodded. "I was about to take a break myself."

Dani flopped into a chair. "Me three." She dropped her head back and circled it to get the kinks out of her neck. The phone rang and she checked caller ID. It was a blocked number, so she let it continue to ring. When the answering device picked up, a voice from a finance company left a number for her to call back.

"That's about the van. I missed the last payment but should get it caught up this month. With the new clients, the cash flow ought to get better."

"So how is your client, that is, friend, Mark doing?" Kevin moved a box and settled on the bench. "Has he been back to see you?"

Dani stretched her arms over her head, a tension-relieving maneuver. "Just to train his dog."

"That's all?" Kevin's eyebrows shot up in disbelief.

"Oh, we had supper together last night. Over at Woody's."

"Aha." Kevin's eyebrows remained at a peak. "Does Dani have a boyfriend?"

She glared at him. "No way. But he does want to take up where we left off."

"Which is where?"

"What is this, Twenty Questions? It's a long story."

"Pardon me," he pouted. "I don't mean to pry."

She sighed. "It's okay, Kev. I probably ought to talk it out with somebody. After Jill's perfidy, I don't trust any woman friends. I figure of all my friends, you probably have the least conflict of interest."

"That's so." A whimsical smile crossed Kevin's face. He reached up and fingered his earring. "He's hunky for a straight. I'd go for him myself if I thought he swung that way. But Mark has hetero written all over him."

"Yeah." She laughed out loud. "That's what I mean. Even if you made a pass at him, he'd turn you down."

"At least." Kevin cocked his hip theatrically. That made Dani laugh harder, which felt great. Liberating. Yeah, this was what she needed to do, even if it did seem as though she was gossiping.

"I'm seeing him in a professional capacity. That's a given. I'm not going to run him off as long as he wants to help him train his dog. After all, I'm not rich enough to turn away a paying customer. If his dog turns out as great as I hope, he'll make a great walking advertisement for my classes. After all, agility training is what I do."

"And very well, indeed."

"That's debatable." Dani grimaced. "Crash gives me a daily dose of humility. Anyway, Mark and I used to be an item. We did everything together." She explained about the blowup. "He gave me his justification, such as it was. I believe him, and it cleared up some things if he's really being truthful. I blame most of it on Jill, though he and I both were too naive enough to catch on to her wedge tactics. I guess he thought I had ditched him, and Jill was right there needing a husband like yesterday, so he felt sorry for her and married her. That lasted about as long as you'd expect, and now he wants me back."

"Do you want to give him another chance?"

She stared into space. "I don't know."

"Is it something you have to decide right this minute?"

"I suppose not."

"Then why not play along? Give him a try. Make him earn the right. What have you got to lose? Does he have any good points, besides being dishy?"

"I didn't just love him. I liked him, too, and that was the best thing. I used to work at the same company where he's running a lab. I was a lab tech but on a different project. Jill was a data-entry person in my department." Dani drummed her fingers against her thigh. "He was kind of shy but really sweet, and the better I got to know him the more I found out what a good heart he has. And depth. He's no dummy either. Went to UF, then got his master's degree from Georgia Tech."

Kevin cocked his head. "All that and he isn't a nerd? Killer."

"I've found myself falling back into that comfort zone, just like nothing ever happened, then something reminds me about him and Jill, and I get all testy and bitchy. I guess I might possibly believe him, that he wasn't fooling around behind my back. But there's that little doubt. She sure was after him, and got him in the end. Maybe I can't really trust him."

"Maybe, maybe not?"

"If I can believe him, he wasn't really playing games. I was out of the picture. And I really did pull back from him. I see that now."

"Have you forgiven him?"

"I'm not sure." She hesitated. "No, not entirely. And should I go back with somebody who dumped me? I do have my pride, you know."

"Ah, yes. Pride."

"With that and several bucks I can get a cup of coffee at Starbuck's, right?"

"Exactly. I repeat. What have you got to lose? You don't have anything else going on, unless you're more secretive than I think."

"So who says I need anybody?"

Kevin snickered. "I know you've been doing nicely on your own. Still, you shouldn't be afraid to have some fun. Take him for a test ride. You don't have to marry him."

"I'm not that way. I don't sleep with just anyone."

"I gather he isn't just anyone."

She frowned. "I don't take these things lightly."

"Dani, I want the same things you do, with a slightly different inflection. My partner took up with somebody else, and I had a hard time with it. Now I'm looking around, and I don't like much of what I see. It's a hard road. Some of those boys are so crazy they have permanent PMS. Bars are the worst. I mean, you can get some ugly buggies there."

"I never was interested in pickups." Dani crossed her index fingers and held them up in front of her face. "Far be it from me to go there."

"You're a wounded soul, Dani. I'd like to see you heal."

"Tell you what. Maybe I was wounded, but I'm fine now, thank you very much. I don't need any healing."

"Whatever you say, sweets." Kevin didn't sound convinced. "When are you seeing him again?"

"He's coming to the agility trial next weekend. He's meeting me here in the morning and we're going together."

Kevin laughed. "Aha. You have made a decision. You're going to try him on for size after all."

"We're just going to an agility trial." She thought about it some more. "Sometimes he makes me feel good and sane, whenever I can forget what happened between us. I blamed him, but he made me realize I didn't give him any reason to stick around. I did shut him out. Oh, I don't know why he really did what he did. I know what he told me. That didn't make me like it any better. But I guess he had his reasons. Yikes." She rubbed her temples. "I think my head is going to explode."

"Cut to the chase, Dani. You're not going in blind. You know the score, and you know what happened last time. Consider him on probation. If he does something you don't like, then you can give him the old heave-ho."

"That makes sense. Maybe that's how I should look at it. Put him on probation."

"Only if you think you can ever forgive him. If not, tell him to take his freakin' dog somewhere else to train. You don't need the cash that bad."

"I haven't smiled this much lately. Come to think of it, except when I've been with Mark. Thanks, Kev."

"Don't mention it. If boss lady ain't happy, nobody's happy." Kevin picked up his shampoo and scissors. "Back to the salt mines, sweets."

"I'll let Jim take care of this stuff while I do my paperwork." It would be a good time to spend a little time with her rehabilitation project, Dolly. Dani went out to the kennel and brought the Golden into the house, noting the dog seemed content enough inside. Dani sat at her computer desk and let Dolly roam while she checked her email and entered invoices. Dolly wanted to cling to her side, nosing her mouse hand so the curser repeatedly skittered all over the screen. Dani laughed the first few times, but the dog's interference became an annoyance.

"Look here, Dollface, you've got to quit messing me up. I've got work to do and you've got to learn to just hang out and let me be."

Dolly started to crawl up into Dani's lap. It didn't work well because the big dog weighed over sixty pounds and didn't fit. Her big front paws hung over Dani's thighs and her chest rested hard across them. Dolly tried lifting a rear leg up, pedaling in vain until she gave up and hung there in between Dani's mid-section and the computer desk.

Dani grabbed the loose skin at both sides of Dolly's head in a rough caress. "Geez. You're as needy as some people I know." Dani took a few moments to give Dolly the extra attention she craved. The poor dog was a love sponge, soaking up kindness insatiably.

"Okay, enough. Lie down and let me work or I've got to put you in a crate." Dani gently shoved Dolly off her lap. Dolly stood looking at her, unwilling to leave her side.

Jim returned from lunch, sauntered in and looked around. "Hi, Dani. Want me to tag and display the new stuff?"

It had become her habit to look him over and try to figure out how he was feeling without coming out and asking. At the moment, he appeared about the same as usual since he'd started the treatments. "That's the plan."

"What's the matter with that Golden?" he asked. "They aren't usually shy."

Dani glanced down at Dolly and saw a changed dog. Jim wasn't a scary looking kid, soft spoken, not imposing, but Dolly's face had taken on a worried look as she stared at him. She crouched down, fear evident in every line of her body. Dani sensed the dog's deep uncertainty.

"She's afraid of men."

Jim kept his distance and squatted down to lower his profile. "Hey, pup. What's the matter?"

"The guy that had her before was pretty mean," Dani said. "I guess she's generalized it to all guy types."

"We'll have to convince her otherwise." Jim pulled a Snausage out of his pocket and offered it to Dolly. She sniffed it but wouldn't take it. He broke it and tossed her half of it. Hesitantly she took it off the floor and vacuumed it in a gulp, watching him warily the whole time. He offered her the other half but she turned her head away, eyeing him sideways.

"If she won't make up to you, she's a hard case," Dani said.

"We'll have to go slow and let her decide to be friends. Kevin can help, too. The more men she can make friends, the better."

"Are you sure it's abuse?" Jim left his hand out, holding the treat loosely in case Dolly decided to take it. "Some dogs just don't like certain people."

Wordlessly, Dani reached down and parted Dolly's neck fur to show him the burn scars. Jim whistled. "Shock collar cranked up to "vaporize"?"

Dani nodded. "It's amazing she isn't downright psychotic."

"I'll give her lots of space, then." Jim sat back on his heels. "Let her make up her own mind."

"Good idea. It takes a lot to get somebody's trust back."

After Jim left the office to turn his attention to the products in the front room, Dani thought of Mark and smiled wryly to herself. She could relate to Dolly's attitude. It would take more than a few Snausages to coax her into trusting Mark again. She watched the wary dog, understanding that it was Dolly's decision whether to accept that Jim wouldn't hurt her. Just as Dani had to be utterly convinced Mark wouldn't turn on her.

"Dollface," she said under her breath. "I think we have a lot in common."

Chapter Seven

Mark drove slower as he neared Jill's neighborhood. She had moved into the boyfriend's abode, a house located in an older subdivision that had mostly gone rental. He always dreaded this trip, leading up to another separation from his buddy Rebel. Worse, after expressing his doubts to Dani, his concern for Rebel's well being had increased. He was tempted to just take the dog home and make Jill come get him if she really wanted to. But he still felt that being cooperative would get him better leverage when he started pushing for more weekend time with his dog.

As for Rebel, he didn't seem to mind either way. The dog had the bad taste to be wild about Jill. Mark heard him shift positions within the crate at the rear of the Blazer. If he had shown any sign of fear, no court order could have forced him to let Jill ever take him.

Jill's misbehavior at Crohn had given him another headache that wouldn't go away. The idea that a bombing in North Carolina and Jill's non-violent sabotage might be connected seemed far-fetched to him. He'd gotten no word from security as to whether the threatening emails had any connection with Jill. But he was going to keep his eyes open for anything suspicious. The idea of more damage to his life's work infuriated him.

If Crohn wanted to press the issue, Jill might not get off with the mere loss of a job after all. Unauthorized release of lab animals could be considered a Federal crime these days. If Jill were truly in trouble with the law, he wouldn't make much of a character witness.

While it was tempting to pile on in hopes of getting Jill thrown into jail and taking Rebel permanently out of her hands, he hoped that kind of vindictive behavior was beneath him.

He'd been excited about the prospect of fatherhood, even though the kid wasn't his. Jill's miscarriage seemed a bigger disappointment to him than to her, judging from her attitude. After her health was cleared, he wanted her to try again, this time with him being the genetic father. She had no interest. Maybe that was for the best, because now he had serious doubts about what kind of mother she would be.

Jill didn't seem to like the constraints of marriage: to be specific, marriage to him. After she got involved with the ARF group, Mark suspected she was on the prowl, because she spent so little time at home. Then one day he came home from work early and found her in the sack with that cockroach, Ted Sturkey. Probably he shouldn't have been surprised, because he'd known Jill was indiscrete from the beginning, but he'd hoped she would settle down with him. Wrong. He'd sent them both packing. It was a scene straight from a melodrama, and he would have thrashed Ted if the scumbag hadn't been willing to slither away, Jill in tow.

Mark filed for divorce the next day. A few days later she committed her act of sabotage against his project. It was as though she'd gone out of her way to hurt him. Yet he had to make nice with her so he could have his dog part of the time. It wasn't right or fair, but he was trapped in the partnership.

At least Dani had listened to his justification, weak though she seemed to think it was, and they'd leveled with each other. More than ever he appreciated her no BS approach. It was a jolting contrast to Jill, who was less than straightforward in her dealings with him

Maybe he could salvage something out of the mess if Dani continued to see him. At least she hadn't dashed his hopes. No, she had seemed reasonable at the end. He wouldn't force his luck and try to press her to accept him. He knew her well enough to realize that if he pushed her, she'd push back. Harder. Best to give her space and let her sort it out.

At Jill's house he pulled into the driveway behind the blue Yugo but didn't get out of his Blazer right away. An unfamiliar car was parked next to the Yugo, a weathered Honda Civic carrying an Oregon license plate. Determined not to overlook anything remotely suspicious, he wrote down the tag number. Then he sat and stared at the run-down brick house, wanting to back out and leave, taking Rebel with him. He certainly wouldn't go inside if Ted was home. So far Mark had been able to avoid committing assault and battery, but all bets were off if he had to deal with Ted.

Fortunately, the house had a privacy fence around the back yard, so Rebel had a safe, shady, if overgrown, outdoor place to exercise. Mark had walked the fence line and tested the boards to make sure it was secure before letting Rebel off lead the first time. He was mildly surprised that Jill and the boyfriend hadn't acquired a collection of animals, considering their activist interests. But then, he suspected that much of their zeal was of a political nature rather than an altruistic one. He was aware that some of the animal rights zealots used that as a front for their generalized misanthropy. Beyond his natural dislike of the guy, Mark figured Ted for some sort of mentally whacked fanatic.

He heaved a deep sigh and unfolded himself from the driver's seat. He went around to the rear of the vehicle and opened it, then unlatched the crate and snapped the lead to Rebel's collar. The Collie jumped out of the Blazer, and knowing the drill, started toward the house. Mark picked up a bag of dog food from where he had stowed it and carried it along.

When he got around to the front of the Honda, a pair of feet sticking out from underneath the car moved, and out squirmed a man, not Ted. The guy stood up, wiping his grease-smudged hands on a dishcloth, staring at him and Rebel. His posture underwent a subtle change, as though he were wound and ready to spring. The look in his cold blue eyes, if not openly hostile, was not friendly. Instantly on the alert, Rebel paused and watched him, head and ears held high. He didn't act friendly either.

"Hi," Mark offered. "Car trouble?"

"Oil leak. But I got it fixed." The accent was anywhere USA, or maybe the west coast.

"Good for you." Mark nodded and continued to the door, not caring to male-bond with this particular individual. Any friend of Ted's was probably not somebody he wanted to know.

Jill opened the door before he had a chance to knock. Like Dani, she greeted Rebel first. The dog acted delighted to see her, wiggling and wagging and pawing at her while she made smooching noises at him and dug her fingers into his short ruff. Then, in typical Collie fashion, he turned back and rubbed his muzzle affectionately on Mark's pant leg as though reassuring him that he wasn't being completely disloyal.

Jill had let her auburn hair grow long, and it hung lank and straight. These days she resembled a refugee from the '60s. She had dark circles under her eyes and looked tired, as she did every time he saw her lately. Sometimes he thought he spotted bruises on her. The vegan diet must promote weight loss, because she had gotten bony. Rather than fashionable, she looked famished. She was still a good-looking woman, but her latest persona, a careless Bohemian style, appealed to him less than the more modish look she had cultivated before they were married. Not that any of it mattered to him, because he was no longer sexually attracted to her, certainly never as much as Dani. She had killed what interest he had ever felt with a series of insults and an outright attack on his project.

She took the lead away from Mark, and he handed her the dog food. "I'd like for you to give him what he's used to," he told her. She set the bag down by the door, curling her lip in distaste. She didn't say anything, but by that look and action she made it clear Rebel wouldn't be eating any of it on her watch.

"I'm serious," he told her. "He doesn't do well on what you've been feeding him."

She shrugged. "I hear you. But I don't agree." Obviously she didn't give a damn what he wanted her to do. Nor had she ever.

"I've started training him in agility, and he needs to be in top form. So I'd appreciate it if you'd do this one thing for me."

She looked interested. "Agility? You ever see Dani?"

"I saw her at a trial. She's a professional trainer now."

"Really?" Jill smirked. "As in personal trainer?"

He heard Ted's voice from inside the house. "Jill! Cut the crap and come in here."

She shot a nervous glance inside. "Look, I gotta go." Was she afraid of Ted? It figured. He was a scary guy. Heck, he looked like a terrorist. Maybe he was one. Mark tried to see inside, but the foyer walls blocked the rest of the house from view.

Speaking of scary guys, the one who had materialized out from underneath the car mumbled "Excuse me" and brushed past them into the house.

"Congenial." Mark couldn't tell if she caught his irony "Friend of yours?"

"He's Ted's guest." Jill leveled a disgusted look after the guy. "His name is Al."

"By the way, you've got the phone line tied up most of the time and I can't get through. Are you on the Internet a lot?"

"We've got cable."

"What's your email address?"

"Why do you need that?"

"I can't reach you by phone, so I'll email you instead."

Ted appeared behind her, scowling. "You got no business talking to her, pal, so get the hell off my property."

Mark pointedly ignored him. "I'll come back and get Rebel Monday after work." He gave Rebel a final pat and went back to the Blazer. He heard Rebel bark once. He ought to take the dog back, court order or no court order, instead of trusting him to that pair. He turned around just in time to see the front door close, and he heard the lock click. How was he supposed to do that, storm the place? Break and enter? Get shot by Ted?

There wasn't anything else he could do right now, so he drove away to his own empty house.

***

Jill led Rebel into the living room past Ted, but he clapped his hand on her shoulder. "What's with Frankenstein?" he demanded.

"He was just dropping Rebel off, that's all."

"Why'd he want your email? What's going on?"

"Nothing."

Al glanced up from his spot on the couch, where he was fooling with a cell phone. He had its parts strewn all over the use-scarred coffee table. "Maybe he wants to prove you clowns were the ones sending him those nasty-grams," he said.

Ted snorted and let go of Jill's shoulder. "No way. He can't do that."

Al snorted back and returned to fiddling with the electronics.

"Put the mutt outside," Ted snapped at Jill. "Last time you kept him inside he ate one of my Birkenstocks. Dogs shouldn't be in the house anyway. It isn't natural."

She moved to comply and slipped by the TV screen, where a commercial about a prescription drug was doing its spiel.

"Damn." Ted threw a screwdriver at the screen, and Jill flinched. It clacked against the glass but bounced off without breaking anything. Thank goodness the screwdriver was lightweight and had a rubber handle, or it might have imploded the TV. "There's that damned Crohn again, pushing their crap." He continued snarling obscenities at the TV while Al chortled at his outburst.

Rebel pinned his ears back and widened his eyes. "Ted, quit yelling," Jill said softly. "You're scaring him." Then she opened the sliding glass door to the backyard and unsnapped the lead. Rebel willingly ran outside. She watched him trot about, sniff and mark his territory. She had so wanted her dog and her man to get along, but it wasn't happening. At first Ted had tried to make friends with Rebel, but the dog wouldn't have any of it. Rebel didn't greet Ted with the same enthusiasm he reserved for her. Or for Mark, she had to admit. The dog avoided Al, which merely showed his good sense. Jill suspected Al was afraid of Rebel, which gave her secret satisfaction.

Ted returned to the project he and Al were working on, which seemed to mostly consist of taking things apart. She had asked him before what it was about, and he'd never explained it to her satisfaction. Maybe she could work up enough nerve to look in Al's computer yet.

Ted looked up from the cell phone and pinned her with his gaze. "I don't want you talking to him."

"Even when he brings Rebel over?"

"Just let him keep the damn dog. Problem gone."

"Rebel's half mine." Of all their arguments, this was one she refused to concede.

"If you go back to Vaughn, I'll kill both of you." Ted said it casually, which really creeped her out.

She didn't show him any fear, just said in a quiet voice, "Who said I'm doing that? You're my man, Ted. Nobody else."

"See that you remember and don't forget. Hey, get that screwdriver for me, will you?"

She bent over, picked up the tool and tossed it to him.

This wasn't the first time he'd made noises about her giving up her share of the dog. Nor would Ted let her bring home any other animals. He said animals belonged outside, in the wild. It seemed strange that anyone who crusaded for animal rights didn't enjoy animals, but that was Ted. His ability to support them both adequately with his stipend and without having a job was another thing she didn't understand but a talent she was not inclined to question.

She ignored Al and sat down on the couch next to Ted, close enough for their thighs to touch. If she made cozy with him he wouldn't talk so mean. "What did I miss? Did Dr. Phil set that oversexed guy straight?"

"His whiney woman is the one he ought to set straight." Ted mumbled into his lap, toward the dismantled cell phone. "What's she got to complain about?"

"Guess he's not as good as you are." She stroked his thigh, wanting to make peace and at the same time hoping Al got an eyeful. Now Dr. Phil was back on, chatting with a new couple. "Screw this. Stupid idiots." Ted grabbed the remote and pushed buttons. "What's on CNN?" The talking head came on with the CNN logo on the screen yakking about some politician. Text crawled along the bottom but Jill didn't bother to read it. She would rather watch Dr. Phil's dysfunctional couple, but it was Ted's TV and he made sure she understood that. She felt her eyes glazing over with boredom.

Ted let out a whoop. "Look at that! They did it again!"

"Did what?" Jill zoned back in and squinted at the text, something about a bomb at a chemical plant in New Jersey.

Al leaned forward in his seat, a rare grin splitting his face. "Blew the hell out of it, I'll bet. The Cabal is hitting them up one side and down the other."

Ted sprang up and punched both fists into the air. "It's the first salvos of the revolution. We're on the cutting edge." He turned around and high-fived Al.

"Hey, Jill. Go get us a couple of beers. We've got to celebrate."

She obeyed, getting one for herself as well. The guys were suddenly ready to party over that news item about the explosion. It added to her suspicions about what they were up to and why they kept her in the dark. She handed Ted and Al their Natural Lights and eyed the wires and plastic things on the coffee table. "You guys making a bomb?"

"You think my last name's Kaczynski? Like I'm the freakin' Unibomber?" Ted took a swig and grinned savagely at her, giving her the idea he liked the comparison. He ought to, considering he was always quoting from the "Unibomber Manifesto." About how being a liberal wasn't good enough, how only radicals could fix the out-of-balance world.

She cocked her head and studied him. With his wild long hair and beard, he might have used the famous eco-terrorist for a model. His hot, dark, bottomless eyes sometimes stared holes right through her. When he got fired up about something, he got really itchy and jumpy. Ted was both dangerous and exciting. Sometimes too much so, and her admiration was lately tinged with fear. "Actually, you look a little like that other Ted." She was careful to smile when she said it. "Did you name yourself after him? The main difference is, you take showers and change your clothes."

"Yeah, and he'd still be out there doing his thing if nobody ratted him out." He laughed, but his eyes were serious. She laughed with him, relieved his mood has swung for the better and didn't take offense.

From the corner of her eyes she saw that Al wasn't laughing but watching the two of them, eyes lazily half shut and unreadable. Most likely they were building a bomb, and knowing Ted's hatred for Crohn Life Sciences, she figured the company complex was the target.

As long as nobody got hurt, she supposed it was a good way to stop the unethical treatment of laboratory animals. Certainly Ted would make sure the animals escaped and weren't blown up by the explosion. Or would he? How was he going to manage that?

The idea of explosives scared her, too. She felt a queasiness that somebody would get killed. She could put faces on those people. The friendly security guard at the front gate, whom she'd dated a few times. He was most likely the sperm donor for the kid she almost had. Thank goodness that situation resolved itself. The receptionist, whose family pictures were pinned all over her cubicle, had always been nice to her. Even Mark had helped her through a bad patch before he got boring and she found more excitement with Ted. None of those people were on her most-hated list. Plus, she might get the blame. Maybe she should somehow warn them they might get blown up.

Should she discuss it with Ted? Dare she? If she ratted them out and they ever found out—

She shuddered.

More and more she wanted to bail out of their arrangement. Her feelings lately oscillated between bored and frightened. Heck, Mark may be boring, but he never hit her, even when he went ballistic over finding Ted and her in the sack. She had become nothing but a scared mouse, like the creatures in the lab, hanging around the fringes of life, unable to pursue her own interests.

Leaving Ted should be a simple matter, except for his threat. No legal ties complicated their relationship as they had with Mark. The only sticky parts were where would she go to live, and how could she afford to eat? She didn't have another man to fall back on.

Before she left, she had to figure out those annoying details. Again her mind settled on Mark despite Ted's threat. Would Mark be interested in taking her back? That might be worth checking out. For the time being, she would sit tight, watch him and Al tinker with their gadgets, avoid getting him mad, and make some plans.

How mad would he get if she did leave him? Was he serious about killing her? In her darker moments, she was afraid to find out.

Chapter Eight

The morning was cool and crisp, another promising day for an agility trial. Dani loved this time of year. A northerly breeze gusted, bringing in more dry air and rustling the nearby pines.

She stood with the course map in her hand, watching the ring crew arrange the obstacles in the pattern the judge had designed. Mostly she was watching Mark, who was one of the volunteers. He had a precise way about him, just like he did at the lab. She liked that earnestness, the tidiness and care he took about most things. As far as she knew, marrying Jill was the most haphazard thing he had ever done. Besides forgetting his cell phone.

So far the agility trial had gone well, but it was still early. Her first run with Jet was successful enough to qualify, which gave him a leg toward his Advanced Gamblers title in this particular venue, United States Dog Agility Association. She had come to expect good things from Jet and always seemed to be able to anticipate what he was going to do. He held more advanced titles under American Kennel Club rules, as Dani had concentrated her efforts at the more numerous AKC trials.

Crash's turn was coming, but predictability was hardly one of his strengths. Being a rookie dog, Crash was entered in Novice, so the closing sequence would be easier than the one required of Jet. Nonetheless, she still had to stay behind an orange surveyor tape and direct him from a distance. The opening sequence was a freestyle affair, with her choosing the route. Each obstacle performed would add points toward a final score.

Mark swung his long legs over the orange snow fence that served as the ring boundary and took his place next to her. As he entered her space his arm brushed lightly against hers, and she was acutely aware of the contact. She stood her ground, ignoring the pleasant tingle. What she couldn't ignore was how fine he looked, the breeze riffling his hair, his blue windbreaker contrasting with the deep brown of his eyes. His jeans clung to his legs, accentuating the trim cut of his frame.

"What do you think?" he asked. "We didn't have to reset anything but a few number cones and the ground tape."

She shifted the diagram so Mark could view it with her, but grew increasingly conscious of their closeness and his body warmth. She imagined his heat radiating through her skin. Having Mark close by gave her a rush, as though he carried an electrical force field with him. She half expected the hair on her arms to stand straight up. Trying to ignore the uninvited sensations, she stepped away an inch, but somehow the gap closed as he moved closer. She reined in that idiotic part of her that wanted to cuddle up to the man and neck.

"The judge might tweak it a little anyway." She tapped the graph against her open hand, forcing herself to concentrate on the next run. "I'll use basically the same plan I designed with Jet. I hope Crash doesn't make a fool out of me. I should just face the fact I entered him in these trials too soon. He isn't ready for the pressure."

"Have a little talk with him first." Mark grinned. "Bribe him. Tell him if he behaves you'll buy him a steak. I'll grill it for him."

"Too bad it wouldn't work. He only knows a few words of English, and 'behave' isn't one of them." Dani wished she didn't have this little flutter of Mark-inspired nerves starting. Plus the anticipated run with Crash, a risky business, had her psyched out. Trish Smart had entered her promising young Australian Shepherd in this class, too, and would probably outperform her and Crash by a mile. Dani had great respect for Trish's handling skill but wasn't sure the regard was reciprocal. Truth was, they just didn't hit it off, and she felt as though Trish was always gunning for her.

That seemed absurd. One-upmanship wasn't a typical sport among Agility competitors. Both of their dogs could qualify or not, regardless of their relative placement. Winning the class was just gravy. The meat was in passing the test.

Of course she wanted to do well. Agility trials were her showcase. If her dogs made her look good, it gave her credibility as a handler and trainer. If Crash made her look like an idiot, it could cost her clients.

She didn't know whether she felt great or just plain nuts. Maybe she would start howling soon. She should start doing breathing exercises to calm herself.

Mark had spent the morning at the trial, but they were not entirely together because she was busy with her dogs while he helped set the courses. Mark had helped her unload her gear when they arrived and together they'd erected her Easy Up canopy. They'd set the crates and chairs underneath their personal shady spot. He'd been there to congratulate her after Jet's successful run. That support had meant something to her. She had to admit that so far she enjoyed having him there even if his presence did keep her off kilter.

"It's only a game, right?" Mark slipped his arm around her shoulders and gave her a squeeze. "He'll do fine. Even if he acts up, he'll entertain the crowd. That's not the worst thing in the world, is it?"

Dani was so focused on his touch that she felt she might jump out of her skin, but she didn't want to show him her reaction. "A close second, anyway. Some of my students are watching. Such a shining example I'd give them, huh?"

"Then give them a lesson on dealing with the unexpected and about controlling as many variables as you can."

"Good one, Mark." What he said offered surprising wisdom. But then, he was a sharp guy, or she wouldn't have taken up with him in the first place. "I'd better walk the course." She left him and joined the influx of exhibitors moving into the ring. She shook off her angst and concentrated on studying and memorizing how she planned to handle Crash.

As the purported brains of the team, she had to know both her route and the most advantageous route for Crash. She and her competitors would be given five to ten minutes to plan their strategy in real time and space, each with the strengths and weaknesses of their particular dogs in mind.

The opening sequence would allow 30 seconds for Crash to perform as many obstacles as he could before the whistle blew. Then Dani was required to send Crash into a simple loop through a tunnel, across the A-frame, and over two jumps from behind the tape. If she could just get him to pay attention, it ought to be an easy run for him.

One thing she had to remind herself: If he didn't have a good enough score to earn a leg toward his title, there was always another agility trial. Sometimes she wished she weren't so competitive, feeling as though she had to prove herself in every single round. It was her pride again, getting in the way of enjoying life.

Trish was doing the same thing as her, pantomiming her motions as she worked with an imaginary dog. "Nice Aussie you've got," Dani told her when their paths crossed. "He ought to eat this course up."

"Thanks." Trish smiled, or was it a smirk. "You running that crazy Border Collie today?"

"Crash," Dani acknowledged.

Trish shrugged as though under-impressed. "I watched him last weekend. I thought he could have used a woodshed moment."

"Really?" Dani hoped the astonishment showed on her face. "I won't risk destroying his enthusiasm by playing whack-a-dog."

"Whatever works." Trish shrugged again, a clear signal that she believed nothing Dani tried could possibly work. "I see you're back with that guy you used to hang around with. What's his name, Mark? You two an item again?"

"We're friends." Dani felt a shimmer of uncertainty. "Actually, he's a client, now that he's got a dog."

"Does he? Well, good luck to you."

Dani excused herself, not wanting to burn the rest of her course familiarization time with small talk or sarcasm disguised as well wishes. What had she ever done to Trish to invite such thinly veiled scorn? Maybe the two of them just weren't meant to get along.

After she squeezed in a couple more walks around her planned course and listened to the judge's briefing, it was time to clear out. Mark stood waiting for her outside the ring. "Got it?" he asked.

She smiled and gave him a thumbs-up. "Now let's see if Crash cooperates." She shrugged. "If he doesn't, I'll try to keep my sense of humor. Laugh to keep from crying."

"Atta girl."

Small dogs ran first, starting with the toy breeds jumping eight-inch hurdles. The ring crew would work through the heights, raising the bars for each height division, up to Crash's class: dogs that had to clear 22-inch jumps. Dani planned to use the next fifteen minutes or so to warm Crash up and get him ready to perform. She hoped it wouldn't turn into a comedy act.

She returned to her set-up area and let Crash out of his crate. He snuggled into her arms, still calm after spending a couple of hours in seclusion and taking in the atmosphere. "Mark said I should bribe you with a steak. Hey, it's worth a try. Crash, pay attention and do your job, and you'll get your payoff, okay? A nice juicy steak. Char-grilled."

His wild gaze locked onto hers and she saw the intelligence lurking behind the goofiness. She imagined a cheerful promise to cooperate. Oh, if only that were so, but it was silly of her to believe he was really telling her any such thing.

The warm-up went well. Dani could have sworn Crash was more focused than the week before. She felt her case of nerves ease. Her confidence returned and stayed with her as she walked Crash to ringside and waited for their turn. She watched the five dogs that preceded them in the 22-inch class go through their runs and noted maneuvers that went right and moves that fell apart for the other teams. A red-and-white Border Collie raced through the course, spilling jump bars and knocking over the tire jump, an enthusiastic but flawed performance. It took the ring crew about 30 seconds to reset the demolished jumps.

Trish and her Aussie made the challenging course look easy. Dani had to give it to Trish: She was a very good handler. She looked like an Olympic ice skater in the ring. Her dog almost blew it once, though, by heading the wrong way. Trish yelled, and the dog slunk back as though the wrong jump had caught on fire, correcting the error just in time. Her run elicited applause and delighted yells from the spectators.

Mark stood nearby, giving Dani room but offering quiet support. It was good to have somebody rooting just for her.

The ring steward called for Crash, and Dani moved to the start line. She tossed aside the lead and positioned Crash at the proper angle for the first jump. He looked into her face; again she felt that deep connection. She led off a few feet while Crash sat waiting with eager impatience, his body taut. Then she released him. It was like letting go of a slingshot.

The next thirty seconds of loosely organized chaos sent Dani into adrenalin pumping action. She and Crash raced through the looping course she had planned with such speed that she was at the frontier of her ability to give him timely direction. He attacked the course, clearing obstacles and racking up points. They hung in that delicate zone of high performance where thought and action synchronized without conscious effort, and it felt like slow motion. The timing worked out with such mystical precision that when the thirty-second whistle blew, Crash was close enough to the closing sequence that they lost no time charging through it. He flashed over the final jump before the cut-off.

The spectators and other competitors clapped and cheered. The judge sang out, "Awesome!" Crash met Dani at the exit gate, grinning, tongue lolling. She had no doubt he was aware he had done well and was congratulating himself on his own brilliance. "Super job, Crash!" She held out her arms, and he leaped into them. She carried the wiggling, panting bundle out of the ring. Ecstatic, still on her adrenalin high, she laughed and told him what a champ he was, collecting his lead on the way out. With shaking fingers she slipped the collar over his neck and let him down to strut on his own power.

Mark met her outside the ring and gathered her into his arms in an exuberant hug. She rested against him for a moment, forgetting that she planned to keep him at arm's length. Then she caught herself and resisted the temptation to snuggle into his warmth and lose herself there. Crash jumped up and planted his paws on the two of them as though he wanted to get in on the embrace.

"Amazing job," Mark spoke so close to her cheek his breath tickled her ear. The sensation evoked delicious memories of previous close encounters, and she let herself dwell there for a moment. "Crash smoked it," he was saying. "You blew their doors off. You made it look like pure poetry."

"It felt good." Dani composed herself and worked up the will to separate from him, though she couldn't stop grinning. "I mean the run felt good, like we were really, truly a team. I've got to hurry and give Crash his treat."

Mark dropped his arms to her waist with obvious reluctance. "In that case, I'll go see if they have his score posted yet."

Dani fled with Crash back to her setup and dug into the cooler, where she found the cheese and hot dog she had brought from home. She fed a handful of the treats bit by bit. He snapped up the food quickly enough, but when she had given him all she planned to, he kept looking at her as though he expected something more.

"Oh, yeah. The steak. It'll have to wait, Crash. I have to get you some tonight."

Crash chuffed, turned away, and slunk into his crate with his back to her. What was his problem now?

Mark walked up, smiling broadly. "His score was 65. Not only did he qualify, but he got almost twice the points he needed in the opening. They didn't have the class rankings posted yet, but I'd like to see anybody top that."

Dani gave Crash's rump a pat through the open crate door. "Good going, pup. I knew you had it in you." Crash swiveled his head around and glanced at her, but seemed subdued, as though he was pouting.

"Told you I liked his style." Mark looked even more excited than she felt.

"What's the matter with Crash?" She gave him another pat, but he didn't even look at her this time. "He doesn't act very happy all of a sudden."

Mark hunkered down. "What's going on, guy? Did you wear yourself out?"

"Couldn't be. He can run all day and be ready for more." She called Crash out of the crate and slipped the loop over his head. "I'll walk him around a bit and cool him off. He shouldn't just pile into a crate after a run. Jet needs an airing, too."

Dani took the dogs up the hill to the edge of the woods bordering the parking area, Mark accompanying them. "Crash seems fine to me," she said. "Not sick or anything."

After letting the dogs exercise, they walked back to the pavilion and checked the tables where the club posted scores. The officials had displayed the sheet listing Crash's class results, and Dani found Crash's name in first place. "Look at that." Mark's voice resonated with pride. Pride in her. "Told you nobody could touch him."

Trish's Aussie took second place. Crash had beaten him by 12 points. Was it a sin to feel such acute satisfaction for leaving one's rival in the dust?

Think of the devil. Here came Trish, giving Mark a lingering look. "Hi, Mark. Good to see you back at the dog wars."

He smiled and nodded back at Trish while she looked over Dani's shoulder at the list.

Dani stifled a twinge of possessiveness although it seemed absurd that she should care whether Trish was interested in Mark. She moved aside to let Trish see, which just so happened to position the woman closer to Mark. "Hmmm," Trish mused. "Not bad. But we'll see how your Border holds up in a Standard run."

"Congratulations to you, too." Dani beamed at her. "It appears both our dogs qualified."

"True." Trish worked up a pleasant expression with visible effort and glanced at some bins full of dog toys. "They don't have the ribbons ready yet. But you get to pick out of the first box. Self service."

"I'll let Crash pick his toy. He earned it. Jet gets one for his run, too, and we haven't picked it up yet." Dani led the dogs to the first bin and picked up a plush toy lizard. She squeezed it and made it squeak. "Like this one?" Crash sniffed it and poked it sharply with his nose, thrusting it away. He didn't protest when Jet grabbed it and chomped on it happily, reveling in the noise it made. "That's for you, since we didn't pick up your prize before," Dani told him.

She poked around in the bin and pulled out a soft Frisbee. "Catch?" She tossed it at Crash and he snatched it out of the air, then spat it out.

"Picky, isn't he?" Mark said.

The Border Collie turned his back on Dani and sat down. "Son of a gun," she said. "He's mad."

"What's he got to be mad about?"

"He thinks I cheated him. I promised him steak, but I haven't given him any yet."

"You think he cares about that?" Mark gave her a skeptical look, as well he might.

"It's really crazy, but seriously, I think he isn't very happy with me right now."

"Like you broke your promise?"

"Something like that. He's acting like two-year-old child that doesn't understand about waiting until later." She frowned. "It doesn't seem possible he knew what I was talking about, but I could swear he's holding me to it. Mark, look at him. He's sulking."

"That's easy enough to fix," Mark said. "You have to keep your promises, so I'll go get him some steak."

"I feel so silly. But..." She pulled out her wallet, but Mark stilled her hand with his.

"Don't worry about that. I'll have it cut into bite-sized pieces. I need, say, a couple of eight-ounce grillers? Then you'll have enough for both of them, all day."

"That should be more than enough." Dani laughed, embarrassed. "You're a good sport, indulging my prima Dona pup."

Mark hurried away, and Dani checked the progress of the remaining classes to see how much time she had until the next event for either one of her dogs. The trial had two rings operating at once, which made for fast progress. In fact, the first of the Standard runs was coming up quickly, and she would have to run Jet in one ring, then Crash in the other. The timing was going to be tight. She grabbed the toys and took the dogs back to their crates so she could study the diagrams, walk the courses and get prepared

Soon after, Jet had a good run, which earned him his Advanced title, as he'd accumulated the other two legs at a previous trial. Within minutes, it was time to run Crash in the other ring. Mark wasn't back with the steak yet, and she wasn't surprised it was taking so long. First he had to drive to a restaurant, then he had to wait for the order, and all that consumed time.

As she led Crash to the ring, she knew he wasn't really with her. The Crazy Crash look was back in his eyes. She scanned the area for Mark but didn't see him. She was on her own, and she felt unaccountably deprived. As before, Trish and her Aussie ran before Crash took his turn, and they did a fast and successful run.

Dani walked into the ring, talking to Crash, but he wouldn't even look at her. It felt like last week all over again. She again considered walking away and scratching the run to save her pride.

Before she had a chance to back out, the scorekeepers gave her the nod and she decided to go for it. She settled Crash into a sit-stay behind the line and led out a few feet, then released him and they were off to the races. Crash was, anyway. He sailed over the first jump, grabbed a plastic number cone from the next jump in his teeth, and tore around the ring, carrying it in his mouth and showing it to everyone standing outside. Dani heard a ripple of laughter.

This time she stood still and watched, feeling impotent, trying to decide what to do next. There didn't seem to be any point in giving chase or even calling him. He was making some kind of point in his own way.

Crash ended his circuit in front of the judge. He skidded to a stop and spat the cone out at the woman's feet, wagging his tail and barking in a play invitation. The judge's face crinkled as she stifled a grin. Arms crossed, she turned her back to him, wisely refusing to reinforce the misbehavior.

Thinking fast, Dani collected herself. They hadn't been dismissed yet, and Crash hadn't technically disqualified himself. She decided to go for it, try to take back control, and complete at least part of the course if possible. It would be a good thing to give Crash a chance to redeem himself if he would let her. She ran over to him then dashed backwards, calling the errant dog and clapping her hands to get his attention.

This time he came with her. She sprinted with him back to the second jump, the one he had bypassed before, and looped him around into position so he could leap over it. To her relief, he obliged her, then she directed him through the rest of the course as though the opening fiasco had never occurred. She made a couple of mistakes due to feeling off balance and failing to compensate for Crash's over-exuberance. It was a ragged, uncoordinated performance. Nonetheless, she felt a surge of triumph when Crash cleared the last jump and crossed the finish line.

***

Mark arrived just in time to see Crash's run. He had left the delicious-smelling Styrofoam container of grilled beef on top of the crate and had come looking for Dani. She was easy to spot in her red sweater. He'd found her standing in the ring while Crash played keep-away with the orange cone. Then, to his amazement, she salvaged the rest of the run. Or maybe Crash finally decided to cooperate.

He hurried forward to meet her as she came out of the ring leading Crash. Mark slipped his arm around Dani's shoulders. "Great save."

"Did you see the whole thing?" She laughed wildly. "What a brat. Guess he showed me, didn't he?"

"You got him back, though, and finished like a champ." He noticed that she didn't seem to mind the contact and gathered her closer, savoring her firm softness before he let go.

"Am I ever glad to see you!" He felt the pleasant impact of the words while she swiped a loose strand of hair off her forehead. "Did you get some steak?"

Oh, yeah. The meat. That was what she really wanted. "It's with your gear. Sorry it took so long. It's early, so I had to settle for breakfast steak from the Denny's in Orange Park."

"His class came up faster than I expected," she said. "I'd better give him some now." They hurried to her set-up. Mark handed her the take-out box, and she doled out a few pieces to Crash, who snapped them up enthusiastically.

"It's a good thing you got it right in the end," she told Crash. "Otherwise I'd have you on bread and water."

The Border Collie turned his head aside. Mark could have sworn that Crash would have given her the finger if a dog were capable of doing such a thing. "It was his little twist of revenge. I think you have a passive-aggressive dog there."

"Not so passive. He looked pretty darned active to me." Dani gave Crash a stern look. "Revenge does not become you, Crash. But it works for me. I could give you to a family with ten cats. How would you like that?"

I'll eat them, too. He licked his chops, looking for more steak. Dani gave another piece to Crash and one to Jet, then set the box out of their reach. "I'd better save some for the next run, Crash. I can't keep sending Mark out for your little indulgences."

"Think he qualified?" Mark asked.

"No way. He ate up too much of the clock with his antics, plus he took the wrong jump once, which would disqualify him off the bat. But that's all right. We finished the course, one way or another." She grinned at Mark, her eyes alive with fun, just as he remembered her from their good times together. "Did I ever thank you properly?"

Before he had a chance to say anything, she stood on her toes and gave him a chaste kiss on the cheek. Perhaps she only intended it as a friendly peck, but the sensual effect rippled through him and made him catch his breath.

"You're welcome." He resisted the urge to throw his arms around her and give her a real kiss, sensing she wasn't ready. "Can I get you more steak? Chicken? You name it."

She laughed. "Now you're offering behaviors, just like Crash does when he wants a treat."

"Hey, I'm trying to earn more positive reinforcement."

"I can see teaching you how to train your dog might be dangerous. Next you'll be using it on me."

"That's fair, isn't it? What's next?"

"Jumpers, just jumps and tunnels. Jet has the same stuff going on but more advanced. He's competing in the other ring. I guess I'll be doing a lot of running back and forth."

He stifled a twinge of disappointment that she would be so busy with the dogs she wouldn't be spending any more time with him than she had the first part of the day. Because he was committed to helping set the obstacles, he was also occupied. He'd have to be content with whatever closeness to Dani he could manage. "Same thing tomorrow?"

"Yep. You coming?"

"Do you want me to?"

She broke into another smile that warmed him through and through. "Sure, if you have the time. If you want, you can run Jet on one of his courses."

"Are you sure?"

"Why not? He's already gone as far as he can at this level, and I can't move him up to Masters until the next trial in this venue. The standard run will be strictly for practice."

Mark knelt next to Jet and scratched him behind the ears. The Sheltie shut his eyes and cocked his head with pleasure. "Will he work with me?"

"We'll give him a try on the practice jump and weave poles. Use some treats to convince him he needs to pay attention to you. He's run for other people before, so I know he'll do fine. Besides that, he likes you. You're the steak guy, remember?"

"Feed him and he'll follow me anywhere?"

“You got it.” She grinned. “You’ve been good sport and a big help.”

“I’ll settle for helpful, at least temporarily. I think I’ll have a T-shirt made with ‘Dani’s Pit Crew’ written across the back.”

Chapter Nine

By late that afternoon, Dani had collected a sheaf of different-hued ribbons, but those she prized most were the five maroon strips her dogs had earned for their qualifying runs. Competition completed, she rested on a folding chair, flanked by her two dogs. She kept telling Jet and Crash what brilliant, wonderful, excellent pups they were. They had scarfed down the last of the steak and cuddled against her, looking as content as she felt. She had talked to a couple of training prospects, and she'd even gotten a promising lead on a new home for Dolly, though she believed the Golden needed more rehabilitation before she let her go.

She shaded her eyes and looked across the field at Mark, who was helping another volunteer move the long, heavy dog walk to a different position in preparation for tomorrow's courses. The rosy glow of success helped her see him in a most favorable light. Watching him work wasn't hard on the eyes, either. His energetic grace and the way he carried his slim yet powerful build pleased her.

Dani had checked on the Collie standard since meeting Rebel, and Mark reminded her of the description of the ideal Collie: "Lithe, strong, responsive, active dog, carrying no useless timber." Substitute "man" for "dog," and that was Mark.

"Hey, Jet, maybe there's something to the old saw that people look like their dogs. Do I look more like you or Crash?" She laughed. "Maybe not. My hair isn't black yet."

Jet yawned in her face.

"The topic doesn't light your fire, I see. Okay, you've had a big day."

She had to give Mark credit. All day long he had been helpful but unobtrusive, supportive but undemanding.

Yes, she had missed him since their breakup, and having him around again made her feel what? Complete? No, it wasn't that. She cherished her self-sufficiency and thought of a male partner as a welcome annex, not as essential equipment. He was matchless as a friend who shared her enthusiasms, triumphs and defeats. He was also right about the chemistry and something else as well. It seemed as though they resonated on the same frequency. From time to time she caught herself knowing what he was going to say before he said it. Wasn't that weird? In truth, it felt intimate and comforting.

The problem lay in the tingle of desire that his nearness set up in her. Today she found it harder to resist those unwelcome feelings and bring them to heel. At least her snappish responses had mellowed. It was clear he wanted her, but what did she want?

Good feelings weren't enough. She wanted to be sure she could trust him. Being able to finish his sentences for him didn't ensure she would ever be emotionally safe with him.

He quit the ring and came over to join her. "We've done all we can do until morning." He eased onto the empty chair next to Jet, who crawled into his lap for another ear-rub. The Sheltie's expression made no secret of his ecstasy. Both dogs were nuts about the man. Dani couldn't afford to be so transparent.

"Your guys did great, didn't they?"

"Five Q's out of six runs." Dani spread out her fingers. "Plus Jet finished his Advanced title. I'll take it."

"Interesting how you figured out what makes Crash tick."

"The steak was your idea. Between us, we created a monster." Dani sighed. "Now he's totally spoiled. Holding out for steak. Unbelievable. Just watch. Next time it won't be just any old steak. He'll be demanding filet or prime rib."

"Then he'll be wanting a union card." Mark reached over to stroke Crash, who had crawled over Dani's legs to get to the man. "Plus overtime pay for working on weekends."

"Don't give him any ideas. He'd make me pay his union dues, too."

"Seriously, has he ever eaten steak before?" Mark glanced at her. "Did he even know what it's like?"

Dani thought about it. "Actually, he's had it a few times. Leftovers from a take-home bag. I cut it up and used it for treats." She gave Mark an incredulous look. "Really. I'm not buying this whole thing. It just played out this way."

He raised an eyebrow. "Whatever you say." Was he being

skeptical of her skepticism?

"You're a scientist," she pointed out. "You're trained to demand empirical evidence and hard facts. So am I. Isn't this ESP mumbo-jumbo getting you a bit off our reservation?"

He stretched out his long denim-clad legs and leaned back, a thoughtful smile playing across his face. "Quantum physics gets downright mystical. Who knows? Maybe the universe is a matrix and we're all connected."

Wasn't it strange that Mark was more willing to accept her quirks than she was? Then she entertained a stray thought of what it would be like to connect with Mark again. He sure looked like somebody she would like to reach out and touch. Even now, after what had gone wrong between them.

She swatted the notion. "Maybe I don't want to be connected. Not that much, anyway. Maybe I don't even want to know what dogs really think."

He gave her a sidewise glance. "No escaping it, Dani. You're connected with Jet and Crash." He ran his hand over Jet's silky head. "How deep do those bonds go?"

"It's not the same thing." She let her gaze drop to the dogs. "Look. I've got to get them home and see if I still have a kennel left. Leaving it in the hands of the hired help for a whole day makes me nervous."

He stood and offered her a hand to help her stand up. "Tell you what. I bought your dogs steak. It just isn't right that the dogs eat better than we do. The least I can do is buy you a steak too. I'll fix extra for tomorrow's shameless bribes, plus pick up some salad greens. Do you have a grill at your place? You can make sure things are all right in the kennel while I fix supper."

It sounded like the makings of a divine evening, but she resisted. "I'm not as easily bought as Crash." She made him wait a beat before she accepted his hand. When they did connect, she found his touch as warm as she expected. She levered to her feet, facing him.

"No," he agreed. "You're not easy. But you are highly prized." He drew her closer; she felt her heart rate accelerate. How she wanted to succumb, to let him wrap his arms around her and go with her heart.

Crash chose that moment to goose her soundly on the butt.

"Hey!" She whirled and scooped up Crash, effectively hugging him between herself and Mark.

He gave the dog an exasperated smile. "Bad dog. I thought you were my buddy." Then he said to Dani, "I'll pick up the groceries on the way over to your place. Ready to go? I'll help you carry your stuff to your van."

It seemed to be a done deal, and Dani didn't bother to protest. The prideful part of her was annoyed with the compliant part, but she mentally told it to sit down and shut up. She was in a celebrating mood, and Mark deserved to be part of the celebration.

***

"Get that wolf out of here." Al glared at the big orange-and-white dog curled at Jill's feet. "He gets on my nerves. I've got intricate work to do."

The beast glared back, then turned and licked his own balls with dismissive languor. Al took it as insubordination, if a dog were capable of such.

Jill didn't exactly jump to his command. "He isn't bothering you. Besides, you can go into that room where you sleep with your laptop and lock the door."

Al stared at her, alarmed. "What about my laptop? Have you been messing with it?"

She shook her head no. "What are you guys up to, anyway?"

"If I tell you, I'll have to kill you." He didn't smile, leaving it up to her to decide whether he was joking. Let her figure it out.

"Do what he says," Ted told her. "Put him out."

She sighed and scowled like a teenager. Moving slow as a snail in molasses, dripping attitude with every move, she moseyed out of the easy chair where she parked her ass most of the day. "C'mon, Rebel." She started toward the back door.

"Not out back," Al said. "I got to do some things out there. Stick him out front."

"No." Jill stopped and set her hands on her hips. "He'll get in trouble if I let him run loose."

Ted snorted. "You didn't feel that way about those lab rats."

"I'll put him in our bedroom."

"If he chews up any of my stuff, I'll kick him out the front door myself," Ted yelled after her.

Al watched her leave the room. He had a job to do and was being paid well to accomplish it. He didn't care whether radical environmentalists or Islamists were the ones paying him, as long as he got the dough. They'd sent him the first couple of increments to get him started on the project, but the Cabal wouldn't pay him off until the job was done and done right. Not only that, but he had to get out squeaky clean. Jill's ex, that Mark guy, had eyeballed him, and he didn't like that.

The emails they had sent to Jill's ex exposed them, too, and threatened to expose him. Worse, that Mark guy was acting too curious for Al's druthers.

He was used to working alone. Ted had proved to be a limited asset and Jill was worthless. He'd tried to keep her uninformed of their plans, but he wasn't sure what Ted might be leaking to her. Ted Sturkey wasn't the brightest bulb in the package. The pair was big on ideology but short on smarts.

Both of them were wearing thin.

***

After dinner, Mark rinsed the dishes while Dani put them away in the dishwasher. The prosaic domesticity of the act felt good and right. Having Dani at hand felt even better. He admired the way she bent over, inadvertently showing him her slim but rounded backside and the glove-like fit of her jeans. It was all he could do to keep his hands to himself.

To him it seemed an excellent ending to a gratifying day. Both of them had accomplished goals: her with Jet and Crash, and him at renewing his friendship with her. She was back to her cheerful, natural self. He believed her brick wall had developed strategic cracks. He dared to hope all he had to do was shake the barrier between them and it would crumble.

He gave her the last of the plates and their hands made damp contact. She slotted the plate in place and poured dish powder into the machine cup while he wiped his hands on a dishtowel. Then he handed her the towel so she could dry her hands, too. "Great evening to top a spectacular day," he said. "I hate to end it, but I guess it's time to go."

She leaned that tempting backside against the counter, her lovely blue eyes contemplative. "Thanks for everything. It was fun having you there." The corners of her mouth quirked into a smile. "And your cooking skills have certainly improved. Dinner was delicious. No hockey pucks or burnt offerings this time."

"Ha. Too bad your memory is so good. I can tell you're never going to let me live it down. I only cremated those hamburgers because you distracted me."

"Yeah, yeah. It was all my fault." She laughed.

"You still distract me."

She looked away and swiped the towel over the back of her neck, a nervous gesture.

"What time should I come by in the morning?" he asked.

"Um, about the same as this morning. Seven or so." She tossed the towel onto the counter.

"I'll be here." He reached across the short space between them and grasped her hand. "And I'll stay close at hand as long as you permit it."

She didn't pull away but gripped his hand in response. He stepped closer and gathered her in his arms. She sank against him, and the physical response he'd been suppressing all day intensified. Her face turned up to meet his, and he let his lips graze hers, then settle into a deeper kiss. She carried a healthy aroma of shower soap and tasted of the dinner they'd just eaten. Maintaining bare self-control, he pulled her yet closer.

Dani pressed her hands gently against his chest, and he realized he had reached her limit, for the present, at least. He honored her unspoken request, broke off the kiss, and relaxed his hold on her. It wasn't easy to do. More than anything he wanted to whisk her up to the bedroom and make love to her. The kitchen table would suffice.

She smiled weakly, her downswept eyelashes hiding what she was thinking. "Okay, tomorrow."

He tried not to read more into what she said. Staying close to Dani for another whole day would be sweet torture, but he'd just have to take it like a man.

***

"Here's what I see us doing." Al turned away from his computer screen and talked in a low voice. Once they'd set up his computer in his bedroom, making it a headquarters of sorts, Ted took to calling the room Command Central, which seemed to appeal to his megalomania. Al didn't care what the fool called it, as long as the cable modem was working. "We got to steal a cargo van, one without windows. Change out license plates."

Ted grinned. "They'll be looking for the wrong tag numbers, huh?"

"Exactly. Then we'll bring it back here and drive it into the back yard. That nice stockade fence will keep the neighbors from seeing too much. One thing you did right was renting this particular house. We'll be able to load it up out of sight."

Al had brought a supply of C4 and detonators with him. His connections had served him well, and he never asked where the stuff came from. He'd been collecting the bulkier, commonly available materials locally. So far, so good.

"Before we mobilize we'll load up the computer and other critical stuff in the Honda. We want to make it easy to take off afterwards, not leave anything incriminating in the house. I'll drive it, and you drive the van. At night they've only got one guard," Al continued. "He shouldn't be a problem, but if he is, I'll take care of him. That little gate won't stop you. You blow through, and I'll be right behind you. You get it situated next to the building." Al pointed to the site map.

Al watched Ted stare at the print, dense as hell but trying to get the picture. "So I get to drive into there with a van full of explosives?"

"You scared?" Al grinned, challenging him. "You'll be okay. All you got to do is park, get out, and run like hell. After you're clear, I'll set it off."

"You're the trigger man all the way, huh?"

"Hey, I'm the expert. I've done this before, never a glitch." He wasn't sure he had Ted's trust, so he laid it on. "Look, buddy, we're were in this thing together. Comrades. Partners in a great cause. I'm the expert and you're a team player."

Ted nodded, looking convinced. "When you think we can pull it off?"

"I just need a van and a few odds and ends. I say Tuesday morning, early."

"We'll do lots of damage, you think?"

"Bring that whole building down and anybody unlucky enough to be in it."

"Yeah. It's on the same side of the building Vaughn works.

Fry him to a crisp."

Ted turned around, and there was Jill standing in the doorway staring at him, a beer in her hand. He knew from the drop-jawed look on her face she'd heard every word.

Al was saying, "Damn, buddy, didn't you lock the door?"

Ted ignored him. "Hey, babe, this is private business."

"Uh, I brought you a beer," she said.

"I didn't ask for one." Ted waved his hand at her. "Get in the bedroom and wait for me."

At first he thought she was going to argue with him, then she looked from him to Al and must have decided not to give them any lip. She slipped out of the room and closed the door just like he'd ordered.

"You know the rules," Al said. "That was damn careless of you."

"She was busy outside brushing the mutt or something. No big deal."

"What about her?" This time Al kept his voice low. "What did she hear? We got to do some damage control, man."

Ted fixed his most intimidating gaze on him. "Never mind her. She's my problem."

After they worked out more details, Ted joined Jill in the bedroom. She was lying on the sack watching a stupid situation comedy, but when she saw him, she switched off the TV. Her expression was serious, grim even. "Where's that freak Al?"

"He stayed in his room. I think he's surfin' the Internet."

"What's this about bringing down Crohn. What's going on?"

"Forget it. Just Al's dumb idea."

"Ted, I thought for a while you guys were working on some kind of deal like that. Good. Damaging Crohn is fine with me. But I don't want any people hurt. I never hurt anybody when I released the rats. What's he going to do to the guard?"

"Knock him out, I guess." Ted shrugged. "Might not have to do anything."

"There are always people working in that building, even at night. If Al blows it up, he'll kill some of them. If it's in the daytime, it'll be a lot of people."

He crawled onto the bed beside her. "I said forget it, babe. Just his dumb idea."

"You sure sounded like you were into it."

"Leave it alone." He wasn't used to her bucking him like this, and he didn't like it. "People who talk about stuff like that are an endangered species. Get my drift?"

Jill didn't say anything. He guessed she got it.

He slipped his hand under the covers and rubbed her thigh. Talking about bombs always made him horny. "Baby, you're what I want to get into. How about a big ole pickle sandwich?"

She laughed nervously at his joke. "I love pickle sandwiches. My favorite."

He worked his hand up higher and felt himself swell into shape, getting ready for sandwich making. He thought about his namesake, Ted Kaczynski, and how his own brother turned him in. Was Jill likely to do that to him?

Maybe he ought to talk to Al about it. Later. Get his opinion. Right now he had better things to do.

Chapter Ten

The next morning, Dani led Jet and Crash to the rear of her van. Both dogs jumped into their crates, eager for another outing. As she latched the second gate, she heard a vehicle turn into her driveway. She glanced over at Mark's Blazer rolling to a stop along the fence line. Right on time. He'd always been punctual.

Dani closed up the back of the van and watched Mark emerge from his SUV. The warm glow of pleasure at the sight of him didn't take her by surprise this time. She had easily slipped back into the habit of enjoying his company, enjoying it too much. Last night his subtle approach had teased her senses and warned her that she could easily slip beyond the brink of emotional safety. He didn't force the issue, causing her gratitude, frustration and confusion all at the same time.

Now he sauntered toward her, keeping his hands warm in his denim jacket, flashing that shy smile she used to find irresistible. Still did, but she wasn't about to let on he had any effect on her.

"Hi, Dani." He stopped in front of her, close enough to touch. "You're looking like a winner this morning."

"Flattery will get you nowhere." She had to grin in response. "But hold that thought." She fingered the cell phone she'd stuck in her own jacket pocket, then held it out to him. "Missing something?"

He took it from her and examined it ruefully. "I missed it this morning, then remembered taking it off at your house." He nodded toward her van. "Need any help loading up?"

"Not much to do. Most of my gear is at the site. I've about got it." She glanced toward the house. "I was thinking about bringing Dolly along to meet those people who were interested in her. The lady said she was coming back to watch. I haven't decided."

"Good idea. I'll walk her around and let her socialize."

"You can try, but I don't know if that will work. She's afraid of men. I bet she'll spook away from you."

"Dogs usually like me."

"I'll give you that." In spite of her better judgment, she liked him, too. "But Dolly might be a challenge."

"What about the family that wants her? Will she be afraid of the man of the house?"

"I told the lady she needs more work, but she was really excited to see Dolly. I haven't met her husband yet. I might be rushing things." She tapped her fingers against the van. "Maybe I'd better just leave her here."

"Why don't we see how she reacts to me, then decide?"

Dani glanced at her watch, considering. "We've got a few minutes to spare. Let's give it a try." She grabbed a lead from the rear of the van and led Mark to the outdoor portion of Dolly's run.

The Golden Retriever met her at the gate, wriggled a happy greeting, and planted her front paws on the chain link fence. Dani was aware of Mark coming up quietly behind her. When Dolly noted his approach she retreated, eyeing him warily.

Dani slipped into the run without allowing Dolly to leave, and closed the gate behind her. She reached down and rubbed Dolly under her chin, talking softly worded nonsense to the worried dog.

"Mark, why don't you come into the run and let's see whether she accepts you?"

He smoothly entered the run and hunkered down to eye level with the Golden, though he didn't try to make eye contact but kept his gaze on Dani instead. He didn't try to reach out to Dolly, either. What he didn't do appeared to Dani like an instinctively savvy approach to a nervous dog. "That's good. I won't restrain her with the lead. Let's just let her make up her own mind what you're about," she told him.

Stretching herself into an elongated crouch, tail tucked, Dolly reached out her head tentatively and sniffed Mark's thigh. He didn't try to rush things by reaching out to her.

"Atta girl," Dani said in an encouraging voice. "He's a good guy, and it's safe for you to go to him."

Mark's smile broadened. "A good guy?" he stage-whispered. "Am I making progress?"

The Golden took another step forward and checked out the

back of Mark's hand, gaining confidence.

"With Dolly maybe." Dani said under her breath.

Mark's soft chuckle told her he wasn't discouraged. To her surprise, when he moved his hand to stroke Dolly's shoulder she didn't flinch away. "There," he whispered. "What a fine girl you are."

"I've got to admit you're right. Dogs do like you, even Dolly."

"Told you so."

"Don't get cocky."

Mark ran his hand over Dolly's back and she continued to hold her ground. "Think we ought to take her along?"

Dani sensed Dolly's tentative approval of Mark, which agreed with the dog's actions. "Might not hurt. We'll take it slow. If she's overwhelmed, we can leave her in a crate inside the van. It's going to be a cool enough day if we leave the windows open, and she'll feel secure there. What do you think, Dolly?"

The Golden appeared to respond to her words with a quick wag, though her tail was still tucked to her belly.

"First, try to put the lead on her," Dani handed Mark the length of leather. "Careful to avoid the scars."

He looped it over the willing Dolly's neck, frowning when he saw the old burns. "Please tell me this was an accident."

"I don't think so. The guy was a lunatic."

Mark slowly rose to full height. Dolly shied but returned to his side, crouching as though ready to bolt if he made a wrong move. "She's trying to trust me," he said. "I think we can be friends."

"She's going to make you earn it."

He gave Dani a serious look. "I expect it will be worth the effort."

She knew he wasn't just talking about the dog and felt an unwelcome thrill of gladness that he was willing to try.

***

After they arrived at the trial grounds, Mark stood aside while Dani coaxed Dolly out of the van and was pleased that the timid dog came over to him right away. Dolly rolled onto her back in a submissive posture, so he knelt down and scratched her belly. She turned her head aside, another display of submission, but she didn't try to flee.

Mark had studied several books on canine body language and was amazed that the tactics seemed to be working so well on Dolly. If only Dani's confidence was as easy to win.

"She's lucky you took her in," Mark said to Dani, who had collected her two dogs from her van and prepared to take them to her area. "I think she's going to be fine."

"Her accepting you is a big step." Flanked by the impatient Crash and Jet, Dani exuded a magnetic glow about her this morning, whether from her inner light or outer cosmetics. Did she exert a special effort to look great this morning, or was it his imagination? If she did, whom was she planning to impress except him? A certain ease had settled in between them. It resembled the feel of their relationship before the bust-up. This time he was determined to carry it as far as she would let him.

"I'll consider Dolly my special project today." Mark stood up and thrust his hand into his pocket, where he had stored some freeze-dried liver. He handed a square of the fragrant, arid stuff to Dolly, who whisked it out of his hand. He laughed when she swallowed the tidbit like a pill. "She says she's starving, and nobody ever feeds her."

"She lies." Dani quirked a smile at him and waved her hand at the substantially built dog. "Feel her ribs, if you can find them underneath the blubber. Are you going to run Jet on his courses today like we discussed?"

"That would be fun, if you don't mind."

"Sure. I'll walk the course with you and help you plan your strategy." Dani smirked. "Uh, that's handling strategy. On the course."

Mark widened his eyes, trying for a guileless expression. "Oh, is there any other kind?"

He led Dolly to the area they had staked out the morning before. He sat petting the nervous dog with long soothing strokes while Dani stashed her two dogs in their crates. Then she left to pick up the day's course diagrams from the officials' table. Dolly leaned against his leg as though drawing support from him. He spoke to her in soft tones, liking the way she took to him despite fearing other men. He found a plush lizard squeaky from Dani's stash of toys and gave it to her. She grabbed it between her jaws and held onto it, squinting in pleasure.

Dani returned and gave Mark the sheet outlining Jet's courses. "I see Dolly got a pacifier."

"Seems to make her happy." He scratched the Golden behind an ear. "She seems more content, anyway."

"Appears she's adopted you."

"Think so?" Dolly looked up at him appealingly and chomped on the toy, making it squeak then dropped it into his lap. He tossed it a couple of feet away and laughed when she pounced on it, her tail finally unfurled from between her legs.

"Look at her, Mark. Frankly, I'm amazed she's so taken by you."

"Why not? She's a fine judge of character."

"Either that or a pushover." Dani grinned and settled into the canvas chair next to him. "Let's have a look at Jet's first course."

He stared down at the diagram, found the start line, and traced out the path on paper with his finger. "It's kind of circular and twisty," he said.

"Let's see." She moved closer to him, so close he felt her body heat. He suppressed an urge to shove the diagram aside, wrap his arms around her, and indulge his impulse to kiss her. How did she expect him to concentrate on anything more complex than primal urges? She withdrew a bit, giving both of them more space, as though she found him just as distracting.

Mark forced himself to study the diagram and plot his path and Jet's. With Dani's help, he broke the sequence down into logical segments and spotted the problem areas where Jet was most likely to bound off in the wrong direction. He reached down with his free hand to maintain contact with Dolly. If only Dani were as easy to charm as the Golden Retriever.

***

Later, Dani walked the course with Mark. "It looks different in three dimensions, doesn't it?" she said after their first round.

He nodded, arms crossed, surveying the layout. "Simpler, actually. I think I can handle it."

"I'm sure you can. Keep walking it until you have it all set in your mind. They give you those number markers, but you'll never even see them while you're running with a dog. Things happen too fast."

"I'm adaptable."

"After you get it all planned out, close your eyes and run the course in your head. You can even go through the motions. It looks like some weird kind of Tai Chi, but that's what the winners do."

"I don't mind making a fool of myself if it can get me what I want." He gave her a slow smile.

"Then you won't have trouble taking your own advice. Just make it your goal to have a good time."

She walked back to where the dogs were crated, leaving Mark to his course strategy Zen. There she found the lady who was interested in Dolly, along with the rest of her family. She introduced her husband, a teenaged boy, and a younger girl. The husband had the look of a guy who'd been dragged there and would rather be playing golf. The kids were more cheerful. Dani had made inquiries about a fenced yard and other qualifications and the people had checked out all right so far. But what would Dolly think of them?

"I'll bring Dolly out to meet you," Dani told them. "Please give her space. She's a little fearful and you don't want to crowd her."

Dani opened the crate and found Dolly curled up in the back of it. She spoke to the Golden as she attached a lead to the collar. Dolly showed no interest in coming out. In fact, her eyes held such a heartbreaking appeal that Dani didn't want to force her. She fancied feeling the dog's dread. She reached into her cooler and took out a piece of cheese. When she offered it to Dolly, the dog turned her head away.

The man said to his wife, "I told you we'd be better off with a puppy."

"But I felt sorry for this doggie when I heard her story." The wife looked doubtful.

Dani rocked back on her heels, considering, not wanting to disappoint the lady but concerned with Dolly's attitude. "Tell you what. She's a little shy, and I don't want to upset her. Let's give it a little more time. You can come by my kennel in about a week. She'll be in her element and won't be as fearful."

"Fine." The husband couldn't seem to agree quickly enough.

"Can I look at her?" asked the boy.

Dani moved aside and he squatted down to peer into the crate. "Hey, doggie," he chirped.

Dolly made herself smaller inside the crate, if that was possible.

"She doesn't like me," the boy muttered.

"It isn't personal," Dani said. "I'm sure she would love you if she knew you better." She glanced across the faces of the woman, her husband and the two kids. "You would have to work with her, but I think she would fit in eventually." She began to doubt her own words.

The husband stroked his nose. "We'll get back with you."

Sure they would. Dani watched the family wander away, knowing they wouldn't be back. "Well, Dolly. Guess that wasn't a match, huh? What did I expect? Too soon to meet the public, huh, girl?"

This time Dolly crept forward and poked her nose out of the crate, looking from side to side.

"I saw those people over here," Mark said from behind Dani. "Were they the ones that wanted to see Dolly?"

At the sound of Mark's voice, Dolly turned and looked up at him, her eyes soft with admiration. Dani nodded. "Yeah. But she didn't want to see them."

Dolly slipped out of the crate and pushed her body against Mark's legs, wriggling her joy.

"I think she's made up her mind. She wants you," Dani said.

"Rebel could use some company." Mark knelt down and cradled Dolly's head in his hands. "So could I. He's not with me all the time."

Dani let out her breath. The growing bond between the man and the dog was unmistakable. "Seriously. Do you want to take her home with you?"

"Seriously yes." Mark grinned and roughed up Dolly's sides. Her tail danced a jig and she twisted around to look adoringly into his face.

"She's been spayed." Dani mused out loud. "Rebel seems to get along with other dogs. I guess you could give it a try. If it doesn't work out, you know where I live."

"I'll take her home with me tonight. We'll be fine."

A sense of relief washed through Dani. Somehow, she knew it was a match.

Dolly trusted Mark without question. Did she sense something

Dani couldn't acknowledge about him?

***

Mark swallowed down the butterflies fluttering up into his throat and moved into place at the start line. Jet raised grave dark eyes to him as though saying he accepted Mark as team captain and was ready to perform. Mark wasn't so sure about his own ability. Even after all that course memorization and planning he had yet to prove he could handle it.

He crunched the last of the mint Dani had given him and swallowed. Mint covers the smell of adrenalin, she told him. Right now he felt as though he needed a handful of mints. He glanced over his shoulder and saw her stationed a little way from the ring, out of Jet's line of vision so she wouldn't distract him. She jabbed a thumbs up and smiled. Knowing she was on his side, at least in this endeavor, delighted him.

He recalled another piece of her advice, to trust the dog to know his job. At least half the team was competent.

Mark moved to the starting line and steadied himself and Jet in front of the first jump. He got the nod from the scorekeepers, and he and the dog were off and running. The action shook off Mark's case of nerves. Once he saw Jet bound over the first jump, the morning's preparation kicked in and he guided the dog with cooler calculation than he'd expected.

Jet raced ahead over a line of jumps, leaving Mark several paces behind, and a beat too late with the next signal. The little dog turned around and barked at him with an air of impatience then decided for himself and started up the teeter, the wrong obstacle. Mark waited for him to safely dismount, then pointed in the other direction and said, "Tunnel!" Jet whirled and whipped into the tunnel, bringing himself back on course. Mark met him at the exit and sent him over the A-frame, then into the weave poles. They got through the rest of the course without mishap, and at the end Jet leaped into Mark's arms.

His elation brimmed over the top when Dani, laughing and smiling, met him outside the ring with a congratulatory hug and a handful of treats for Jet.

"I hope I didn't do too embarrassing a job." He felt flushed with excitement and didn't want to break off contact with her.

"You did fine! Jet knows his job and you're a fast study. That was spectacular for a first try." She affixed the lead onto Jet and Mark set him down. "Let's cool him down. You, too!"

***

They trotted to the field nearby before they slowed to a walk. Mark slipped his arm around Dani's waist. She let it rest there and closed the space between them, liking the feel of his warmth. "I don't want this weekend to end." His warm voice caressed her like a kid glove.

"Come on over to my place after the trial." She wouldn't come out and say it, but she didn't want the weekend to end either. "My turn to fix dinner. I'll stop and get some Chinese take-out. That's my idea of cooking."

Naturally he accepted.

Being with Mark for the past two days had brought a level of joy she hadn't experienced in a long time. Certainly she wasn't immune to his charm. It must have overcome her Mark-proofing antibodies. Was she a fool to even consider letting him have another crack at her?

Chapter Eleven

At the end of the day Mark helped Dani break camp and load her gear into her van. They headed back to her place, with a brief stop at the Chinese take-out place she liked. At home she only had to unload the dogs and the cooler because the rest of her gear could stay in the van, ready for the next excursion. Soon after, she sat at her kitchen table with Mark rehashing the day's events over Hot and Sour Soup and Beef with Broccoli.

"Crash was half and half today, just like yesterday. Playing hide and seek inside the tunnel was his latest joke," she said. "He still wants to pull an occasional trick on me. I don't know if he'll ever outgrow that. He likes playing up to the audience."

"It's part of his charm." Mark spooned a second helping of fried rice onto his plate. "He's an original. I kind of like him the way he is."

"Good thing. I don't think he's going to change." Dani sat back in the chair, the edge off her hunger. "When do you get Rebel back?"

"After work tomorrow. I'd like to take Dolly home tonight."

"I don't see any problem with that. She's crazy about you. So am I."

One of Mark's eyebrows shot up.

Realizing what she'd just said, Dani clapped her hand over her mouth. She took a deep breath and mumbled, "Or just plain crazy."

Mark's slight smile kept him looking hopeful. "What are you doing tomorrow night?"

"Um, I've got a class at the community college."

"What kind of class?" He held a frozen smile as though hiding disappointment.

"Self-defense for women."

Mark gave a low whistle. "Should I be afraid?"

"Be very afraid." Dani laughed. "Tonight's lesson is about breaking arms. Last week we covered eye-gouging."

"Ouch. Now you tell me. Am I in danger?"

"Not so far. You've been a perfect gentleman."

"It's a strain, considering how you affect me."

Restless, Dani pushed her plate side. "You're coming for a private lesson Tuesday, right?"

"I wouldn't miss it." His smile deepened. "We make a good team, don't you agree?"

"That sounds like a leading question."

"You realize you're going to have to beat me off with a stick if you don't want me around."

"I'm getting that clue."

"I'm not trying to force anything. I just like being with you."

"I know. You've been considerate. I have to give you a lot of credit." But she knew all she had to do was say the word, and he'd jump her bones. Moreover, her bones were ripe for jumping. She crossed her legs and told that primal part of herself to sit and stay. "But I'm not ready."

"'Not ready' beats never." He quirked an eyebrow. "Do I have to do more penance? Or have you completely sworn off men?"

She smiled sweetly. "Or maybe I already have a lover?"

Mark smiled slyly. "Your groomer?"

She laughed out loud. "He's awfully cute, but I'm not his type."

"If you do have a lover, he chose to make himself mighty scarce this weekend."

"Maybe he's on a business trip." She laughed when his smug look faltered, then sighed. "I confess. It's the first two."

"Good. I'll do the penance, then I'll persuade you to unswear off men."

"This could be a good thing." She stared up at the ceiling as though in deep thought. "Let's see. I could use another kennel slave. How about seven years at hard labor, then we'll discuss it."

"Don't I get time off for good behavior?"

"We'll discuss that, too." Dani got up and worked on putting away the plates and the boxes of leftover food. As he did the night before, Mark cleared the table and helped her with the few dishes. He ranged alongside her, brushing his body inadvertently against hers. She supposed the touch was accidental, anyway. She tried to ignore the sensation his nearness produced. She stuck a plate into the dishwasher then stood and faced him.

She knew the look on his face, the sleepy-eyed yet intense watchfulness of desire. Knowing full well what she was doing, Dani wrapped her arms around him and pulled him closer. He felt wonderful pressing against her. He groaned in his throat then they were kissing deeply. She ran her hands over his waist and up his back, reveling in the lean, muscled feel of him. She felt his erection press against her, and his hands cupped her rear and pulled her closer to him.

Dani nuzzled her cheek against his light stubble, admitting to herself he'd won. She was a goner, and she rejoiced inside. Maybe he was the winner, but she felt as though the victory was really hers. Life with him back in it was going to be ecstasy.

"Let's go upstairs," she murmured.

"No eye gouging? No arm breaking? What about the dogs?" His voice sounded husky in her ear.

"The couch, then. It would take too long to move the dogs around."

"By all means let's not waste any time." He gave her a throaty laugh. "I don't want a cold nose poking my butt."

She broke into laughter, too. "Cocky, aren't you?"

He trailed kisses down her throat. "Can you think of a better way to cap a most excellent weekend?"

She led him by the hand to the guest room and sat down on the couch. He settled next to her and wrapped his arms around her. "You don't need this tee shirt on, do you?" He ran his hands underneath her shirt and gently tugged it upward.

Dani allowed him to slip it off her head, lifting her arms to free them from the fabric. Then she ran her hands under his shirt. "It's like strip poker, only both of us have winning hands. You have to take your shirt off now."

He slipped out of his shirt and unhooked her bra. Freed, her breasts spilled into his hands. He kissed each of them and stroked them until the nipples stood up. Dani reveled in his touch. He was the only man she'd ever known, and returning to intimacy with him felt like a homecoming. He suckled at her breasts and she felt liquid fire burn in her center. She ran her hand down and felt his hardness, his readiness for her.

"Lie back," he murmured, and she complied. The rightness of it completely overcame any vestiges of mistrust, and she let her guardedness dissolve into oblivion. Still wearing his jeans, he pressed himself against her. Raw want flooded her being. Then he lowered his lips to hers and she felt his hot tongue exploring her own lips. She parted them and took him in, letting him probe, answering with her own teasing thrusts.

His hand reached down and unbuttoned her jeans. She did the same to him then pushed his trouser tops down, releasing his pent-up organ. She wrapped her hand around it, feeling the smooth, taut skin. He groaned again. "Don't stop me now."

A tiny voice of reason penetrated her overwhelming desire and her hand stilled. "Mark, I don't have any protection."

"So what? Don't stop doing that. It feels so good I could fly apart in delight. Listen. We're going to get married anyway."

"We are?" She let go and started to push him away but didn't have the will.

His gentle kisses trailed down her throat. "I love you, Dani. Always did."

A burst of joy leaped through her. "I love you, too, Mark. This time it's forever."

Off came his jeans, and hers, then he caressed her, stoking her fire at its source. His hand moved aside and he entered her with one motion, filling her with the aggressive press of his maleness. Worries about the risk of what they were doing were nothing compared to the rise of sensation he created within her. She pushed against him in urgent rhythm as he brought her to a peak of hot fire. He cried out as he came to his own peak, his thrusts matching her grip around him. Then, spent, he gathered her into his arms and kissed her face all over.

"I've been had," she murmured.

"Ah, wasn't it grand though?" he whispered in his ear.

She laughed softly. "This is how women get in trouble."

"No trouble. I told you. This is for keeps. We belong together."

She hugged him close, thinking it might just be true. She had never felt closer to any other human being than this. The moment of passion had come too soon for her druthers, but the sated way she felt right now, it was long overdue. Celibacy did have its drawbacks.

“Kevin might be right about one thing.”

Mark kissed her neck. “What’s that?”

“Maybe this will improve my disposition.”

He chuckled. “Nothing wrong with your disposition. I love you, woman.”

Dare she say it? She had never stopped loving him. Her resistance to him had been nothing but fear that she would find that love all over again only to have it snatched away.

His cell phone rang out The William Tell Overture. Mark glanced down where his jeans lay in a heap on the floor. “Never mind that. I’ll let voice mail catch it and call back.”

“Are you spending the night?”

“Is that an invitation?”

She traced his lips with her finger. “The horse is already out of the barn. We might as well enjoy it, right?”

She felt him, still inside her, start to harden again. He moved in a gentle rocking rhythm. “I can’t get enough of you,” he murmured.

They took their time, moving with less urgency, and to her amazement, it was just as delicious. When they finished, wrung out and satiated, he relaxed on her and covered her with his sheltering body. She hadn’t been so happy in a very long time.

“Think you’d better find out who called?” she asked.

“I guess.” He rolled off her and she reached for a box of tissues next to the couch. Still naked, he groped for the phone and pulled it out of his pants pocket. He checked the last number called and frowned.

“What’s the matter?” she asked.

“Strange. Never mind.” He pulled on his pants and left the room, cradling his cell phone. Dani made her way to the bathroom, carrying her clothes. She didn’t have a robe in this room and still had dogs to check on, so she had to get dressed.

When she finished, Mark was sitting on the couch fully clothed, an odd look on his face.

“What’s the matter?”

He scrubbed his hand over his face. “Something’s come up. I have to go home.”

“Oh, nuts.” She sat down next to him and laid her hand on his thigh. “Is everything okay?”

He looked away. “Nothing I can’t set straight.”

“I’ll miss you.”

“I’ll see you Tuesday.” He laid his hand over hers and nuzzled her neck. “We’ll pick up where we left off.”

“I can’t wait,” she admitted.

He gave her a lingering kiss before he left. Dani watched him drive away in his Blazer, then remembered that he’d left without Dolly.

What on earth had taken him away so abruptly, oblivious to his earlier intentions, and why wouldn’t he tell her what was going on? Another tiny voice piped up in her head, the one that warned her she was a fool to trust him.

She returned to the room to tidy the evidence of their lovemaking, then noticed he had left his cell phone on the couch. Maybe she ought to get a chain and attach it to him permanently. Might as well call him now and remind him he’d left it. Besides, she wanted to ask him about when he wanted to come back for Dolly. She called his house to leave a message on his answering machine.

Chapter Twelve

Jill wandered around Mark's house, touching his possessions, fantasizing about what it would be like to live there again. It was much nicer than Ted's house, which was a rental in a run-down neighborhood. She had always liked the woodsy natural setting of Mark's house, especially when it was their house. Ironic that he didn't hold her awed reverence for nature but lived here, and Ted was the ecologist who lived in the plastic, ticky-tacky development.

She wondered where Mark had been when she'd called. He didn't sound too happy to hear from her. She wondered if she stood another chance with him. He'd said he couldn't talk on the phone and he was coming straight home to hear what she had to say. That was the best thing. She'd be able to talk to him in person. Maybe she could get him to come to bed with her. A man was easiest to persuade when he was thinking with his second brain, the itty-bitty one located between his legs.

Ted didn't know where she was, and she hoped he wouldn't miss her and come looking. He and Al were all tied up in whatever it was they were working on. They'd gone off somewhere and she didn't even have to make up a story about where she was going. Maybe she wouldn't ever go back, if Mark let her stay. Sure it bothered her that Ted would want to kill both of them, but staying with him seemed even more dangerous. Mark could protect her; otherwise, she was on her own.

Ted's threats and Al's lurking presence had her scared in general, never mind specifics about Ted being jealous of Mark. For sure they planned to do something violent. How had she, a pacifist, managed to get herself mixed up with killers? Okay, maybe they weren't killers yet, but they appeared to be getting ready to pull something deadly.

Despite his warning, she'd risked turning on Al's computer before coming here. Everything, absolutely everything, was password protected, and she had no idea how to get in. She'd gotten nowhere with her investigation.

Going to the authorities wasn't part of the picture. She'd had enough trouble with them after getting caught releasing those rats. She hated the jack-booted thug police.

Mark's phone rang, and Jill picked it up immediately. "Hello," she purred into the mouthpiece.

The caller didn't say anything right away. "Hello," Jill repeated.

Just before she decided nobody was there and set down the receiver, a vaguely familiar woman's voice said, "Hi, I must have the wrong number. I wanted to speak to Mark Vaughn."

Jill thought fast. A girlfriend? Better nip that right away if she could. "Honey, it's the right number, all right. This is his wife Jill."

After another long, processing silence, the woman on the other end said, "Jill? This is Dani."

Dani? Was he back with Dani? Oh, yeah. He was doing agility with Rebel now. And doing bedroom agility with Dani besides? Not good. She really had to work on this before Dani stole him back. "Oh, hi. How you been?"

Dani's voice sounded shaky, confused. "I thought you were divorced."

"Oh, that. We're working things out. I moved back in."

Dani was silent so long Jill thought she might have fainted. "Hey, Dani. You still there?"

"Mark just left my place."

"Well, hell. That sorry lying sack of shit." Jill didn't have to fake it to seep rage into her voice. Damned if she was going to let Dani get her hooks into Mark again. Damn her for even trying. "He told me he had to go in to work today."

"He went to the agility trial with me," Dani said flatly.

"Did he now? How about yesterday? He said he was working Saturday, too. I guess the SOB is two-timing me." Jill was starting to have fun with her scenario. "He's doing it to you, too, from the sound of it. We ought to get together and beat the crap out of him."

"Tell him he left his cell phone here." The click on the other end signified the end of the conversation and the line went dead. Jill allowed herself a hopeful smile and set down the receiver. "No sense of humor, darlin? Too bad." The old playbook still might work because Dani was so freakin' gullible.

***

All the way home Mark mentally kicked himself for his procrastination He should have changed his locks long ago, but he'd never seen this coming. He'd let Jill keep a house key because she'd persuaded him she might have to get to Rebel in an emergency. That excuse was finished.

Jill had let herself in, called him from there, and now she was waiting for him. What did she want from him? At first he feared something was wrong with Rebel, but the put-on sweetness in Jill's voice made him realize right away that it wasn't an emergency. Whatever she wanted, it had ended an idyllic evening on a dissonant note. Giving up Dani's invitation to spend the night irked him, and he worried that Dani might take it wrong, too. But how could he tell her why he had to leave? She wouldn't take that well, not at all.

With a jolt, he realized he'd forgotten to bring Dolly home with him. That was how much Jill's call rattled him. He didn't turn back to get her because it was important to confront Jill immediately.

He still couldn't believe Dani had invited him into her bed and made love to him. It seemed like a wonderful dream, but it was real enough. He'd even mentioned marriage and she hadn't exactly freaked out. They could work out the arrangements between her business and his career. He didn't see any conflict. He could rent out his house and move in with her. Her house wasn't big, but they could add on if they wished. Or else she could hire more help and move in with him. He wouldn't quibble. He wanted the woman and didn't care about the details.

Was Jill going to somehow interfere? It was now clear she was behind his breakup with Dani two years ago. How blind had he been not to realize it? So much for believing the best of some people.

He drove up his driveway and spotted Jill's Yugo parked in his spot just as when they were still married. He pulled up next to it, unfolded out of his Blazer and strode into his house.

Jill met him at the door with a broad smile. She ran her tongue over her lips in that sexy way she had. She had fixed herself up and looked prettier than last time he saw her, not so sallow and sullen, as though she'd carefully prepared for the occasion. Did she really think him that susceptible? "Hi, Mark. How was your weekend?"

"Fine. Great. Look, what's going on? Why did you let yourself into my house?"

She shrugged. "Why don't we sit down and talk about things?" She led him into the living room and parked herself on the couch. Her short skirt rode up, exposing some thigh. He knew her well enough to realize she was out to seduce him. The idea disgusted him. Besides, his loyalty to Dani would have given him the good sense to turn down the invitation even if he hadn't just made love to her.

He remained standing. "Did you bring Rebel?"

"You don't get him until tomorrow. You know that."

"That's something I'd like to change." Mark forced a smile, trying to relax and strike a balance, let her know she couldn't con him and yet not antagonize her. She still had that bit of control over him in Rebel. "I'm going to want him some weekends."

"We can talk about that." She absentmindedly stroked her thigh. "I was thinking we could see more of each other, too."

He crossed his arms over his chest. Was she serious? At one time he was attracted to her, liked her, didn't mind helping her out in a grand gesture despite the cost to him. He'd even tried to make a life with her. But he'd been entirely disillusioned and no longer understood why he'd ever gotten mixed up with her. "What about Ted?"

"That isn't working out. Ted is a real dickhead." She gave him an earnest look. "You were the only man who ever treated me right. I know now what I was too dumb to see before, what I really had in you." Tears welled up in Jill's eyes. "I'm sorry I did that to you, Mark. I wouldn't ever do that again."

It was a fine performance. He'd learned enough to know that was all it was. Much as he'd like to laugh in her face, he'd better not insult her because she still had Rebel half the time, and she had the power to make the shared custody difficult for him. He took a deep breath. "Jill, you're an attractive woman, but I've moved on. I'm seeing Dani now. We've got a relationship going, and I'm happy. I want to see you happy, too, but I don't think I can give you what you want. The only thing we have in common any more is Rebel."

"So it's working out with Dani, huh?" Jill wiped a tear from her eye.

"I'm in love with her."

An odd, hard look crossed Jill's face, contradicting the tears. "I hope you can keep her. She does tend to run hot and cold, if you'll remember."

Almost certainly Jill had something to do with that. "Back then she was going through a lot of stress. Her grandmother practically raised her, and Dani had to be there for her while she was dying. She's fine now, and I'm confident we're solid."

Jill's expression held in a smirk that made Mark uneasy, but he wasn't sure why. She didn't seem inclined to move from the couch, either.

He continued, "I'll come by tomorrow after work to pick up Rebel. Maybe then we can talk about working out a different schedule."

"We'll see." Jill finally got up. "I don't want to make problems for you. That isn't what the arrangement is about. I just want to have my share of Rebel. I don't want to lose him." She looked down and wiped an eye with her finger. "Losing the baby was bad enough."

Mark shifted on his feet. "Nobody's trying to take Rebel away from you, Jill. I want to train him for agility, and I need certain days for him."

"If we got back together, it wouldn't be any problem, and we wouldn't have to split custody."

He shrugged. "That's a point." *When hell freezes over.*

"Sure. See you tomorrow." Jill sidled up to Mark and rubbed her body against his on the way out, like a cat in heat.

She might have been in heat, but she left him cold. He escorted her to the door and watched her drive away. She had taken his news about his renewed interest in Dani with surprising calm. He'd have to watch her. She certainly didn't have his interests at heart.

He closed the door and walked into his empty living room, missing Dani already. He couldn't even see her tomorrow night because she had that class. He'd have to wait until their Tuesday night appointment. Was it too late to call her? It would reassure him to hear her voice. Maybe it wasn't too late to go back to her place. He wanted to pick up Dolly anyway. That was a great excuse to go back, maybe stay the night as he'd intended before the rude cell phone call.

He glanced at the telephone and it made him think of his cell phone, which needed to be recharged. When he reached for it, the spot on his belt was vacant. Then he recalled setting it down on the table after Jill's call. He must have left it at Dani's again.

***

Jill certainly had poured cold water all over Dani's warm afterglow. She felt like a fool for letting down her guard with Mark so soon. Not only had she let down her guard, she'd invited him inside the gates to ransack her heart. Was he really playing a two-timing game, or was Jill up to her old tricks? How could she know for sure? Could she take Mark at face value, or was he hiding a secret desire to stay in Jill's good graces while he dallied with Dani? In any case, he sure was quick to run back to Jill when she called.

Just because a man made love to a woman didn't mean he was committed to her. Was his talk of marriage merely a ploy, a way to keep both women on the hook? He'd said he loved her, but those words were easy to mouth. And Jill was at his house in the middle of the night. What should she do? Should she cut and run, tell him she was finished with the uncertainty, or should she wait out the situation and find out who was on the level, Mark or Jill?

She picked up his cell phone and punched the buttons that revealed the number of the last incoming call. There it was, Mark's home phone number. When he took that call he'd skittered off to hide the conversation from her. No wonder, because Jill was calling from his own house. That made sense and explained why he'd been such in a hurry to run home.

What should she say to Mark? He couldn't deny Jill was at his house. She had the proof.

Her own phone rang and she knew without looking at the caller ID that it had to be Mark. She stared at the ringing phone as though it were a poisonous snake, then picked it up. "Yes?"

"Hi, Dani." His voice sounded mellow and sexy, but she wasn't about to be seduced again. "I miss you. How are you doing?"

"Fine. Just fine." Bitchiness snapped in her own voice.

He hesitated. "I forgot a couple of things."

"I should say you did. I'll leave your cell phone at the front desk and you can pick it up at your convenience."

"Dani, what's the matter? Are you okay?" He didn't sound mellow any more, but alarmed. Did he sense she was onto him? Should she let on she knew Jill was with him?

"Did Jill tell you I called?"

He paused again. "No. She didn't."

"Well, she told me some interesting things."

"Such as?"

"Is she listening in?"

"She went home. Back to Ted's." His voice hardened. "What interesting things did she tell you?"

"That she was living there. With you."

"You believed that?"

"Should I?"

"You ought to have more faith in me than that, Dani." He sounded offended, turning it around on her. "Do you really think I'm capable of that kind of deceit?"

Of course he would deny it. "I don't know. I do know she was waiting there for you."

"Without my permission."

"She sounded very much at home."

"You could come over and inspect the house." His voice was cool, measured. "See if you can find Jill, her clothes or any of her stuff. If you won't simply take my word for it, there's a bigger problem between us than I thought."

"Maybe there is."

"One more time. She let herself into the house last night and left as soon as she found out she couldn't get her way with me."

"Why didn't you level with me before you blew out of here?"

She heard him catch his breath. "How would you have taken that news?"

"At least you would have been honest with me."

"Would you have been any happier about it?"

She found it difficult to speak and didn't want him to know how upset she was. "I have to go."

***

Mark stared at the receiver, set the phone down and slumped onto the couch. Hot and cold, Jill had said. There went Dani again, ready to quit him at the first hint of a difficulty, real or fancied. The conversation had blasted to hell the euphoria her acceptance and their lovemaking had induced. She had cut him off as though she'd rather believe Jill's lies over anything he had to say.

He punched in her number again. She didn't answer this time. He listened her recorded message, then said levelly, "Dani, we need to talk, in person. I'm on my way so we can discuss this face to face."

She finally picked up the phone, sounding flat. "Don't. It's too late."

Too late. Mark clenched the receiver. "This is too important to put off."

"Come if you must. I'll leave your phone inside the screen door. Don't bother to knock, because I won't come to the door."

The line clicked on her end and he listened to silence. He sat back in the couch and scrubbed his hand over his face. Jill had done it again, wedged herself between them. But why was Dani so willing to let her do it? Was it just an excuse to distance herself from him? Maybe Dani was afraid of him, afraid of getting involved. As far as he knew she hadn't gotten attached to anybody else since they had broken up before. It was starting to look like a pattern, one he didn't like. Dani was too quick to think the worst of him, and this was just one more time she made as though she wanted to run out on him.

Maybe he was the one who ought to run.

Chapter Thirteen

The next morning Dani found time to stay in the office attacking the long overdue paperwork, a welcome distraction. Her dogs lounged at her feet, obviously tired from the stressful weekend. She had brought Dolly inside as well. Jim's medication had gotten the better of him, and his mother had called in sick for him. Fortunately, it was quiet for a Monday. Dani should have been able to concentrate, but she was far too upset.

The weekend was memorable for success, enjoyment and a great letdown. Lulled into feeling easier with Mark, she'd no longer felt the need to push him away. Her cold rage toward him had diffused like morning frost in the noonday sun. For a time she'd believed that holding onto her hurts didn't benefit her in any way she could name. It seemed too much effort to question his every motive and guard her every emotion.

Yes, she'd wanted him. Wanted him in every way possible. So much for staying detached and protecting herself. Her heart was wide open, all over again. She was the one who let it happen, and he certainly hadn't put up any fight. If she hadn't opened the door, he wouldn't have been able to push through. She couldn't blame him for making love to her when she practically asked for it.

Then that short, shattering conversation with Jill brought back every doubt, every suspicion she'd ever harbored. Was Mark really a two-timing snake? Wasn't she right not to feel safe with him? She ought to be able to find out for sure. It should be easy enough to check up on him. But from the way he'd reacted, he would resent it if she actually needed to verify his denial. If life with Mark was a constant routine of trying to figure out were she stood, she didn't need it.

Kevin came to the door and leaned one hip against the jamb. "Excuse me, sweets, but I could use a little help." Dolly raised up and stared at him, tail tucked, a far different reaction than Mark elicited from her.

Dani felt a surge of annoyance that Dolly liked Mark better

than Kevin, who had a fine way with most dogs. "What's the matter?"

"I have a Corgi with talons from hell, but she won't let me clip them. I tried the grinder, but she came unglued at the noise. I need your magic touch."

Dani got up from her computer desk and followed him into the grooming room. Crash lifted his head, noting her departure. Dolly licked her lips, still with a worried look, but didn't bolt.

In the playpen lay a little black and tan Pembroke Corgi, curled into a self-protective ball, a strained, distrustful expression in her eyes. Dani could relate. She reached down and stroked the Corgi's rough fur. "What's her name?"

"Cindy. She doesn't want her feet touched. Watch it. She might snap."

Cindy sniffed Dani's hand. "Ticklish? Or are you afraid?" Dani picked up the chunky little dog and cradled it against her chest. "May I see your feet?" Dani gently touched Cindy's forelegs and worked her way down to the toes. The dog reluctantly endured the examination, wincing when Dani touched her feet, but didn't show any resentment. Kevin was right about the nails. They were too long for Cindy's health, curving far beyond the pads. "Those feet are going to splay if we don't tame the claws," Dani said.

"She's a new client," Kevin said. "My guess is her mama hasn't ever cut her nails."

"My guess is Cindy wouldn't let her anyway." Dani sensed, though of course it was just an assumption, that Cindy's nails had been cut beyond the quick earlier in life and she feared a repeat of the painful experience. "Cindy, it's like this. Your nails have to be trimmed a little, or you won't be able to walk right. Sometimes it pinches a bit, but then it's over with. If you relax and hold still, we can get it done fast and it won't hurt too much."

"I can muzzle her. It might be the safest way to go," Kevin offered.

Dani shook her head, thinking it would upset Cindy even more to be helpless. "I'll take my chances." She took a deep breath and let it out, settling into a regular, unhurried rhythm. She held onto Cindy, cupping her hand around the dog's underjaw, while Kevin took a paw and massaged it. He crooned to her, trying to keep her calm. It was a rare dog Kevin couldn't sweet-talk into letting him have his way with it. He didn't often need help from her. Dolly was the only other exception Dani could think of.

"Careful not to cut into the quicks. That would confirm her worst fears. Just take a little off the end for now." Cindy flinched in her arms. Kevin gave Dani a withering look. "Okay, okay. Never mind. You're a pro," she amended.

Still, it was easy enough to make a mistake even when the trimmer was being careful. Cindy squirmed but didn't fight hard enough to prevent Kevin from cutting each nail. When they finished, Dani held Cindy for a little while longer, stroking her. "See, no blood. And you've still got all your toes. That wasn't so bad, was it? Do you trust us now?"

The Corgi was still apprehensive, not knowing what else was coming, not knowing whether she could relax and trust these humans. Dani was having trust issues of her own.

"Ah, Dani, thank you for having a word with Miss Cindy," Kevin said. "I knew you could get her to understand we weren't planning to cut out her liver. They always listen to you."

Dani set Cindy onto the grooming table and gently held her there to make sure she didn't jump off. Was it true she had a special rapport with dogs? A knowing that went beyond the usual training and observation? If so, she ought to enjoy a great advantage, but owning such a gift could be a great curse as well. Did she really want to know what her dogs thought of her? It might be just as bad as knowing what subterfuge lay behind a person's smiles. Maybe she ought to try reading Mark's mind. Yikes, did she really want to go there?

Not any more than she wanted to intrude into a dogs' mind, even though animals didn't know guile. A dog would let her know its opinion, unsparing of feelings.

Kevin took over with Cindy, parting and brushing her thick coat. "You've been mighty glum today, sweets. Is your love life taking a bad turn? I was hoping you'd get lucky over the weekend."

Dani deliberately misunderstood. "Didn't you see all the ribbons my guys won? I'd say I got really lucky."

"Dani, you know what I mean." He stroked his beard and wriggled his eyebrows. "How's Mark?"

"He's fine." She crossed her arms over her chest. "We're good friends, and we had a nice, friendly time at the agility trial."

"Good friends. That's lovely. Then why are you so grinchy?"

Should she voice her doubts? Why not? She did feel safe with Kevin, more so than with Mark. She'd told him enough about her history with Mark that he might understand where she was coming from. Kevin wasn't going to get her into an emotional entanglement, nor was he going to make a play for Mark. Really, it would be a hoot to see him try. "I called his house to tell him he forgot his cell phone, and his ex-wife answered."

Kevin stroked his beard. "Didn't you tell me she lived elsewhere? Did she say why she was there?"

"She claimed things weren't working out with her boyfriend, and she had gone back to Mark. She acted mad because he was at the agility trial with me instead of at work like he'd told her."

"Did you ask Mark for an explanation?"

"He acted insulted that I believed a word she'd said."

"Do you?'

"It's more complicated than that. I was having trouble trusting him anyway. Now Jill is back in the picture, and she claims she's living with him again. He was testy when I brought it up. Guilty people do that, blame the person who dares to question them. So do innocent people." She shook her head. "I don't know if we can make this work."

"Dani, you've been skittish about him from the start. Do you want it to work?"

"We had a nice weekend together. We were really getting along. He was changing my mind about him. Then Jill made me rethink the whole thing."

"Didn't she run you off before? Are you going to let her do that again? I thought you were more of a fighter than that."

Dani stared at him. "He was too easy to run off the first time. He didn't waste any time getting together with her once I was out of the picture." It was the same pattern all over again. In a way, she wished he'd overridden her insistence he not come straighten out things between them last night. "Kevin, he's the one that's not much of a fighter. I tell him to back off and he won't push."

"Maybe the poor guy mistakenly thinks no means no."

"Whose side are you on, anyway?"

"Yours, sweets. When are you seeing him again? Tonight?"

"I have another self-defense class tonight."

"Ah, you're the one that's the fighter."

"Want to see a demonstration?

"As long as it's not up close and personal."

"Come, on, Kevin. I need to practice." She grinned and shifted her weight.

"Are you going to knee me in the groin?" Kevin lowered his hand protectively. "Back off, sweets."

"Trust me." Dani widened her eyes. "I won't hurt you. I'll just show you." She sidled close to him and slipped an arm around his shoulders. "I have to get real close, like this. Get friendly. Say things like, 'What a fine looking rapist you are.'"

Kevin tensed and gave her a strained smile. "Oh, yeah?"

"I bring up my other hand to cup his cheek, but instead," Dani pointed two fingers at his face. "I stick my fingers in his eyes." She released him and backed away, spreading her hands. "Works every time. The instructor guarantees it."

"Have you tried it for real?"

Dani sighed. "Nobody's attacked me yet, so I haven't had a chance to practice."

"Chin up, sweets. Maybe you'll get your chance yet."

***

Ted loved how the plan was starting to come together. He opened the drive-through gate to let Al bring the stolen cargo van into the back yard. He had lifted a license plate from a different vehicle to further confuse anybody looking for the van. He doubted they would look very hard for the old wreck. Even the balding tires weren't worth salvaging.

The privacy fence had so far screened their activities from the neighbors and should continue to protect them from scrutiny. The neighbors mostly kept to themselves anyway. Al finally had all the ingredients collected and ready in the utility shed.

He noticed Rebel wander out of the open gate and yelled at him to come back in. The damned dog ignored him as usual, just kept going. Ted thought about getting Jill to fetch the beast, then remembered she'd just now taken off to pick up groceries. So she said. He'd check the mileage on her Yugo after she got home and see how far she'd really gone.

"Close the gate," Al called out.

Ted shrugged and complied. He wasn't about to chase down Jill's stupid dog. Nor did he want to leave the gate open, exposing the red-hot van to the view of anybody walking down the street.

***

After work, Mark pointed the Blazer toward Jill's home to pick up his dog. He steeled himself for another encounter with Jill the spoiler. At least he was onto her this time.

Still, was it fair to blame Jill completely for Dani's eagerness to believe the worst of him? Was it possible that he and Dani were getting along so well that she had to find justification for backing off? He wasn't a shrink. All he knew was he wanted Dani.

They had plenty of unfinished business. He still needed to pick up his cell phone. Plus she still had Dolly, and he'd paid her in advance for Rebel's agility classes. Would she have the nerve to expel him from class?

He left 103rd Street and turned into the subdivision, following a red pickup truck. The driver of the pickup accelerated ahead, faster than the posted limit.

Mark rounded the last corner before Jill's house, and a flash of orange and white movement in the road just beyond the pickup caught his attention. To his horror, he made out Rebel trotting down the middle of the lane toward the speeding truck.

Mark screamed "Stop!" to the other driver, even though he certainly couldn't hear, and leaned on the horn. He willed his Collie to get out of the road, out of the way. Was his dog going to be killed right in front of his eyes?

Then the pickup veered around the oblivious dog, barely missing his flank, and accelerated away. Mark breathed "Thank you" out loud, then pulled over and slammed on the brakes. He jerked open the door, slid off the driver's seat and called the dog. Rebel frisked to him, apparently unhurt.

Mark grasped Rebel's collar to make sure he wouldn't dart away and guided him to the shoulder of the road. "You dodged a bullet that time, buddy." Suddenly weak-kneed, he sat down on the grass and clung to his dog, trembling with relief.

And rage. The only reason Rebel would be roaming the streets was because somebody turned him outside. "What's going on with Jill?" he asked the dog. "Has she completely lost her mind?" Was this carelessness on Jill's or Ted's part or a deliberate act?

He hustled Rebel to the rear of the Blazer, opened the doors and let him jump into the crate. He secured the crate door. Once Rebel was safely contained, Mark got back in the SUV and continued to Jill's house. He pulled into the driveway and stared at the house. Her car was gone. Only Al's Honda sat in the carport.

Mark strode to the front door and rang the doorbell. Nobody came, but he heard a TV blaring inside. He banged on the door with his closed fist, bruising his knuckles. That was a waste. He'd rather bruise them on somebody's chin.

He waited an interval, then gave up and returned to his Blazer. He backed out of the driveway and headed home, his knuckles white on the steering wheel.

"Tell you what, buddy." He glanced over his shoulder, directing his words to the rear of the SUV. "I'm not going to let her risk your neck any more. You're staying with me where you don't have to eat tofu and won't get squashed on the road. Let her sue me. This is war."

***

Business picked up in the afternoon, and Dani had to rush to make it in time for her self-defense class. She fed her own dogs then realized she was starved. She opened the refrigerator and shoved the contents around until she found something edible, a take-out box of barbecued pork from a few nights before. She sniffed it suspiciously, deemed it acceptable, and popped it into the microwave.

Dani poured herself a glass of water and took the warmed leftovers out of the microwave. Her dogs acted interested, pressing close. "You've had your dinner, guys. Go lie down." The three of them acted as though they didn't understand a word of it and ringed close around the table. Dani shooed them out of the kitchen and closed the door.

The leftovers were surprisingly good, and the meal bolstered her strength. The taste and smell of the barbecue reminded her of her talk with Mark a few nights ago. She'd thought they'd made some progress toward clearing the air, but the fog had set in all over again. Never mind the unsettling conversation with Jill; maybe she had never forgiven him for marrying Jill. Without forgiveness and trust, their relationship had no future. Could she simply take his word for it that he was truly finished with Jill? What about the next time Jill jerked his chain. Would he do another fast recall?

The doorbell rang, jolting her out of her reverie. All three dogs barked as though they believed she was too deaf to hear it herself. Was that Mark? Hadn't she told him the phone would be inside the screen door? Still chewing, she wiped her mouth, and waded through the excited dogs clustered in the foyer.

Mark stood there looking harried and held his cell phone up, showing her he'd found it. "Thanks. Got a minute? Really. We have to talk." The sight of him had the wrong effect. Her insides went mushy despite her resolve to steel up.

"That's about all the time I have. What's the matter?" Alarmed at his grim demeanor, she stepped aside and let him in. The dogs swirled around his legs, Dolly shyly wagging and sniffing Mark's fingers. He reached down and stroked her head, his posture relaxing slightly. Dolly jumped up and licked his chin, the bravest thing Dani had ever seen her do.

Mark shifted his gaze to Dani and caught his breath as though he'd been running. "I just came from the house where Jill's shacked up with that Ted slime bag. They let Rebel run loose. Just like those lab rats."

"Oh, my God. Is he all right?"

"He was running down the street and almost got hit. But I've got him now. He's in the Blazer."

She let out her own breath in relief. Now matter how she felt about Mark right now, she empathized with his concern. Another reality struck her. If Rebel wasn't living at Mark's house, neither was Jill, unless he was lying about that, too.

Maybe the compulsive liar among them wasn't Mark. He didn't appear to harbor that sort of deceit, and it would have taken a novelist or a discredited news anchor to invent the whole situation. She made a decision to take him at his word until she found out otherwise. "You can't let him go back there, court order or not."

Mark's face was taut with anger. "I'd see Ted in hell first. Jill close behind."

"Who let him out?"

"Doesn't matter. Jill's car wasn't there and nobody answered the door. Whoever let him out could do it again. They have a perfectly good fenced back yard, and Rebel isn't an escape artist.

I doubt he climbed or dug out."

"In this day and age nobody with a brain lets a dog run loose. Are they nuts? I mean really, really out of their freakin' minds?"

"Dani, I'm still so mad I can't see straight." His voice leveled and he sounded calmer. He expelled his breath as though he'd been holding it. "Sorry. I had to vent." He looked down at Dolly, who had backed up in response to the angry sound of his voice. "You, too, Dolly. Sorry I yelled." He knelt down, and Dolly came up to him to rejoin the other two dogs, sniffing his hand, a soft yearning look in her eyes. "Dani, do you still want me to take her?"

"Is it a good time?"

He let out his breath and shook his head. "I need to get some things straightened out first. How about if I pick her up tomorrow?"

No matter what her conflicted feelings about Mark, they didn't have anything to do with his rapport with Dolly. "Okay."

He locked eyes with her. "At the same time, I'm coming for a private lesson with Rebel."

"What if I say no?"

"Dani, I'm the one who ought to be spitting mad. I've done nothing wrong, but you're making a federal case out of it. Maybe I was wrong to think we could get back together if you don't want to believe in me." He turned toward the door. "I'll let you go to your class. Bye."

She watched him stride back to his Blazer. Was she really in the wrong, or was he just laying a guilt trip on her? She wasn't used to being told off by Mark and wasn't sure how to take it. She had a fleeting impulse that she should call him back inside and apologize for giving a moment's credit to Jill's word.

Not yet. What if she her instincts were wrong again? Could she trust any of her own instincts? The niggling doubt remained in the back of her mind.

***

Jill pulled up at the house and carried her groceries inside. Rebel didn't greet her; then she remembered that Mark was supposed to pick him up this afternoon. She hoped he and Ted hadn't gotten into a fight. All they had to do was look at each other and they wanted to have a slugfest. The living room looked tidier than usual. The guys had finally picked up some of their high-tech junk. Well, ta-da for them.

She opened the sliding glass door and stuck her head out. Rebel wasn't there either, but what was that gas-guzzling van doing in the back yard? She walked outside and Ted came from the back of the van and met her. "Go back in the house, babe."

"What's the van for?"

"Al borrowed it." Ted's voice dropped to an excited whisper. "He's got stuff to haul."

"What stuff?" She remembered the conversation Ted told her to forget and how the men celebrated the car bombing of a pharmaceutical plant. Was that what Ted and Al were up to? She couldn't see inside the van to know what they were hauling. She didn't want to know, either.

"Yeah, we're going to go on a little trip. You ought to pack up. Your clothes, anything you just can't live without."

"What trip? Where?"

"Yak, yak, yak. What is this, twenty questions? What's for supper?"

"I'm working on it." She looked around the yard. Al emerged from the shed, watching her, then slipped into the house. "Where's Rebel? Did Mark pick him up?"

Ted shrugged. "Beats me. I've been out here all afternoon."

"But the front door is locked. Mark couldn't have gotten him without your letting him in."

"The mutt wasn't in the house. He took off when we opened the gate to drive the van in."

"What? You let him out?"

"I didn't let him out. He let himself out. You know the dumb mutt won't come when I call him. I didn't worry about it. I've been busy."

"Geez, Ted. I thought you gave a flip about me and you know I love that dog." She slammed the door on the way in, and Ted followed. She whirled on him. "I've got to call Mark and make sure he got him."

"Oh, hell. I told you not to talk to that prick. Anyway, what are you worried about? He's a dog. An animal, not a baby. He can take care of himself."

Jill retreated into the kitchen, picked up the phone, and

defiantly punched in Mark's number. It rang a few times before the answering device picked up. "Mark, you there?" she whispered into the receiver. He didn't pick up, so she hung up and called his cell phone. All she got was the "no service" message. Either the battery was dead or the phone was turned off.

The men had gone into Al's room. She unloaded the grocery bag. Soy milk, soy cheese, granola, tofu, organic carrots and cucumbers. She couldn't even think of fixing supper when she had so much on her mind.

Rebel's safety was only one of her worries. The more she contemplated the guys blowing up Crohn, the worse she felt about it. Violence wasn't the answer, and she didn't want anybody she knew fried. Now with the men holed up in Al's room, and now that she had an excuse to call Mark, maybe she ought to do something about it, short of ratting them out to the company. It might blow up their plans as well, but at this point she questioned the ethics of their project. Maybe it would be better if they failed.

Again she picked up the kitchen phone and punched in Mark's home number. She'd talk to Mark, then she would leave Ted cold. Let him fix his own damn supper. He'd told her to pack, so she would and didn't have to answer any questions about it. She didn't need this kind of grief. If Mark let her move back in, great. If not, she'd find her own digs, far away from Ted and Al.

This time Mark answered. "Mark, this is Jill. Did you pick up Rebel?"

"Why wasn't he in his fenced yard?"

"You got him?" Relief made her weak-kneed even though Mark sounded pissed off enough to eat snakes. Damn Ted for not caring what happened to Rebel. At least Mark did.

"Who let him out?" Mark demanded.

"Ted did. He's all right, isn't he?"

"I'm looking at him. Lucky that truck barely missed him. No thanks to you and your boyfriends."

"Mark, it won't happen again. I swear."

"Damned straight it won't happen again. And tell that scumbag Ted something for me. Tell him if anything had happened to my dog, right now he'd be staring straight up at a hospital ceiling. Got it?"

She dropped her voice really low so the guys wouldn't overhear back there in Al's room. "You're right. He is a scumbag, and I've just about had it with him. If you put his ass in the hospital and kick Al's ass back to Oregon, that would be fine with me." Before he could react, she added, "Look. There's something else I have to tell you."

"What, Jill?"

His voice was so cold she almost changed her mind, but she said it anyway. "Um, can you be sick for a few days, like, not show up for work?"

Another pause. "What's going on?"

"Don't ask any questions, Mark. Please?"

"Come on, Jill. What's your game? Besides trying to torpedo my relationship with Dani. For the second time. What did you tell her?"

Damn. He was onto her. "Not much. You know what a suspicious mind she has."

"I know your conniving one. What are you plotting now?"

"I can't tell you. Just do what I say."

"What's going on? Are you planning to blow up the place next? First destroy the cancer project, then the whole company?"

She caught her breath, realizing she'd screwed up and he'd guessed right. "Never mind, jerkface." She slammed down the phone and stood for a while chewing her thumbnail, trying to decide whether he was just blowing smoke about guessing what was going on. She didn't dare confess to Ted what she'd done. He'd kill her.

From the sound of it, Mark wasn't going to let her move in with him either.

Let him get his sorry ass blown sky high. See if she cared.

***

Al set the phone back in its cradle. He'd listened to the whole conversation. Ted had been with him in Command Central watching him eavesdrop.

Al folded his hands over his belly and sat back in the lawn chair he used at the computer desk. "Ted, me boy, that bitch of yours is a loose cannon."

Ted looked like he was about to explode, figuratively speaking. "What's she up to now?"

"Where shall I start? Your honey just told Vaughn he ought to put the 'scumbag,' that is, you, in the hospital. Then she told him he ought to miss work for a few days. That sure set him to asking questions. Sounds like he might have made the leap and figured out somebody's going to attack Crohn."

Ted's face lit up like a Roman candle, but it wasn't as pretty. "You're shitting me. That sorry–" He jumped up and ran out of the room.

Al followed lazily, interested in watching the drama unfold. He wasn't worried yet. A little damage control, and he would be fine. He didn't believe Vaughn would be able to do much with what he heard Jill tell him, especially if they acted right away and nipped this problem before it got out of control.

He would have to move up the timetable. He'd scrap their plans to carry out their mission during work hours for maximum damage. They couldn't wait until the next day. He had most everything in place, the van packed with plastic explosives and hardware that would turn into shrapnel. They would have to pack up the computer and personal effects because he wouldn't be returning to the house after the job was completed, despite what he'd told Ted. His useful idiot Ted appeared ready to roll, but he'd better watch the clown to see he didn't go postal before the deed went down. Al had a few contingency plans perking in his mind.

Al prided himself on being a neat freak about his job. He believed in cleaning up after himself.

***

When Jill heard Ted's heavy footfalls in the hallway, her instincts warned her to flee. She lurched toward the kitchen door, but he grabbed her by the arm before she could slip outside. Her strength was no match for his. He dragged her back into the house.

"What the hell did you call Vaughn for?" His eyes blazed hot, lips compressed, but he wasn't yelling. That was the scariest part.

"Hey, let go." She tried to squirm free of his hurtful grip.

"Hold still." He hit her open-handed on the side of her face, and it stung. "I warned you," he raged. "Anything I hate, it's a traitor."

Tears came to her eyes, and she turned away from him. "What's the matter with you, Ted? You knew I had to call him about Rebel."

"Yeah and tell the jerk I'm a scumbag. And tell him to lay low from work for a few days. You been in cahoots with him all the time? Betraying me?" Ted's calm voice wasn't fooling her. He was about to explode.

"Honest, Ted. That isn't so."

Al stood in the hallway, smirking. Her heart sank deeper, if that was possible. "Giving him a heads-up so he can foul us up." Al added. "Who else you gonna talk to? The freakin' police?"

"No. I swear." She sagged in Ted's grip. "I just didn't want him to get hurt, that's all."

"A real heroine," Al said. "A whistle-blower."

"No!" Jill squirmed some more, then stopped when she felt Ted harden his grip and saw his free hand come up again in warning. "I'm with you guys all the way. I was just scared for him, but he made me mad and I don't care what happens to him now."

Al leaned against the counter and folded his arms. "Tell you what, darlin'. We'll let you off the hook if you'll help us out."

"Sure, Al." He sounded so reasonable, she felt a surge of hope. "Whatever you say."

"We gotta discuss it first. Just Ted and me, in private, like."

Jill managed a smile. Her hopes lifted another degree. "You guys go ahead and talk. I'll stay right here."

"Ted, hold onto her while I get some duct tape." Al sauntered back down the hall.

"Duct tape? Geez, Ted. You aren't gonna let him truss me up, are you?"

"Can't let you make any more crank calls, babe, can we now?" He said it right into her ear. His grip on her arm was so hard it would leave bruises, if she lived that long. She hugged herself in fear.

***

Ted took Jill into the bathroom. He didn't feel like being gentle, so he first taped her mouth shut so she wouldn't holler. He trussed her up so tight he hoped her joints popped loose. He felt like killing her but controlled himself because he and Al needed to make plans first. Then he went with Al into Command Central and shut the door. The bugs were crawling on him again. He tried not to scratch his arms as he sat on the bed. His gut had tightened into a fist. He crossed one leg over the other and didn't even try to stop his foot jiggling.

"Calm down," Al said. "You look like you're about to go through the roof. I need you to have a cool head."

"I need a joint, man. Good, strong stuff."

Al shook his head. "A reality check is what you need."

"What are you gonna get her to do?"

"Here's the deal. First we got to pack up the rest of our stuff and put it in the Honda. Computer, clothes, anything we need. Sweep the house, make sure we're not leaving anything incriminating. Then we'll all three of us go down to Vaughn's house in two cars, mine and hers. He's home now, and we'll make sure he's still there before we go. It's got to be tonight. Tell her we got to get his ID pass, promise her we won't hurt anybody. After we cruise on in, we waste them both. Then we'll come back here and get the van and anything we might have overlooked, do our job at the plant, and get the hell out of Dodge."

Ted licked his dry lips, then found his voice. "Now you're talking. I can't wait to waste Vaughn."

"Ted, my man, let me remind you that we're soldiers. We have a duty here. We have to do things in an orderly way to succeed."

"You don't think I can handle it?" It seemed as though more bugs were making his skin crawl, and he rubbed his arms.

"You ever done anybody before?" Al's face snaked into a grim but comradely smile. "You've got to keep a cool head."

Ted scratched his neck and thought about Jill and her ratting him out to Vaughn. He'd been suspicious all along that she still wanted that button-down creep, and he'd been right. Besides, she had gotten to be a real drag lately. An albatross around his neck, getting in the way. Not getting to kill her would be a real let down. As for Vaughn, he hoped he could take his time on that one, make him squirm.

Al kept talking. "If we make it look good, like a breaking and entering, nobody has to connect us. We'll jimmy a lock after we do 'em, take any money or good electronics he has sitting around. Nobody will notice for a while. Didn't you say he lives in the woods?"

"His house is way off the road down a long driveway. No neighbors close by. We could drive in and out, nobody's likely to see us. If we use Jill's car, nobody would think much of it anyhow. What are we going to do, leave it there like she went to see him?" Ted was starting to calm down, thinking better, warming to the idea of a sensible plan. "Yeah, we'll leave in your car. I don't think he has an alarm system."

"No problem. He'll let Jill in, won't he? We'll do it tonight. Soon as we can."

"Jill has his key." Ted shifted positions as he thought out loud.

"Think he changed his locks since they split up?"

"He let her keep it for the mutt's sake. For emergencies. I didn't like it but figured it might come in handy some time."

"You figured right. We could get it all done in one stroke." Al's confidence was contagious.

"Yeah. The van is loaded." Ted started to feel the excitement again and a return of his sense of purpose. "We can pull this off."

Chapter Fourteen

Jill's call disturbed Mark so much that he called plant security. Mr. Snyder was gone for the day, but Mark spoke to the guard and asked him to be extra vigilant. The guy sounded more bored than alarmed.

He hoped he wasn't just crying wolf, but more and more it appeared she and Ted were up to no good as far as Crohn was concerned. She'd tried to warn him. Of what? Were they going to attempt some violent act of sabotage against the plant? Should he call the police, too? What was he going to tell them, that his ex-wife told him not to go to work for a few days? What would they think that was about? It sounded less than damning, even to him.

He called Mr. Snyder at home, knowing he at least would take him seriously, but all he got was an answering device. He left a message. He tried the regional vice president, but the line was busy. No use going over to the plant. What was he supposed to do? Stake out the place? He was a scientist by training, not a policeman.

Still, he had to keep trying. He called the police dispatcher and told her the little bit he knew. Afterward, he realized what he told her wasn't convincing. Would the police bother to follow up on it or dismiss him as a crank?

Restless, wanting to go see Dani in spite of their recent unpleasantness, he wandered into the kitchen for a snack, Rebel padding after him. He poured himself a glass of milk but made a face at the first nasty-tasting sip and spat it into the sink. "Sour," he told Rebel. "Guess I haven't been spending much time at home." No, he'd been seeing a lot of Dani instead, and he feared Jill had added enough acid to curdle their relationship. Was his newly rediscovered love for Dani so tenuous that it couldn't withstand a challenge? He poured the remainder of the milk down the drain and tossed the carton into the trash can.

Too bad. He really did want a glass of milk and some chocolate chip cookies. But then, fresh milk was only as far away as the convenience store. Come to think of it, he needed a fill-up for his SUV, too. Also, he could no longer allow Jill to walk into his house any time she chose. She hadn't given him cause to worry about having access to his house until yesterday. She'd been merely indifferent, not vindictive. He didn't want a repeat of that unsettling surprise. It was past time to install new locks on his doors.

He checked his watch. It was only eight thirty. He could still make it to the Home Depot before closing time. He'd better pick up the locks and change them tonight.

He considered taking Rebel along for the ride but didn't see the benefit. He would simply have to leave him in the vehicle at every stop. He didn't expect Jill to cause any problems over Rebel until he refused to take him back to her on the designated day, which wasn't until Thursday.

"I won't be gone long," he told Rebel. "You might as well stay here and be comfortable." He considered leaving Rebel loose in the house, then remembered the chewed chair leg and realized that might be a bad idea. He crated Rebel in the living room with his rawhide bone to keep him busy and left, locking the door behind him.

***

On the way to Mark's house, Jill sat next to Al, who was driving. Ted led the way in her Yugo. Al had explained the deal, that they were going to go see Mark and get his ID pass. He promised they would just leave the two of them tied up a while, until they got their business done. He assured her they weren't out to hurt anybody, just an evil corporation that deserved whatever it got. They had only the best of intentions for the environment and the world.

She didn't believe him. The handgun positioned in his lap didn't square with his pacifist line. She was scared enough to puke.

At least they'd removed the duct tape. It was too dark for anybody in another car to see her trying to signal for help. Given the chance, she could walk or even run. She thought about opening the door and diving out when Al slowed down for a turn. But she might get herself run over trying that stunt. Plus she didn't doubt he'd use that gun on her. Frozen with indecision, she just sat trembling.

"Your job," Al told her in a reasonable voice, "Is to get him to open his door. You have to convince him you are only here to see your dog."

"He won't buy that." Jill swiped the sweat-damp hair from her forehead. "He's real pissed about finding him outside."

"He'd better buy it, pissed or not. Be convincing. We'll do the rest."

Both drivers cut their lights as they climbed the long driveway. Once they got past the dark tunnel of trees, Mark's post light illuminated the rest of the way. They pulled up and stopped in front of the empty carport.

"Where's Vaughn's SUV?" Al asked her.

She shrugged. "How am I supposed to know? So he isn't home. He didn't tell me where he was going."

"He answered the phone just a few minutes ago."

"Go figure."

Jill watched him slip on a pair of plastic gloves from a box behind the front seat. Then he took out a dark blue ski mask and fitted it over his head. He looked scary, his hollow eyeholes like the ones in a skull. He looked like one of those terrorists on TV who was about to whack some poor guy's head off. Jill started to open her car door, trying to decide whether she could give him the slip, but right then Ted came up and jerked her door wide. He was done up in a ski mask, too, which gave her a fresh case of the creeps. Her heart thumped like a jackhammer.

"Where's your key?" Al asked. "You need to get us into the house."

She swallowed past her constricted throat. "Aren't you going to try the doorbell first? Maybe his car's in the shop." If only that was the case. Maybe if she could give Mark some warning, he could save them both. He was a big, strong guy.

"You do it. Get out."

Jill fumbled in her purse, wanting to stall.

"Hurry up," Al snapped.

She closed her hand around the key chain and took it out. Feeling weak, she managed to step out of the car. She walked toward the front door, Ted and Al closing in behind her.

The men stood aside, out of sight of the peephole and the

window as she rang the doorbell. After a short pause, Al ordered her to use the key.

The key still worked. She turned the knob and eased the door open. Al shoved her inside. The men charged into the house like a SWAT team on TV, Al with his pistol drawn.

The foyer light was on, but Mark didn't appear and Rebel didn't run up to greet her either. Then she heard him barking from inside the house.

"Where does he keep his ID badge?" Ted asked.

"Bedroom. On the dresser," Jill managed to choke out of her dry mouth.

"Let's go."

She headed into the living and found Rebel in his wire crate. When she spoke to him he quit barking and wagged his whole body rattling the metal frame. His face shone a grinning, innocent welcome. Would he defend her if she turned him loose and the men tried to harm her?

She started toward the crated dog, but Al snapped, "What the hell are you doing? We came for Vaughn's ID card, not the damned dog."

Jill knew better than to disobey. "Not now, Rebel." She slunk down the hallway toward the master bedroom, aware of Al and Ted following. She walked into Mark's room, glanced at his unmade bed and wondered where he had gone. Maybe he was with Dani. Not that it mattered. She had more important things to worry about, like her own neck.

She moved over to the dresser and fumbled through the bills and receipts scattered over the top of it, searching for the card among Mark's clutter. The old familiarity soothed her, a comfort in her near panic. She'd shared this bedroom with the man for over a year, and they'd gone through some serious stuff together. He'd never been mean to her like Ted, and she wasn't afraid of him. She should have known when she was well off and stayed married.

She opened the top drawer, but it wasn't there either. Only underwear was in the next one down. "It's not here. He's probably got it with him." When she turned around, Al wasn't there, just Ted. "Can we go now?"

"Wait for Al," he said.

She couldn't read his face because of the ski mask. The look of it added to the unnerving situation. "Ted, take that thing off. You look like a freak."

Then Al reappeared. The two men stood there in their ski masks like it was *Halloween* or something. Maybe *Friday the Thirteenth* or *Nightmare on Elm Street*. But this wasn't a movie. It was for real.

"Think we ought to wait for Vaughn?" Ted asked Al.

"Let's go." Jill didn't want to sound like she was begging, but she would if it helped. "I'll do whatever you say." It frightened her even more that she couldn't see their faces.

Al ignored her like she wasn't there. "We have bigger fish to fry. No telling when he'll be back. We got to hurry. We're burning too much time. It's getting too complicated. We could sit here all night waiting to ambush that jerk."

Jill shifted toward the door, hoping to edge past the men, maybe run for it.

"No way." Ted and Al seemed to be talking in code. They knew what was going on; she didn't.

"If we leave her here, he could put two and two together and bring the cops down on us," Al pointed out.

"Not if we make it look like he did it." Ted shifted on his feet. "That'll keep him busy."

Leave her here? Do what? Jill suddenly knew for sure why the men were talking about her as though she didn't exist. Soon she wouldn't. The only hopeful thing, the guys were so sure she was cowed they weren't bothering to restrain her, just blocking her path a little.

"Really think that'll work?" Al finally seemed to notice her, and that wasn't good. "We got to be flexible. Let's just keep her with us for now and put her in the van."

Jill chose that moment to eel past the men and run down the hall toward the front door.

***

Al rushed after Jill, caught by surprise at how fast she had moved. But Ted was ahead of him and snagged her from behind before she hit the door, the same way he had earlier back at his house. It looked like an instant replay.

With one hand Ted grabbed her mouth and with the other he

had her by the throat, so after the first squeal she didn't make another sound. For such a weak sister, she fought him hard. Al had to give her credit. Her hands clawed at Ted's hands and she thrashed about kicking his shins, making strangled noises. Ted's voice was husky with rage. "Stop, damn you," he snarled. Al figured she wasn't going to stop so Ted was going to kill her right there whether that was the smart thing to do or not.

His mind raced through probabilities like a runaway computer. He almost got in there to force Ted to ease up so they could do it right, but from the out-of-control way Ted was going after her, he figured the bastard was liable to turn on him, too. Crazy, dangerous jerk, a stupid loose cannon like the Incredible Hulk. Al fingered his pistol butt in its holster under his sweatshirt, wondering if he was going to have to tangle up this whole unraveling deal even worse by shooting Ted, just to save his own neck.

The dog tore at the crate, growling and barking so loud Al feared he'd alert someone, even though the neighbors weren't close by. He thought about shooting the dog, too, but didn't want to risk gunfire bring somebody down on them. Besides, killing the dog would queer a shot at framing Vaughn.

Now Ted had both hands around her neck and her eyes were wide open, staring. Ted grunted with the effort of clamping his fingers hard, shaking her like a terrier shakes a rat, and Jill's struggles weakened. She shuddered and relaxed, but Ted still ground down on her.

"Take it easy, man," Al said. "She's dead."

Ted dropped her. She collapsed limp on the floor and he stood over her, breathing hard. He flexed and unflexed his hands, looking down at the crumpled woman. Her eyes were still wide open. Al knelt down and felt behind her ear for a pulse but couldn't find one. He noted she had let her bladder go, and her pants were damp.

"You just lost your virginity, pal." Al nodded at the dead woman. "But now we've got a mess to clean up. That wasn't even close to how we should have handled it." His mind was planning ahead. They could load her into one of the cars and drive off like they'd never even been there. Put her body in the van and blow her up along with the Crohn building. Make it look like a suicide bombing, just like Hamas did in Israel. Yeah, that would work.

Ted ripped off his ski mask and gulped in air. His contorted face was gray and he made a gagging noise.

"Suck it up, man," Al told him. "I'm sure as hell not going to clean up after you."

The dog was still carrying on. Ted stumbled over and kicked at the crate. "Shut up."

Al flinched at the sight of the raging beast's long snapping jaws. "He wants to get a piece of you."

"Give me your gun and I'll shoot him." Ted's eyes flashed hot.

Ted seemed to have gotten over his shakiness. Now that he had he tasted a kill, apparently he wanted more. The guy was a maniac. A no-brainer, and would get them both busted if he kept it up. Trouble was, Al needed a helper to get the job done. Somebody in this team had to stay sane, and it was a lead pipe cinch Ted wasn't the one to do it right.

"Not so fast. Think, man. For once in your life. Would Vaughn kill his precious mutt?"

Ted snorted. "Probably thinks a whole lot more of the mutt than his ex. But the cur is sure making a fuss."

"Dogs bark. So what? Leave him alone, whichever way we handle this. He ain't talking." Al kept his hand on the handle of his pistol. "We need to put her in the Yugo and take her with us."

"I don't like that." Ted shook his head. "Driving around with a dead body? That's nuts."

"You're going to be driving around with a great big load of explosives anyway." It was Al's turn to snort. "What difference does a body make?"

"I want to get Vaughn."

"You want to shoot yourself in the foot, hanging around here. We left the Honda sitting outside, so if he drives up before we move it he'll know it isn't just Jill visiting. It's a surprise party without the surprise. If he has half a brain, he'll wait outside and call the cops."

"Here's the way I see it." Ted wouldn't let it go. "Jill let herself in, found her trying to take something, maybe the hound, and they had a fight. He killed her. Men kill their exes all the time. Now let's get out of here."

The phone rang. Al whirled and stared at the receiver on the end table. He held up his hand to make sure that cretin Ted didn't answer and waited. Three more rings, and the answering device picked up with Vaughn saying leave a message, yada, yada, yada.

A man's voice crackled through. "Mark, this is Snyder at Crohn Ops Security, returning your call. What's going on? I also got a call from Security. Is this a bomb threat or something? I'll call you on your cell phone." Then the caller hung up.

"Damn," Al said.

"Shit, shit, shit," Ted sputtered. They stared at each other.

"Your girlfriend really screwed us over," Al told him. "I told you. This business is getting messier all the time."

"How was I to know she'd pull a whistle-blowing act? If I'd known that, and if I'd known it was so easy, I'd have gotten rid of her days ago."

"We need to get back to the house and get that van rolling."

"Yeah. Let's go. Ted headed toward the door.

"Just a damned minute. We got to take her with us, and I'm not lugging her alone."

Ted turned and ran his gaze over the body then back to Al. "I say we frame Vaughn."

"That won't fly. We leave her here, he'll blame us, and the cops will want to come talk to us, maybe as soon as tonight whether they think he did it or not. You want the cops at our doorstep with a search warrant? They might still show up anyhow, after what Jill let on. Let's just take her and get the hell out of here. We'll stick her in the truck and blow her sky high."

Ted didn't say anything more but helped him hustle the body out and throw it into the Honda. Al covered it with a blanket so nobody could look inside and see her. Then he backed out of the driveway with the lights killed. Ted followed in the Yugo. To Al's vast relief, they didn't meet any other cars when they pulled out into the street.

***

Mark parked in front of his house and grabbed his packages off the passenger seat. When he started to insert the key into the doorknob, he found the door slightly ajar. He recalled locking the door and shutting it firmly behind him. Burglars? Jill? Had she done the unexpected again and snatched Rebel?

He pushed the door wide and looked inside. The lights were on, just as he had left them. He wished he'd been more on top of things, wished he'd changed the locks sooner, wished he'd seen the need to take Rebel with him this time. He'd really thought Rebel would be safe tonight.

To his relief, Rebel's barking greeted him the minute he charged inside. "Jill!" he called out. No answer, and the dog quieted down, whining frantically. Mark rushed into the living room and found Rebel still in his crate where he belonged. But something was wrong with the dog. He visibly trembled as though feverish. His eyes showed white around the edges and foam dotted his lips. His head drooped as though he'd been beaten. Or was he sick?

"What's the matter, buddy?" Mark set his packages on the floor, unlatched the crate and let Rebel out. The Collie rushed to a damp place on the tile floor and sniffed it. Then he slunk out and raced out the front door, which Mark had left open. Mark chased him outside. Rebel ran around in circles on the driveway, sniffing and growling.

"Rebel, come!" The Collie glanced at him, then lowered his head again and continued his frantic quest. Mark ran after him and grabbed him by the collar. "What are you doing? What happened while I was gone?" Rebel leaned away from him, whining as though he was determined to keep searching for – what? "Let's go back inside and look around. See if anything was stolen. Thank God they didn't harm you."

He made a circuit of the house, Rebel pressing against his legs, obviously distraught. Mark couldn't find anything missing, though it appeared the receipts and mail on his dresser might have been moved around or displaced. An ugly feeling of unease persisted.

Back in the living room, he listened to the message on his blinking answering device. He returned the call, and this time Mr. Snyder answered on the first ring. Mark recounted Jill's strange conversation about avoiding work for a few days.

"I was going to tell you tomorrow," Mr. Snyder said. "Those threatening emails went straight to Ted Sturkey's account. He and your ex-wife were the ones sending them, not only to you but to some of our other people."

"I'm not surprised, but I hoped it wasn't her," Mark said.

"We expected Homeland Security to question them by now. Anyway, we've already taken extra steps to protect the plant."

Mark hung up the phone, his mind racing. Today at work he'd seen the barriers being constructed around the building. Would they be enough to protect it? What were Jill and Ted plotting? An attack on Crohn was an attack on him as well. Had they come to his house and why? To plant a bomb? Did they want to personally harm him?

He snatched a paper towel from the kitchen and wiped up the damp place on the hardwood floor. It smelled like urine, but he hadn't noticed it before he left, and Rebel had been confined to the crate. Another mystery. Who had come into his house and taken a leak?

He made another inspection of the house, found nothing untoward, then sat down on his couch. Rebel crawled up to lie next to him, letting out a deep groan. Mark mentally ran through his earlier conversation with Jill. There had to be a connection, but he couldn't be sure what. Tonight was turning out to be entirely too strange. Mark stroked the dog's head. Rebel's expression was sad, pleading. "Something happened here, and it stressed you out big time. You could tell me what it was, if only you could talk."

***

Dani had no sooner returned home from class when the telephone rang. She let the answering machine catch it, but when Mark's strained voice came on, she stared at the receiver. "Dani, I really need to talk to you. Call me no matter what time it is." He was being persistent, trying to wear her down. Then he added, "It's about Rebel."

That persuaded her to pick up the phone. "I'm here."

"Good. You're home."

"Yeah. I just walked in the door." She didn't mention how satisfying it was to pretend she was decking Jill during her self-defense class. "What's the matter with Rebel?"

"Things are getting stranger and stranger. You're going to think I'm nuts, but I believe something happened here while I was gone for a little while, but I have no idea what."

"Such as?"

"I don't know. That's the trouble. Rebel is acting really screwy. He's frantic." Mark hesitated. "I hate to ask, but it's too much to talk about over the phone. Would you mind coming over? I need your help."

"With what? If he's sick you ought to take him to the emergency clinic."

"I don't need a vet. He isn't sick, he's upset. I need you. In person. If you can't come here, I'll bring him over there. Whatever it takes."

Driving over to his house this late was so not what she wanted to do right now. But he certainly sounded desperate, as though Rebel was in some sort of mysterious trouble. "Why, Mark? What do you want from me?"

"I'm bringing him, then. We're on our way," he said.

"Wait." If he came here, she couldn't control when he chose to leave. But if she went to his house, she could leave whenever she chose. "I'll be right over."

***

Al pulled up to Ted's house and waited for the idiot to open the gate so he could drive the Honda into the back yard. Jill made a quieter passenger in her present condition. Actually, she was better company as a corpse than as a whiney live companion, except for the urine smell.

Al preferred going solo. He was looking forward to being on his own again.

He'd been thinking the whole way back from Vaughn's house. He didn't expect any authorities at their house, not yet, despite the call he'd intercepted from the Crohn security chief. Still, they'd better not burn too much nighttime. Jill's tip-off had really screwed them over, but he hoped not fatally.

He pulled out of sight from prying neighbors and cut the engine. He opened the door and levered himself out to meet Ted. "No door slamming, hear? We leave all the doors open and keep it quiet. Don't want to disturb the neighbors."

Ted bent to look into the car.

"She's still dead," Al said in a low voice. "First thing is to get her into the van. Then we got to make sure we've got the essentials. We might have time to come back and get the Yugo and the TV, if everything goes OK."

"Tonight's the night, then." Ted faced him.

"Tonight or we're absolutely in deep shit. If security's too tight, it'll blow the whole deal. You want to spend the night at a no-tell motel with that red-hot van full of explosives and your dead girlfriend sitting outside your room? Or dump her body and take a chance on a hunter finding it?"

"I'm ready. I'm primed." Ted bounced on the balls of his feet, breathing hard. "After all this work I'm not giving up. Let's go for it right now."

"All right," Al allowed. "I'm itchy, too. But we got to do it right."

Chapter Fifteen

When Mark met her at the door, holding Rebel by the collar, Dani took a step back as a physical assault of sadness nearly decked her. She closed the door and Mark stood aside, looking bleak. "Thanks for coming. I appreciate it," he said.

She tried to ignore Rebel's suffocating despair so she could observe his body posture objectively. The dog stood curling his body against Mark's legs, tail tucked, the corners of his lips drawn back in distress.

"I think Rebel saw something terrible happen while I was gone," Mark said. "I wasn't away long, a little over an hour."

"I've got to admit, he's a wreck." She sank to Rebel's level, partly to accommodate her own weak knees. His dark brown eyes looked into hers, and she felt her own well up. She took a deep breath. "I see what you mean. He's sad. And angry."

She wasn't sure how she knew that, but she did, certain as the sunrise.

They moved into the living room and settled on the couch. Rebel crawled up between them, curled into a miserable ball and rested his head on Mark's thigh. The dog's depression struck her in waves, like a physical force. When Dani closed her eyes, she could almost see it, dark brown in color and draped like a cloak. It matched her own darkest moods.

Whoever said dogs didn't have true, real emotions was ignorant. Dogs might be less complicated than people, not as intellectually endowed, but they suffered and enjoyed the same spectrum of feelings as humans, including grief. If she could put a name to what he projected, that would be it.

Rebel shifted his gaze toward her. Again the intense sadness punched her in the gut. This time she imagined seeing two figures locked in an embrace. No, fighting, one holding onto the one that looked like Jill and shaking her savagely by the neck. What could that be about? She caught her breath and tried to throw off the fright of knowing something she shouldn't. She glanced warily at Mark but decided he wasn't one of the combatants.

She fought off her angst by taking a distracting look around the living room. Mark had changed little since her last visit here, a couple of years ago. She saw none of Jill's influence, a reassuring observation. Dani was starting to feel foolish for being so quick to believe Jill's claim that she was back with Mark. No, it appeared she had merely moved into his life and left quietly, taking most of her personal baggage with her. Or perhaps Mark had purged the house of all things Jill. Somehow she knew that if she searched the house, she still wouldn't find many of Jill's leavings there.

"I want to bounce this off you, all right? Here's what I do know." Mark told her about the threatening emails he had received, the strange phone call from Jill, his attempts to warn the Crohn security people about his suspicions of pending sabotage, and his conviction that someone had entered his house while he was gone on errands.

"The door was unlocked and open, yet I know for a fact that I locked it behind me. I came in and found Rebel still in his crate, but he was a basket case. I need to know what happened."

"Shouldn't you call the police instead?"

"I tried to get them interested, but nothing's missing that I can see. The dispatcher asked me if I forgot to lock my door."

"What about your suspicions? Those ugly emails you've told me about. Haven't you figured Ted for some kind of eco-terrorist? Is it possible that has anything to do with this?"

"Maybe. Still, this calls for the unconventional. Given your talents, maybe you can find out from Rebel."

He wasn't joking. She was sure of it. She took another deep breath and shut her eyes. "My talents?"

Mark dug his fingers in Rebel's ruff and leaned close to the dog's ear. "Tell her, buddy. Tell her what you saw."

"Mark, come on. This is crazy. You're overwrought. " Jill tried to suppress her rising uneasiness. "He's not a Disney dog."

"But you can get things that dogs are thinking."

"Yeah, sure. I'm really a Vulcan. I do mind-melds, too." She lifted her hand to her head, pushed the hair aside and forced a smile. "See my pointy ears?"

"Please try to talk to him."

Was it possible she could tap into Rebel's memory and learn what was bothering him? Did it center around the image of the man attacking a woman, which was how she had come to interpret it?

Did she even want to know? How could she separate her own wishes and assumptions, her own thoughts, from anything she might receive from Rebel? During her easily explained flashes of intuition others might misinterpret as telepathy from dogs, she had seen no lightning bolts, heard no voices, seen no signs or visions, save the fleeting impressions of intense sadness and of the apparent death-struggle. Usually whatever she perceived seemed no different from her own thoughts, as though she herself were drawing those conclusions from her own mind.

Whatever it was, she wanted no part of it. She feared the uprisings from her subconscious that she usually managed to clamp firmly in place.

Mark was watching her every move with an attitude of quiet expectation. "What if I make us some coffee?"

"That would be good." She understood he was backing off, giving her space. Such an intuitive guy ought to be able to talk to his own darned dog.

He moved away to the kitchen and left her alone with Rebel, who stayed put on the couch. What would it hurt to try? Was she really afraid this exercise in futility would send her over the edge? She wasn't that loosely wrapped, was she?

She shut her eyes and concentrated on her breathing, using the little bit of Yoga she'd picked up from one of those For Idiots books. Now wasn't that a perfect fit?

She tried to clear her mind. That wasn't easy, with all the thoughts like malevolent weasels chasing their tails in her head. She watched the chaos for a while, then ordered the weasel-thoughts to go away. She would deal with them later. One by one they faded. One thought persisted, though: an irrelevant recollection of her nightmare, a shattered, smoking building outlined against the night sky.

She tried to shake that off and let her thoughts shift to Rebel, mentally reached out to him, spoke to him in her mind. She pictured him, pictured herself, and sought to unite them. Should she grip his skull and try to do a Mr. Spock number? She almost laughed out loud at the notion, then banished that image like the weasels.

What about it, Rebel? What happened to get you so upset?

As before, she felt the dampening effect of great sorrow, but this time, no reply and no images. Maybe Rebel didn't want to talk about it. Fine. Call the project a failure and let it go at that.

Dani startled when the coffeemaker gurgled, and she opened her eyes. Mark stood in the kitchen door watching her. His questioning expression prompted her to say, "I'm trying, but he isn't talking. This is silly. It's a waste of effort. Why don't you try? He's your dog. Maybe he'll talk to you. It couldn't be any bigger a failure than what I'm getting."

"Rebel, you can tell her," Mark said. "Tell her what you saw."

This time, with the sadness, Dani felt a jolt of feeling sharper and edgier. She caught her breath in real, palpable fear but didn't understand the source. Probably she should have stopped there, but she stayed with it. Behind her closed eyes she saw the struggling figures again, playing like a movie in her head. A third figure stood by. One of the fighters and the bystander each had their heads obscured by something like a ski mask, but the woman being attacked could have been Jill. Dani wasn't sure.

Then it hit her, the same way it hit her when her mother and father were killed in that accident years ago, the loss punching through the disbelief and straight into her heart. The tears she'd been suppressing welled up and flowed freely. Dani choked on a sob that came out without her permission.

"What's the matter?" Mark knelt in front of her and gripped her arms in his hands. She accepted his comforting embrace without a struggle.

"It's the grief," she told him. "I know that grief. It's mine, too."

"Then stop trying to communicate with him. I had no intention of putting you through something awful." He reached for a napkin on the coffee table and handed it to her.

"I dropped my defenses to let Rebel in." Dani wiped her eyes. "I don't know whose emotions I'm feeling. This is ridiculous. I'm not a crier."

"I'm sorry. I had no idea what I was asking."

"It's all right." Dani looked at Rebel. He had fixed his deep brown-eyed gaze on her, which struck her as unusual, because most dogs tended not to stare at human faces unless specifically taught it was a desirable behavior. She got the distinct impression he was indeed trying to tell her something. "Now I have to get to the bottom of it. If that's the worst of it, I can stand it. I'm all right." She managed a watery grin. "Just get me a box of tissues, okay?"

He returned quickly with the tissues, and she wiped her eyes once again before closing them.

Now, behind her closed eyelids, a woman lay on the floor. The sadness intensified, but this time she was able to experience it more objectively and not personalize it so deeply. Nonetheless, she had to move the napkin to her face to blot new tears.

The movie in her mind played on. The attacker pulled something off his head. Dani saw wild dark hair and a full beard.

The woman on the floor — or ground — didn't move. Was she dead? What on earth was going on here? How should she interpret it? The pervasive feeling of sadness intensified. Had she witnessed somebody's death? Another feeling surged: rage, focused on the hirsute man.

"Mark." She felt dead calm now. The sharper feeling of righteous anger had overcome the spate of grief. "I did see something. It's upsetting."

"Are you okay?" He sat next to her and slipped his arm around her back.

She nodded. "It's really strange, and I'm not sure how to interpret it." She drew strength from his warm presence. The personal issues between them had to wait because this felt important. "Or whether I'm making it up." She described the action she had visualized.

"Ted has a beard, dark hair and he's fairly tall," Mark said. "What does the other guy look like?"

"He didn't ever show his face. But he seems stockier."

"Could be Al. That's the guy I met at Ted's house, the one the second car belonged to. He's shorter and clean-cut."

Dani knitted her brow. "None of it was that clear. I don't even know for sure what I saw. If I credit the emotions I feel, I could swear it was a murder."

"Jill? Ted murdered Jill with that Al guy standing by?"

"That's one way to interpret it. If I was really getting something accurate, that is. Or maybe I'm a novelist in the making? Or your dog has a wild imagination. Or there's a spaceship nearby beaming mind-bending rays at me?"

"You're right," he said. "This is bizarre."

"Supposing this is good information, not mind junk, what do we do with it?"

Mark rubbed his forehead as though trying to clear it. "The coffee must be ready. Maybe that will help us think."

For the first time Dani noticed the rich smell of fresh coffee. "Geez." She rolled her eyes. "At this point I'm ready for tequila shots. Do you have the same creepy feeling I do? Like bad vibes?"

"Ever since I came home. Maybe it's a shared psychosis, huh?"

She sat with Rebel while Mark fixed the coffee. The dog lay with his eyes half shut, his chin resting on his forepaws. She could have sworn he looked relieved, as though telling a listener what bothered him released some of his despair.

When Mark brought her a cup, she took a sip. "Milk and pink stuff. You didn't even have to ask how I like it."

"Of course I remember." He took his place back on the couch and set his cup on a napkin upon the end table. "Okay, what you saw might or might not be significant. If it is insignificant, we disregard it. If it is anywhere near accurate, we have to investigate it. Agreed?"

"We?"

"I hope you're still on board. If it's not costing you too much."

"Mark, you are pulling me down a road I don't want to travel."

"Humor me for a minute, okay?"

"That's what I've been doing since you called. Humoring you."

"I appreciate it. Believe me." Mark let out a deep sigh. "I need somebody to bounce my ideas off who isn't going to run for the hills."

"I've got my track shoes on."

"I notice you're still here."

"I did suspect it was a ploy to get me to your house so you could seduce me again."

"It wasn't, but that's not a bad idea."

"Unfortunately, the topic is far from sexy."

"So you know I'm on the level."

"Mark, I've decided that duplicity is not your strong suit." Now that was a breakthrough. Dani shifted on the couch. "I'm trying to take this at face value."

"I'll try not to strain my shaky credibility." He gave her a lopsided grin. "Do I detect another truce in the making?"

"Tell me what you think is going on."

"Let's assume, just for argument's sake, you got that experience, or whatever you want to call it, from Rebel. Let's further assume it's an accurate picture of what happened here. Ted killed Jill. Okay, then they must have taken the body with them. But why would he kill her? It makes absolutely no sense. He might have been abusive, but I'm not sure. What do we do with information like that?"

"If you call the cops, they'll either pat you on the head and say sure, sure, or else they'll Baker Act you and you'll end up in a nice safe place with no sharp objects for a few days. I might even get to join you there." Dani snickered. "Wouldn't that be fun? In any case, I doubt they'd take you seriously. There's nothing concrete here. No physical evidence. Just a Disney dog, a crazy woman who talks to him, and a loony guy doing the cheerleading."

"I made my boss want to check my head for a tinfoil hat when I talked to him earlier. I don't need to bring in the cops, too." Mark grabbed the napkin and a pen off the table. "We ought to be able to figure out how to handle this scientifically."

"Applying science to this? Come on, Mark. This is la-la-land."

"Duke University takes it seriously enough to offer study in parapsychology."

"Considering some of the crazy things universities offer, that's no endorsement."

"Let's make a flowchart." He wrote Jill's name in the napkin's center. "First, we make a hypothesis. Ted killed Jill in my house in front of Rebel, with his buddy looking on, and they removed the body. Obviously, they took it with them because it isn't here. We won't even try to hypothesize a motive yet, but one possibility is they didn't approve of her phoning me last night."

"In spades," Dani said. "Why not go there? Look what her call triggered. You took it as a tip and warned some people. It could have hurt their plans if they really were up to no good."

"True. But that's something to consider later. Right now we need to test the first hypotheses. Is Jill okay?"

"Don't you have her phone number? See if you can talk to her."

He reached for the phone and entered her number. She watched his face and listened, straining to hear the faint sounds from his end of the receiver. She counted ten rings, then eleven and twelve. Mark set down the receiver and checked his watch. "Eleven thirty. That didn't prove anything either way."

Dani shrugged. "So nobody is home, or they aren't answering the phone. Third possibility, they have call waiting and are ignoring the beeps. Do they have an answering device?"

"I don't know. I only called Jill once in a while, and she always seemed to be home."

Dani didn't doubt him this time. In this incredible situation, Mark was gaining credibility with her. Ironic.

He jumped to his feet. "I'm going over there."

"I'm going with you. I can't stand not knowing." She shivered, as though it mattered to her whether Mark could meet harm at the hands of murderers. "And I don't think you should go there alone."

***

On the way to Dani's house to drop off Rebel, Mark tried to order his jumbled thoughts. Something strange was going on tonight, but trying to sort it out was like eating egg drop soup with a fork. At least he was doing something positive. Warning Crohn security was one thing, checking out what Rebel and Dani seemed to perceive was another.

He was the one who insisted Dani try to talk to Rebel, so he was the one who ought to be the true believer. But how could one not doubt the validity of what she had supposedly gotten from the dog? The emotional storm she had suffered made him doubt the wisdom of his talking her into trying to communicate with Rebel. He'd been amazed by her reaction and concerned he had somehow done her injury. But she had regained control with admirable strength.

Dani sat quietly in the passenger's side. If she could read Rebel's thoughts, could she read his as well? In that case, she would know he'd been on the level with her and that he never wanted to be apart from her again.

"Are you getting anything else from Rebel?" he asked.

Dani looked over her shoulder toward the rear of the SUV, where the Collie lay in his crate. "Not now. I guess he said his piece, and I don't feel like working at it right now."

They left Rebel in a run next to Dolly's, then drove on to Ted's house. Jill's Yugo was parked in the driveway, as usual. Mark edged up behind it and turned off the engine. He stared at the dark house. "The other guy's Honda is gone, but I don't know whether he was living there or not."

"We could knock on the door, ring the doorbell. Throw pebbles at her window." Dani offered. "You know, something normal."

Mark left the Blazer and went to the front door, aware of Dani right behind him. He rang the doorbell then rapped his knuckles on the door. He stood there for about a minute, then said to Dani, "Banging on her window would be the next step."

"Which one is hers?" Dani asked.

Mark shot her a glance. "I have no idea. Let's try them all."

He strode to from window to window, rapping at each, Dani following. Nobody came to door or window yelling at them to cut it out. When they got to the back gate, He tried to open it, but it only rattled. He shook his head. "Padlocked."

"Which should stop law-abiding citizens like us," Dani said.

Mark looked around. "We can check the other side, see if there's a gate. It's a six-foot fence. I could get over it if I drove the SUV over and I used that for a leg up."

Dani scouted the other side and came back. "No gate over there."

"Then let's roll." Mark got into the vehicle and drove around to the gate. He parked alongside and fished out a flashlight he kept under the seat. Feeling like a sneak thief, he retrieved a pair of gloves also stored under the seat and slipped them on. Then he got out and climbed onto the roof. He grabbed the top of the fence, jacked himself over the top, and jumped down into the back yard. He froze, waiting for any reaction from inside the house.

"What's back there?" Dani whispered from the other side of the gate.

"There's a metal shed that wasn't there a couple of months ago." He cast the flashlight beam around. "That's about it. I see tire tracks on the grass, so somebody's been driving back here. I'm going to check the door and the windows."

To his surprise, he found the sliding glass door unlocked and let himself in. "Jill!" he called out.

No response. He hit the switch next to the door and flooded the room with light. If Ted had invaded his house, turnabout was fair play. He swiftly moved through the house, from one bedroom to another. The beds were empty, as devoid of human life as the living room. The furniture looked bare. The house smelled like a locker room He made his way to the front door and let Dani in.

"Nobody home?" she asked.

"Not unless they're hiding in a closet or they got really small."

Dani wrinkled her nose. "I guess we'd better check those places, huh?"

Again Mark toured the house, Dani shadowing him. He opened the closets and looked under the beds. In one closet he found Jill's clothes but none that might belong to Ted. "What do you make of that?" he asked Dani.

"He split and she didn't? Or else Ted is a nudist and doesn't own clothes?" Dani gave Mark an odd look. "I don't like this. Her clothes and car are here, but Ted's stuff is gone, like he left her. What about that other guy, Al?"

"He had a Honda. I don't know for sure he was living here."

An inspection of all three bedrooms turned up nothing else that interested them. In the kitchen he found the unopened bag of dog food he'd brought over, stuffed inside the pantry. The living area was as unrevealing. "I've only been inside once, and that time I got the bum's rush because I only came through to make sure the backyard was secure for Rebel. Ted was kind of cool to my presence, to say the least. Anyway, I don't see anything different."

"Jill liked crossword puzzles." Dani pointed to a book of

puzzles and the comic section of the *Florida Times-Union* scattered on the coffee table. She rifled through the pile of paper. "Those must have been hers, too. Nothing of Ted's?"

"If he left, he abandoned the TV. She had a computer, but I didn't see one here."

"She could have pawned it." Dani shot him an odd look. "Do you realize we keep referring to Jill in the past tense?"

Mark shifted, restless. He didn't like being here among Jill's things and Ted's leavings. "I'm ready to get out of here. What do you think?"

Dani shrugged a shoulder. "We haven't proved a thing."

They left through the front door, and Mark drove the SUV away from the fence so Dani could get in the passenger side. He backed down the driveway and onto the street, then at the stop sign threw the gear into park. "You know what? I need to go up to Crohn and make sure everything is okay. If Ted were really going to pull something, the way he's vacated this house makes me think he'd most likely do it now. I doubt he's just going to turn a few rats loose. Want me to drop you off?"

She shook her head. "I want to see this thing through."

He should have objected. It might be a dangerous mission. But he didn't. Her company was a gift he could not turn down.

Chapter Sixteen

Ted parked the van in his usual surveillance spot within sight of the Crohn complex. He glanced over at Jill, strapped in the passenger seat. Her head lolled to one side as though she were asleep.

"This is it, babe." He didn't care that she couldn't answer. "We're about to pull this thing off."

Al walked up to his door, and Ted rolled down the window. "She behaving herself?"

"I'm not getting much lip out of her." Ted giggled, feeling high. He slapped Jill's cold cheek. "Hey, babe. Speak up. This is your big moment."

Al shot him a snotty look. "Whenever you're ready to quit farting around, we need to talk about how we're going to pull this off."

"I'm listening." Ted peered off into the distance. Cars were parked in the entrance and exit lanes next to the guard shack. "I've never seen them block the lanes like that."

"Your girlfriend's call must have made them nervous."

Ted turned to Jill. "Bitch." He backhanded her cheek again. She was starting to get stiff and didn't move much

Al continued, "Never mind the blocked lanes, and screw the guards. The chain-link fencing won't stop the van. You can plow right through." He swept his hand toward the Crohn complex. "They're starting to install concrete posts. We have to do it tonight or forget about it."

Ted stared where Al pointed. "Son of a bitch. They sure are. When did they start doing that?"

"Not because Vaughn called them tonight. They didn't have time. They weren't working on them last week. They must have gotten spooked by the deals in North Carolina and New Jersey. They had to have gotten started on installing them over the weekend. Maybe today."

Ted nodded. "Jill turning the rats loose made them nervous,

too."

"Exactly. She was nothing but a liability all the way. Next thing she was going to have the Feds coming down on her." Al squinted into the distance. "When I drove by, it looked like they had some road cones up, closer to the building."

"Big deal. Road cones won't stop the van either."

"All the stuff they've got up won't stop anybody that means business," Al said. "Not what I see so far, anyway."

"Stupid." Ted laughed out loud. A scattering of cars dotted the parking lot, close to the building entrance, but it appeared the road cones kept them away from the first lane. "All they're doing is inconveniencing their night shift."

"Look here." Al ignored the small talk. "We won't waste any more time, give them any more chances to fortify. We'll break through over here, far enough from the guard shack so they can't do a thing. You gun it through and run it up to the building. Leave it in gear, jump out and run for it, and I'll pick you up. Then we'll detonate. With any luck we'll bring the building down. For sure we'll do a lot of damage."

Ted felt feverish. His skin crawled. His foot twitched with excitement. He was really pumped, ready for action. He'd been planning this for a while. It was finally happening. "Think they'll come after us?"

"They'll be so busy with the explosion they won't be chasing anybody. It'll be a first class distraction while we make our getaway." Al patted his jacket pocket. "I have our new papers with me. We're all set, and once we hit I-10 west, they won't be able to trace us."

Yeah, they'd been over this before. The only part that made him nervous was getting out of the van, avoiding getting stopped by guards, and trusting Al to detonate it after he had safely cleared the blast area. They'd move on out, ditch the car and steal another one. They'd go underground with the new identities the organization had provided. Ted realized he'd have to shave, get a haircut and otherwise change his appearance, but it might be fun to travel incognito. They could come up for air and soldier on after things cooled off. "Yeah. Let's do it."

***

Al followed Ted's van, lights out, in his Honda but hung back at a safe distance outside the fenced compound, just like he told Ted he would. He had the cell phone in his hand, the number set and ready for him to punch the button that would trigger the blast. He smiled in anticipation. He loved this part. The adrenalin rush made his senses tingle. It beat the Fourth of July all to hell.

He watched Ted rev the van and blast it through the fence as though the metal fabric were made of fishnet. The fencing snagged on the van's bumper and crunched under the tires. The posts ripped out of the ground and bumped along on either side of the van. Sparks flew as the metal scraped along the asphalt.

Al U-turned the Honda around 180 degrees so it pointed away from the complex, ready for a fast getaway. He swiveled in the driver's seat to watch the action. The guard came out of the shack hollering and waving his arms, but didn't give chase to the van right away. Sensible of him because he couldn't stop it on foot anyway. The van finally broke free of the fencing and sped up. It careened toward the building.

Al wrinkled his brow when he realized the van wasn't driving straight but was fishtailing out of control. Did the fencing blow out the maypop-plagued tires? Then the van jumped the curb, skewed sideways and crashed into a light pole. It jerked to an abrupt stop well short of the building. What the hell?

Barriers they didn't see? Stop sticks? Or Ted's persistent incompetence.

The parking lot lights illuminated exhaust spewing from the van. The engine roared, protesting Ted's attempts to gun it in reverse. The van rocked back but wouldn't go any farther.

Al swore, but he couldn't give it any more time. He hit the "Talk" button on the cell phone and heard the music of the number tones, then the other end ringing. He floored the accelerator and burned rubber.

The Honda was well on its way before the explosion rocked the little car and seemed to propel it forward faster. A fireball lit up the landscape behind Al, and he had to duck and squint to protect his night vision from the flash in his rearview mirror.

"Rest in pieces, useful idiots," Al said under his breath. "You outlived your usefulness."

***

Mark's Blazer rounded the last curve before the Crohn complex service road, bringing the main building into view, illuminated by the parking lot and security lights. Dani saw the sky light up, the building outlined in the blast, and her recurring nightmare came alive. She felt the boom in the vehicle frame as much as heard it.

Between the shock of recognition and the shock of the explosion, she froze in her seat, hand clutched around the cell phone. She braced herself when Mark slammed on the brakes and pulled over to the shoulder of the road.

"Oh, my God," she finally breathed. "It's real." Smoke rose from the front of the building, but the scene wasn't quite faithful to her dreams. The building still stood, though it might be damaged. She saw no gaping holes in the façade, at least in the light from the parking lot. Lights shined steadily in the windows, a sign that the power hadn't been interrupted. The clarity and lack of reflection in the windows suggested that glass had blown out.

"The Fourth of July happened months ago." Mark's voice was grim. "I don't like the way this is shaping up."

Dani tried to apply logic to the scene in front of her. Burning parts of something lay all over the parking lot though the building seemed mostly intact. She took a deep, shaky breath. "I've seen this before, in a dream. But it looked worse. Much worse, like Oklahoma City."

"I've seen things like this on the news, but it was always somewhere else," Mark said. "This one I'm taking personally."

Separately, the events of this night were strange enough. Linked together, it didn't take a conspiracy theorist to see an ominous trend. A phone call that might or might not have been a tip off of a sabotage in the offing, intruders in Mark's house, an overwrought dog who might or might not have witnessed a killing, Dani not quite sure she received those images, Jill and her boyfriend AWOL. Now what appeared to be an explosion near Crohn was the cherry on top of the banana split.

A car approached, not preceded by the usual sweep of headlights. As it hurdled toward them, the lack of blinding headlights made it possible to make out in the SUV's lights a cream-colored compact. She got to see that much as the car swerved by, fishtailing so close it almost sideswiped Mark's Blazer.

Mark whipped the SUV around.

"What's going on?" Dani said as he hit the accelerator.

"I think it's Al's Honda."

Dani flipped open her cell phone. "I'm calling the cops."

"Tell them we're on his tail."

***

Furious, Al negotiated the corners away from the scene of his aborted mission. Certainly the van hadn't gotten close enough to the building to bring it down. It probably shook the structure and blew out a few windows. In a day or two, the damage would be repaired and the company would be no worse for the incident. Plus there wouldn't be a next time, at least not by this method. The concrete posts would be solidly in place within days, leaving the building even less vulnerable.

He'd gotten an advance and an interim payment, but that was probably all he would ever see from this fiasco. His full payment on the botch job might never be forthcoming. Goes to show that even his expertise and planning wouldn't make up for the bumbling of idiot helpers like Ted. He was well rid of him. He calculated Ted didn't have time to get out of the van and run from the blast. The C4 explosive shockwave struck at the speed of sound, and that was the only thing he could count on.

Through his disappointment, Al's mind continued to click along, task-oriented as usual. His first need was to clear the complex without being fingered. Then he would ditch the Honda, steal another car and boost a license plate from a third. He must do what he could to confuse anybody who might be onto him. He hadn't actually lied to Ted about the fake ID's. He'd had to show Ted his, even though he never intended to give it to the jerk.

Who could identify him? Not Ted and Jill. They were silenced. Vaughn had seen him but didn't know much about him, even his last name. All his handles were aliases anyway. He hardly remembered the name he'd been born with.

He noticed headlights behind him and thought about the SUV he'd met on his way out. Was it possible the driver had turned and followed him?

Al slowed at the Normandy Boulevard intersection and turned right, as he'd planned. He could take Chaffee Road from there and hit the Interstate. But if the vehicle behind him followed, he'd start to get nervous. Not until then. He had to slip into a quiet residential area where he could find another car. But first, he had to find out whether somebody was really tailing him.

***

Dani punched in 911. When the dispatcher answered, she babbled, "There was an explosion at Crohn Life Sciences. We're following a car that was rushing away from the scene. We think the bombers are in it, and we're following."

The dispatcher put her through a maddening slow process of giving her name, address phone number, Crohn's address, and other minutiae. In the meantime, she kept the other part of her attention on the chase. Mark wisely hung back but kept the Honda well within sight.

"We're headed northeast on Normandy Boulevard." She described their location to the dispatcher, whose lack of urgency made Dani wonder if she and Mark were going to get any help from Jacksonville's finest. Were they on their own?

Just then she noticed the blue strobe of a police car rush down the road they had just left, followed by a fire truck, sirens screaming.

"They're headed toward the complex," Mark said. "Look. I'd better let you off at a convenience store or someplace safe in case this gets too hairy."

"A convenience store at this time of night? I'm safer riding shotgun." Dani kept the cell phone against her ear, continuing to relay their location to the dispatcher.

***

With mounting disgust, Al realized the SUV had turned with him down Normandy. Typically it was a busy roadway, but the late hour made it less so, and he was now sure he was being followed. He whipped down a side road, taking the turn on two wheels. When the vehicle behind him turned as well, he knew.

Could it be the SUV Vaughn drove? Could it be the corporate robot was the one on his tail? On one level, it made sense. The beefed-up security at Crohn led him to believe Vaughn might have warned them of Jill's suggestion that he skip work for a few days. If they connected the dots.... This was not good. It was also possible Vaughn had been concerned enough to personally come down here in the middle of the night and see if anything was going down. Nosy asshole.

Stealing a car was out of the question with somebody on his

butt, watching his every move and threatening to come down on him. Who knew whether Vaughn was armed? It was legal to carry concealed weapons in Florida, and even grannies took advantage of that right. Al had a gun, but he'd rather be sure his assailant was unarmed, just to make sure the odds were in his favor.

Right now, his best bet was to shake his pursuer. He killed his headlights, whipped abruptly onto another street, and floored the accelerator.

***

Mark barely had enough time to turn and follow the darkened Honda around the corner. He realized he was at a disadvantage because the small car was more maneuverable. He didn't dare take a curve so fast he risked rolling his Blazer. It wasn't big, but it did have a higher center of gravity than the car.

The actions of the Honda's driver verified Mark was following somebody who had been up to no good at the Crohn complex. How much damage had Ted and Al accomplished? Dread filled him with thoughts of nightshift workers buried under tons of debris. Terrorists usually went for maximum mayhem. If the damage didn't seem that severe, it probably fell short of the bombers' intentions. Damn if he was going to let that murderous pair get away. He accelerated to keep up with the recklessly speeding car, praying nobody was out on the streets this time of night.

Except for the occasional streetlight, the darkness of the rural area was deepened by the heavily wooded lots with houses and mobile homes set far off the road. Few lights were on within the houses, though a few yard lights gleamed. It was like driving through a blacked-out tunnel.

He didn't even glance at the speedometer. He didn't want to know.

Dani tried to make out the name of the cross street to relay to the dispatcher. Fortunately she seemed to be maintaining a cool head though he was concerned for her safety. He had no business bringing her along on a chase after a what? A terrorist? Still, it was a good thing for him she'd come along. Their teamwork allowed him to follow Al's car. He would have a hard time talking on the phone and driving like a maniac at the same time.

One thing he knew, he wasn't going to give her up again, not without a fight.

But he'd have to deal with that after he finished this particular battle.

***

Al was sweating despite the coolness of the night. He couldn't shake the SUV by turning corners, and he couldn't get out of its driver's sight either. The asshole behind him seemed unshakable. If he was in contact with the cops, Al could be in serious trouble.

He multi-tasked well enough to curse Jill's betrayal as he drove. She could no doubt be blamed for every single thing that had gone awry tonight. That one phone call had cascaded the screw-ups into a fiasco beyond belief. For the thousandth time he regretted not insisting Ted kick her out of the house. But that could have caused the loss of his helper before he needed to get lost. This job was a loser from the start.

It was looking more and more likely he'd have to use the loaded Glock he'd stowed next to his seat. First he'd try to scare the bastard, slow the SUV down, or put it out of commission. He had little hope of actually hitting anybody under these conditions.

He swerved around another corner, righted the wheel, and rocketed away. He groped for the pistol with one hand while he stayed the course with his other on the steering wheel. Wrecking the car was not an option. He clasped his hand around the grip. Now he was in charge of the situation.

He headed down the straightaway for the next few blocks. It would give him a chance to at least put the SUV out of commission. With any luck he'd hit the driver, too.

It wasn't easy to drive and shoot behind him at the same time. It was near impossible to get any accuracy. He risked looking backward and fired through the rear window. The deafening crash made his head ring and exploded the window. He heard a lesser crash as he sideswiped a roadside mailbox. Al corrected the wheel and turned around to try another shot at his pursuer.

***

Dani saw the flash and heard the whine of a bullet ricocheting off the SUV body. "He's shooting at us!"

"Get down." Mark swerved, a move she realized was an evasion attempt. The tires on her side skidded and chattered on the grassy roadside. She hoped he could avoid the drainage ditch that yawned dark just to her right.

Dani sank lower behind the console but held onto the cell phone with one hand and told the dispatcher what was happening. She refused to duck so far she couldn't see where they were going. After she delivered the news of the gunfire to the dispatcher, she relayed to Mark, "The police say to back off and let them handle it."

"Where are they, then?" Mark asked. "I can't let him get away."

"They claim they just sent a couple of patrol cars." Dani read street signs off to the dispatcher as they passed them. The self-defense class she was taking offered advice that was useless in this situation. The instructor would advise her to break off the chase and forget about the whole thing. On second thought, that advice would be the height of practicality.

She licked her dry lips and kept feeding information to the police.

***

Al got off the third round but at a price. Just as he turned back around to face the front, he realized the road took a hard turn to the left. He found himself barreling straight ahead toward a stand of trees. With no headlights he hadn't been able to predict the curve. He hit the brakes and tried to whip the car around and hold the road. He dropped the Glock on the floor so he could handle the wheel. Tires screeching, the car skidded and slid sideways. He realized he wasn't going to make it but tried to aim between the trees. Before he got to the woods, the car nosedived into an unseen drainage ditch.

The abrupt stop threw Al forward and deployed the air bag. Slammed in the chest by the plastic force, Al was momentarily stunned. He regained his senses and groped for the Glock. Where was it? Did it get stuck under the air bag? Lights from the pursuing car closed in. Time was about to run out.

Forget the gun. He had to run for it and disappear into the darkness on foot. He could get into those woods beyond the ditch and get lost.

Al threw open the door and stumbled out.

***

Mark stopped the Blazer behind the disabled Honda. He told Dani to hunker down behind the dash and opened the driver's door. Staying low, he remained in his seat, the engine running, brights trained on the wreck. He knew the driver had a gun, and it would be crazy to rush him. But at this close range, the headlights could effectively blind a shooter and wreck his night vision.

Dani continued to inform the police dispatcher. "He crashed into the ditch. No, we've stopped and we're watching him. I only see one man. He's moving around in there. I can't tell if he's injured. Hey, he's getting out now."

Mark started out the door at the same moment the Honda's occupant spilled from the car. The driver's stocky build caused Mark to believe it was Al. He didn't see Ted in the car or outside it. The driver climbed up the far side of the ditch, his hands appearing to be empty. Had he lost his gun? No blue police strobes in sight, and the perp was about to slip away. Mark couldn't let that happen. He hit the ground running.

Al stumbled and staggered toward the woods. Mark crossed the few feet to the ditch in a few bounds and scrambled to the bottom. His running shoes splashed into the stream. He swarmed up the other side, slipping on wet sand, but heaved over and poured on the speed.

Al glanced briefly over his shoulder then kept running. He didn't seem to be much of a runner; perhaps injured in the crash. Mark still didn't see a gun. Maybe he was getting lucky and Al really had lost the weapon. Mark's football training from high school kicked in automatically; his long strides rapidly closed the short space between them. He snatched at Al's shirt and grabbed him around the waist, tackling him.

Mark didn't expect Al to go down without a fight and didn't enjoy being right. Al twisted around, slugging, swearing. He landed a blow to Mark's chin that clacked his jaws shut so hard Mark saw jets of light pulse through his vision. Mark reached up and grappled for Al's wrists to immobilize him. Al's knee came up, barely missing Mark's crotch. Mark tried forcing the heavier man down, but Al's flailing, twisting, kicking action threw him off-balance. Mark lost his grip.

He lunged forward for another tackle.

Trying to hold Al down, he realized the terrorist had reached down his calf and pulled out a knife. Mark gripped the knife arm by the wrist and bore downward, trying to avoid Al's efforts to twist his arm free and stab him.

***

Dani pocketed the cell phone and picked up the only potential weapon she could find, a big, heavy flashlight. So much for her self-defense class. Common sense told her this situation called for using whatever was at hand. She raced after the two men and caught up to them struggling on the ground. The flash of a blade warned her Mark was in danger, though he was trying to pin the man's hand. Praying Mark wouldn't shift into her trajectory, she slammed the flashlight against the back of the man's hand. He yelped, but instead of dropping the knife, he reached for her with his free hand.

That wouldn't do. She brought the metal canister down hard on the man's head. He loosened his grip enough for Mark to get the knife away from him and fling it aside. Dani picked up the weapon.

"You okay?" she asked Mark.

"Fine. You brained him pretty good." Mark pinned the man down with his full weight. Relief surged through her. Just the idea of Mark's being injured made her heart ache. Delayed reaction hit her. She trembled. She would have been devastated if anything happened to him. A deep thankfulness enveloped her. He was fine. Nothing was going to separate them again.

The man they'd pursued squirmed on the ground, still trying to escape Mark. She switched on the flashlight, amazed that it still worked, and shined it into his dirt-smudged face. Nobody she knew. He closed his eyes against the light. "Hold still, whoever you are," Dani ordered.

"It's him. Al," Mark said.

The blessed sound of sirens approached, blue lights flashing. "It's the cavalry. Five minutes late. What timing."

Then the cops were yelling at the three of them to freeze. Suddenly it seemed to Dani a good thing she didn't have a gun. She was glad to turn the situation over to the cops, but how hard would it be to convince them that she and Mark were the good guys? She remembered the cell phone she had thrust into her pocket and hoped the dispatcher was still holding the line open.

***

Mark let go of Al and raised his hands, relieved that

reinforcements had finally arrived. Al crawled out of reach, scrambled to his feet, and took off running again.

"Halt," yelled the cop, but Al kept running. A policeman released a German shepherd that took off after the running man. "Freeze!" yelled the K9 handler. Mark stilled and so did Dani. The dog ignored them and charged past, intent on catching Al.

It didn't take long. The dog leaped up and tackled Al as effectively as Mark had but held the terrified man down, roaring savagely, probably scaring the guy more than hurting him. The police converged, one of them covering Mark and Dani, the other trotting off to separate Al from the canine cop.

Mark didn't like the way the officer had his gun ready, poised to shoot. "Hey, you can put that down. We're the good guys."

Dani held out the knife. "I'd like to get rid of this. I took it from that guy over there. He pulled it on Mark. Tell me what you want me to do with it." Her voice was amazingly calm.

"Slow and easy," instructed the patrolman. "Set it on the ground. The flashlight, too."

Dani did as instructed.

A third policeman came forward and picked up the knife. "We'll check that out later. Now, lie on the ground. We've got to search you both."

"Officer, she's the one that was talking to the dispatcher the whole time we were following the Honda," Mark said. "There's no reason to treat her like a criminal. She has the knife because she saved me from getting stabbed by that guy."

"Just do as we say. You, too. Lie face down."

Listening to the crackle of the police radios, Mark lay on the chilly, damp grass. He tasted blood from a smashed lip and was beginning to feel the bruises Al had inflicted on his cheek, thighs and torso during the scuffle. His soaked feet were going numb from the chill. He submitted to being cuffed and searched.

They treated Dani like a criminal, too. Infuriating. At least she didn't get roughed up. She'd been cool and brave throughout. Indispensable. God, he was proud of her.

She told them to find the cell phone in her pocket, and the officer groped it free and spoke to the dispatcher, who by some miracle was still on the line. Chalk up one for their side.

The K9 officer escorted Al toward the parked police units,

holding onto his arm, his dog prancing at the ready beside him. Al was handcuffed and looked even worse than Mark felt. The headlights showed a dirt-smudged face and torn shirt. "I'm glad you caught these two, Officer," Al said. "They were following me and harassing me for no reason. It's because of them I crashed my Honda. He ran me off the road. Then he tried to beat me up. And you turned that vicious dog on me and he chewed up my arm. I need to go to the hospital, and I'm going to sue every last one of you for excessive use of force."

So that was what Al was going to try? Lies and more lies, finger pointing at him and Dani? "He was shooting at us," Mark countered. "I don't know what he's done with his gun, but it must still be in his car. Ask him why he ran."

"We've got somebody looking in his car now," one of the cops said.

Mark's cell phone rang inside his jacket pocket, but his hands were immobilized by the handcuffs. "Hey, would you let me get that?"

"I got it." The policeman fished out the phone and flipped it open. "Yeah? Officer Bryant speaking." He listened for a moment. "He's right here but can't get it right now. Who's this? Uh, Snyder from Crohn? All right. I'll tell him."

Officer Bryant shut the phone. "Said he's the security chief at Crohn. He's all worked up about the explosion. He wants you to call him back."

"Why wouldn't you let me talk to him?"

"First things first. What's your story?"

"I had gotten a vague sort of threatening phone call and told Mr. Snyder about it. He was going to heighten security. We were headed toward Crohn when we saw the blast." Mark nodded toward Al. "We saw him driving away." He turned back to officer Bryant. "How much damage was done?"

"I don't know about any of that."

One of the officers walked over from the parked cars carrying a bag with something in it. "He's the one driving the Honda?"

Mark said, "The Blazer is mine, and Dani here was with me. That man your dog ran down was driving the Honda."

The officer held up a plastic bag with a handgun and a cell phone inside then turned to Al. "Sir, we are taking you down to the station for further questioning." Then he read him his rights.

To Mark and Dani he said, "The dispatcher verified you were in telephone contact. We have to take you in to the station so you can make a statement."

"Fine," Mark said. "Would you mind taking off these cuffs?"

Chapter Seventeen

Hours later, after the police had taken their voluntary statements and they were free to go home, Dani let Mark into her house. "I want to see Rebel right away," he said.

"You need your war wounds looked after." Dani inspected his split lip. "Did you get hurt anywhere else? Think I ought to take you to a Doc in a Box?"

"I'm fine. Let's go out to the kennel. Can we bring him into the house?"

Together they walked out to fetch Rebel. "We still don't know what happened to Jill," Mark said. "Maybe the police will find out something that will bear out what we think Rebel told you. Or not. Until Jill turns up dead or alive, we won't know."

"What do you think?"

Mark just shook his head.

"I know what I think." Dani opened the door to the building, and the warm earthy scent of confined animals met her. The shuffle of wakeful dogs reassured her in its normalcy. "It's like I watched an actual murder."

Mark followed her into the building, and his nearness also reassured her. "However the facts turn out, it wasn't a one-shot thing, Dani. You have a gift, and I hope you try to develop it."

"I'd like to develop the ability to know what's real," she conceded.

"Jill's phone call was real. That's for sure. I'm kind of surprised she cared enough to warn me."

Dani noticed he still referred to Jill in past tense, and so did she. Both of them knew she wouldn't be found alive.

Mark's cell phone played its theme. He pulled it out of his jacket pocket and opened it. "Mark here."

While he handled the call, Dani opened the gate to Rebel's run, gently pushing him aside so she could slip inside without letting him out to disrupt Mark's phone conversation. Dolly stuck her nose against the fence, wanting her share of attention, too. "In a minute, Dollface."

Dani sat down and let the Collie nose her ear while she roughed up his neck. "Are you feeling better?" She sensed Rebel's confidence in her, though he was grieving and uneasy in the unfamiliar surroundings. This time she accepted the insight for what it seemed to be, instead of trying to explain it away. Whatever she sensed from the dog, it just was, and it didn't need any rationalization.

How could any evil come from listening to the heart of one of the most honest creatures God ever created?

Having finished his phone conversation, Mark joined them and greeted Rebel over the gate. The Collie danced his welcoming two-step greeting. Dani opened the run gate and let Rebel out. The dog rushed to Mark and buried his long head between his master's knees, then wriggled through while Mark rubbed his flanks. "He's sure glad to see you," she said. "Fortunately, he didn't seem too upset that we left him here. Any news?"

"That was Mr. Snyder, the security chief at Crohn. He had some information he wanted to share."

"Well, out with it. The cops were pretty close-mouthed. I hope nobody at Crohn got hurt."

"Apparently nobody in the building."

"Do you still have a job?"

In the stark kennel building lighting, his battered lip made his grin look lopsided. "Hey, I'm a genuine hero."

"I think so. Thank God you weren't killed. When you took out after Al, I thought that was a possibility." She recalled her terror when she thought he would be harmed, and her frantic efforts to find a weapon, any weapon. Fortunately, the flashlight turned out to be sufficient.

He shrugged. "They think when the van crashed the fence it blew tires so the driver lost control and crashed into a light pole. The van didn't get close enough to destroy the building. Some windows were broken and the shrapnel made a mess, but there wasn't any structural damage. Mr. Snyder took my phone calls seriously and had the building evacuated, so there wasn't anybody inside. The security guys had been briefed. They knew they shouldn't interfere with a vehicle doing the things that one was doing. The guys on duty were smart enough to duck behind their shack when they saw the van zero in on the building, so they didn't get hurt."

"Was Al the guy driving the truck bomb?"

He shook his head. "The guards didn't see anybody get out of the truck, though somebody was certainly driving. One of them noticed the Honda loop around and speed away. I guess it could have been Ted in the van. Funny, I never took him for a suicidal maniac. Just a garden-variety maniac. The police are holding Al on stolen vehicle, firearms and assault charges, possibly for domestic terrorism. Did you notice how interested they were in his cell phone? I overheard them say they were turning it over to the bomb squad. Plus they found a laptop in his car they're taking a look at."

"Has anybody seen Jill?"

He shook his head again.

"I hope she's all right." Dani meant it though she doubted Jill would be. "Even after what she pulled."

"I'd sure be glad to see her alive. Alive and far away from me."

Dani crossed her arms. "Siberia would be nice."

"I'll tell you one thing." He dropped an arm protectively around Rebel's shoulders. "Even if she surfaces, she won't ever get Rebel back. If she wants to see him, she'll have to make a supervised appointment. I'm calling my lawyer in the morning."

"I shouldn't have believed a word of what she said, that the two of you were back together." Dani rubbed her temple. "I guess I was afraid of leaving myself open to disappointment, and she fed my fears. In retrospect, it seems kind of stupid."

"She could be convincing." Mark smiled ruefully. "She fooled me a few times."

"I'm immune to that nonsense now." She smiled back at him.

"No more hot and cold?"

"Totally hot." She put her arms around him and snuggled up to his warmth, enjoying the feel of his strong arms gathering her in. "I'll settle for a hug for now, considering your sore mouth. Al sure got his licks in."

"Didn't you see the other guy? I got my licks in, too." She felt the rumble of his chuckle against her chest.

"Hey, I was impressed. If it hadn't been for you, Al would be in Georgia by now."

"Amazing how much I remember about tackling from high school football." He pulled her closer. "I was sure glad to have you along, even if I was worried I'd gotten you into trouble."

"Fastest cell phone in the Southeast." She turned her face up and grinned at him. "We make a passable team. But you know, we gotta talk. Tonight had to be the worst in the history of dating. A car chase, fighting, getting hauled in by the cops."

"Will you let me make it up to you?" His warm breath grazed her ear.

"We could explore that possibility." She drew him closer yet and buried her head against his chest. "By the way, I don't think you ought to go home tonight. You're exhausted, and Rebel seems content here."

"Should I check into the Motel 6?"

He nibbled the same ear, and she shivered in delight. "Nothing wrong with my place, is there? I've got everything a motel has, plus a warmer bed."

"I accept." He kissed her lightly. "Nowhere I'd rather be, even if I have to share it with Crash and Jet."

"That's not what I had in mind."

"I have a feeling I'm going to be spending lots more time here," he said. "If it's all right with you."

"More than all right." She sighed. "No use fighting it. I want you back in my life."

Chapter Eighteen

Mark knelt with Rebel, waiting for their turn to run the practice course. They were third in line. He watched the black Labrador retriever taking its shot at conquering the sequence. He grimaced when the handler executed a clumsy move and inadvertently pushed the dog off the jump he was supposed to take. Then he had to bring the dog around for another pass, all of which would have cost him penalties in faults and time in a real agility trial.

"I promise I won't get in your way like that," Mark whispered into Rebel's ear. The Collie was watching, too, his body taut with excitement under Mark's restraining hand. Mark told himself the agility club's summer fun night didn't even count for titles, but he still wanted them to do well.

Dani came up behind him and laid her hand on his shoulder. "Remember your own advice. Just go out there and have fun." She bent down to kiss him, and he rose to meet her. Then she flashed a grin and slipped back to the bleachers.

His lips still warm from the kiss, Mark moved forward another slot as the Lab exited the ring and a German Shepherd started the course. Sure, he would have fun. It was Rebel's public agility debut, and he didn't know how the rookie dog would do with his equally rookie handler, but one thing he did know. When he finished his run, he would get to take this terrific dog home with him and he would never again have to give him up.

Only a couple more minutes lapsed before it was Rebel's turn to try the course. Mark strode with Rebel into the ring and set the dog in a sit-stay about ten feet in front of the first jump. He removed the slip lead and tossed it aside. He left Rebel sitting and strode into the position he had already planned to take that would allow him to run parallel to Rebel's projected path.

"Okay, hup," he called out and took off at a run, watching Rebel spring forward, gather himself and sail over the first jump. Mark guided the dog at a gallop along the route of obstacles, over the A-frame, through the chute, over jumps, then onto the pause table where he told Rebel "Down." Rebel dropped to his elbows and his rear sank into a sphynxlike crouch. Mark exhaled "Stay." After a count of five, Mark sent him over the next jump and to the teeter. Rebel ran up, tipped it, and trotted down the other side. Rebel cleared the last three jumps in a series of bounds and crossed the finish line. Mark's fellow agility enthusiasts broke into clapping, and someone let out an appreciative yell.

Jubilant, Mark called Rebel to him and hugged the Collie exuberantly. Rebel grinned and wagged, eyes sparkling. Every line of the dog communicated joy and his willingness to do it again. Mark retrieved his lead from where a helper had hung it near the ring gate. He secured Rebel and walked out of the ring straight into Dani's arms.

"Great run! I'm so proud of both of you!" Dani let go of Mark and knelt down to give Rebel a congratulatory ruff-rub and a treat.

"Where's mine?" Mark asked, laughing. "Am I always going to play second fiddle to my dog?"

"You've got to wait for yours. It's way too public here."

"That's too bad. I can't keep my hands off you." He slipped his arm around Dani's waist and together they watched the rest of the class compete. She snuggled against him and for the zillionth time he marveled at how abruptly his out-of-kilter world had corrected its spin.

Trish Smart walked over, her Aussie in tow. "Nice run, Mark." She glanced at Rebel. "Awesome dog, and you did a nice job with him."

"Thanks." He gave Dani a little squeeze. "I've got a great teacher."

"Hi, Trish," Dani had stiffened when Trish appeared, but now he felt her relax. He believed she now knew it was safe to trust him because neither of them would let anybody get between them again. Trish was attractive and flirtatious, but Dani ought to realize she wasn't a threat. In truth he never did have a roving eye, just got confused for a while.

Trish's dog pushed forward to sniff Rebel. "Leave it, Speedo." She gave the Aussie a sharp jerk, and he curled back to her. "I hear you two got hitched. That was quick."

"Just two weeks ago." Mark thumbed the gold wedding band that matched the one Dani wore. "I moved into the boarding kennel house and I'm going to rent out my house in Middleburg. Maybe I'll sell it." He didn't mention that he could no longer bear to spend the night there, and Rebel had also made it clear he was uncomfortable inside the house.

"Didn't I see you on the news?" Trish jerked her dog's lead. "Down, Speedo." The Aussie dropped like a rock and turned his head sideways in a submissive posture. "Didn't you have something to do with that explosion at Crohn Life Sciences?"

"Not as a perpetrator." He offered her a wry smile. "I've been a witness on the case. Dani and I helped capture one of the terrorists."

"No kidding." Trish ran her gaze over Dani.

"Mark did the capturing. I just helped," Dani said.

"Exciting," Trish said.

"Too exciting." Mark was tired of the notoriety. "Thank goodness things are getting back to normal. After what they found on his computer, I think he's going to be in jail for a very long time."

"Wasn't there a suicide bomber or something?"

He exchanged a glance with Dani. "Something like that. It's pretty unclear whether it was suicide or murder. They did DNA tests to identify them, so at least we know who they were. The guy they captured isn't talking about how they ended up in the van."

"Weird. Well, I've got to go find out what Speedo's time was. The lazy bum knocked a bar, so he didn't do so great." Trish made a face. "I guess it's back to heavier bars so they sting when he hits them. See you."

After she walked away, Mark said to Dani, "It's too bad we can't tell anybody what Rebel saw. Not exactly admissible evidence, huh?"

They started back toward their set-up, Rebel frisking along at the end of his lead. "It's a good thing you weren't home when they came to your house. I think they would have killed you, too." Dani shuddered.

"Only reason I can figure they murdered her was she tried to warn me and they decided she was a liability. By making that call she probably saved some lives, including the nightshift workers.

It's a shame we can't give her the credit."

"After all the trouble she caused, she did try to do the right thing in the end," Dani agreed. "Because of that I've been able to forgive her for all those shenanigans, too. It's a good thing Jim's cancer is in remission and he doesn't have to depend on new drug research. For the time being, anyway."

"Aren't you running Crash soon?"

"Yeah." She grinned. "I made a deal with him. He can blow a run every so often for fun, as long as he does it right the rest of the time. He won't tell me which one, so it'll be a surprise. I've got to keep my sense of humor."

"Ah, you're talking to your dog." He raised an eyebrow. "And admitting it?"

"Listening to him, if you want to know the truth." She rubbed her cheek thoughtfully.

"I've decided to look into this further. I found out about an animal communication seminar, and I want to go."

This was news to him. "They have dog talk seminars?"

"Seems lots of people can communicate with animals. Most of them don't make anything of it. I can certainly understand that. Others want to learn, even if they've never consciously experienced it. I suspect people do it all the time but don't realize it."

"Hmm. Think they'd let me come?"

"You want to go, too? Why not?" She flashed her one of her million-megawatt smiles. "After all, you're the one who made me admit I was getting what Rebel had to say. You might even be better at it than I am."

Mark let Dolly out of her crate and sat on the floor, letting both big dogs try to fit onto his lap at once. Dani tossed a rope tug toy next to him and Rebel pounced on it. He gleefully showed it to Dolly, who started to grab for it, but the Collie turned his head and pulled it out of reach. Dolly persisted, lunged forward and snagged the end. They settled into a rambunctious game of tug, Rebel knocking over a chair in his exuberance.

"Okay, break it up." Laughing, Mark snatched the middle of the toy. "Leave it."

Both dogs let go but stood staring at the tug now dangling from his hand.

“Dolly sure has come along,” Dani said. “It’s good to see how much she trusts you now.”

Mark just smiled. Dolly sat looking up at him, eyes full of adoration. And there was Dani, willing to spend her life with him.

She leaned close, eyes warm with love, and kissed him softly on the cheek. “I’ve got to say, you’ve earned it.”

About the Author

Lydia Filzen has written two award-winning Civil War novels, FIRETRAIL and PERFECT DISGUISE, under the name Lydia Hawke. Her non-fiction work and photographs appear frequently in Clay Today and Civil War Courier with her byline Lydia Filzen. Her dog-related short stories, GETTING IT and ANGUS, THE VAMPIRE SLAYER have been released as a "Dollar Downloads" by Echelon Press. She is an avid history buff and lurks about Civil War reenactments trolling for stories and great pictures. Also, she shows champion Collies in conformation and agility. Lydia is a member of various writing organizations, Collie Club of America, Pals and Paws Agility Club, Greater Jacksonville Collie Club and Greater Orange Park Dog Club. She owns DesJardin Electrical Service with her husband, Larry. In her spare time she… Spare time???

Check her websites at www.lydiahawke.us and www.lydiafilzen.us, or email her at lydiafilzen@comcast.net

Civil War novels written as Lydia Hawke, available through your favorite bookstore:

Firetrail ISBN 0-9766449-7-5 published by Global Authors Publications
Soon to be a feature-length movie by Forbesfilms! Check http://forbesfilm.com.

Perfect Disguise ISBN 0-9766449-0-8 published by Global Authors Publications

Doggy short stories written as Lydia Filzen

Getting It! and ***Angus the Vampire Slayer***

Available as Dollar Downloads from Echelon Press
www.echelonpress.com

Printed in the United States
61364LVS00005B/256-264

9 780976 644910